THE
FREEDOM
FACTOR

THE
FREEDOM
FACTOR

GERALD N. LUND

DESERET BOOK COMPANY
SALT LAKE CITY, UTAH

© 1987 Gerald N. Lund

Deseret Book is a registered trademark of Deseret Book Company.

Library of Congress Cataloging-in-Publication Data

Lund, Gerald N.
 The freedom factor.

 I. Title.
PS3562.U485F7   1987   813'.54   87-15548
ISBN 0-87579-098-4 (hard)
ISBN 0-87579-961-2 (paper)

Printed in the United States of America

10 9   8   7   6   5   4   3   2   1

CHAPTER 1

"Ladies and gentlemen."

The television news reporter, a stunning blonde with a glitzy smile, was looking earnestly into the camera set up on the steps of the United States Capitol.

"This is Senator Benjamin Hawkes, senior senator from Massachusetts and co-sponsor of what some are calling the most important piece of legislation of this century." She half turned, smiling at the slender, impeccably dressed man standing at her elbow. "Good morning, Senator."

"Good morning." The senator looked directly at the camera and gave the several million people who might be watching the easy, relaxed smile that had been a major factor in winning him five consecutive terms in the United States Senate.

"Senator, the Hawkes/Larkin bill calls for the most sweeping governmental reform since the signing of the Constitution. How do you predict the vote will come out this afternoon?"

He chuckled softly. "Oh, I think we'll win."

Bryce Sherwood, who was standing slightly behind Hawkes in the crowd that had gathered quickly, felt a quick flash of irritation. What did Ms. Glitzy expect him to say?

"It takes a two-thirds vote to pass a proposed amendment to the Constitution, Senator. The media count shows you one or two votes short of the needed sixty-seven at the moment."

The senator smiled warmly. "Well, Kathy, the media have been known to be wrong."

1

She pounced on that. "Does that mean you have senators who have changed their vote?"

Senator Hawkes cut her off smoothly. "Only the next two hours will tell for sure. That's why I've got to get inside and keep things moving." He turned. "You know Bryce Sherwood, my legislative assistant. He helped me draft the bill. He can answer any questions you have about it."

Bryce groaned inwardly as Senator Hawkes pulled him forward. "I need you!" he hissed into Bryce's ear. "Hurry!" He turned back to the camera, waved and flashed a quick smile, then slipped through the circle of people.

The smile on the newswoman's face had slipped slightly, but she hitched it up as Bryce stepped forward. "Mr. Sherwood, for our viewers who may not be familiar with the Hawkes/Larkin bill, could you briefly summarize why it is so significant?"

Bryce nodded thoughtfully, trying to look appropriately somber and yet pleasant at the same time. "Well, actually this bill simply proposes that there be a twenty-seventh amendment to the Constitution. Since a similar bill has already passed the House, if Senator Hawkes's bill passes today, the proposed amendment will then go to the states for ratification, and, as you know, three-fourths of the states must pass it before it becomes law."

"Yes, of course."

Bryce leaned forward slightly, getting more earnest now. "Again and again in recent years, we've seen how the government can get bogged down in a stalemate between the president and the Congress. Right now, there is no way to break the impasse except to wait for new elections. In this day and age, waiting up to four years to form a new government can be catastrophic."

"And the new amendment will change all that?"

Bryce laughed easily. "Well, to say 'all that' may be a little optimistic, Kathy. I'm not sure we'll ever completely do away with the warm and loving relationship that traditionally prevails between the White House and Capitol Hill."

There were a few appreciative chuckles and nods from the surrounding crowd.

"But under the new amendment," he continued, "Congress can pass a resolution of no-confidence in the administration. If two-thirds of both houses concur in this no-confidence vote, the government is dissolved and new elections are held within six weeks."

Suddenly a reporter standing on the sidelines broke in. Bryce remembered that he was from the *Washington Post*. "Mr. Sherwood, critics of the bill say it does away with some of the checks and balances set up by the founding fathers. What's to stop the Congress from throwing the president out every time he wears a tie they don't like?"

Bryce laughed. "Well, John, I know you know the answer to that, but it's a good question. Many people don't understand that this amendment has an important set of checks and balances of its own. First, you'll note that I said that if Congress passes a no-confidence resolution, the government is dissolved. That doesn't mean just the administration is dissolved. It means Congress too. Every senator and representative will have to go back and face their own constituents for reelection as well. That should make them think twice before voting to turn the president out."

He took a quick breath, warming to the subject now. "But there is also a second set of checks and balances, and in my opinion, this is the most exciting thing about the proposed amendment. It makes government directly responsible to the voice of the people. Remember that a vote of no confidence by the Congress doesn't mean there will necessarily be a new president, only new elections. The people may disagree with Congress and put the president back in office. Then he comes back with a real mandate to govern. Or if the people think it is time for a change, the new president comes in ready to try something new. Either way the stalemate is broken."

The cameraman swung around as another reporter at Bryce's left broke in. "So this really does put government back into the hands of the people, doesn't it?"

Before Bryce could respond a feminine voice behind cut in sharply. "Which people? The rich and powerful?"

Bryce swung around and was mildly surprised. From the acrid bitterness of the voice, he expected something very different than what he saw—an attractive, well-dressed brunette in her mid-twenties. He smiled directly into her angry eyes, wide and green and disturbingly lovely. "The people I think he was referring to are *the people*, as in 'We, the people.' That's in the preamble to the Constitution, in case you were wondering."

The crowd quickly sensed the potential for an interesting confrontation and stepped back enough so the woman was put into the front row facing Bryce. The newswoman was motioning quickly to the cameraman to get both of them in frame.

But if Bryce had meant to throw his opponent onto the defensive, he was wrong. She smiled right back at him, sweetly, but her eyes were crackling. "As a matter of fact, I was reading the Constitution again this morning. And when was the last time *you* read it, Mr. Sherwood?"

That won her a few guffaws from the crowd, and Bryce flushed.

She pressed her advantage. "Don't you find it a little intimidating to try to rewrite a document that took some of the finest minds in American history several months to create? But then," she went on, before he could answer, sarcasm dripping from every word, "I suppose graduating *magna cum laude* from the Harvard Law School does qualify one to sit right up there with George Washington, Thomas Jefferson, and Benjamin Franklin."

Bryce had not taken three national titles in college debate or won ninety percent of his cases in court by being slow on the uptake. He shook his head, seemingly puzzled. "You obviously have the advantage of knowing more about me than I do about you, Miss . . . ?"

"Adams. Leslie Adams."

"And which newspaper are you with, Miss Adams?" he asked pleasantly. "The *Washington Hatchet?*"

There was a ripple of approving laughter. The crowd had stopped to watch an interview and gotten a prize fight instead.

Now it was she who flushed deeply. "I'm not with a newspaper. I'm a volunteer worker with a citizen's group called Save the Constitution."

"Ah, yes," Bryce said, understanding now. "The STC. No wonder you're a little depressed this morning." He looked around innocently. "I suppose you have American flags edged in black in case we win today."

"That's right!" she retorted bitterly. "Flash the boyish grin, spread a little cutesy humor around. But whatever else we do, let's not focus on the real issues."

Bryce caught himself. It wouldn't do to be too brutal with her. Not on national television. He turned back to the blonde newswoman and the camera and noted with satisfaction that it swung away from Miss Adams. "I agree," Bryce said pleasantly. "Why *don't* we focus on the real issue, which in my mind is this: Is it time that big government becomes more responsive to the will of the people, or do we continue to lumber forward into the future with a government that grows more cumbersome and unworkable every day?"

He glanced quickly at his opponent, then turned away, before the flashing eyes could fire back at him. "And with that, I too had better excuse myself. There is a very important vote coming up in an hour or so, and there is much yet to be done."

The newswoman, glad to have the ball back in her court, nodded smoothly. "Thank you, Bryce. Good luck to you on what will prove to be a very important vote for all of America."

Bryce lifted his arm in farewell and started out of the circle. On impulse, he turned back to face the dark-haired young woman. "I wish we could continue this," he smiled. "I haven't had this much fun since my last root canal." Again he waved and pushed through the crowd, not unaware of the good-natured laughter rippling through the group, nor of Leslie Adams's tight-lipped glare boring into the back of his head.

Outside, the heat was stifling. It was the first week of August, and the temperature stood at ninety-seven degrees, the humidity only four points lower than that. Tourists, queued up to enter the White House, wilted like parched corn in a West Texas drought. At the far east end of the Mall, the gleaming dome of the Capitol shimmered as though it were slowly evaporating in the summer sunshine. Tourists dutifully followed their guides through the Capitol rotunda, sensing but not understanding the hush that had fallen over the building. And in fact, for a moment it seemed the whole city paused, cocking one ear to catch the proceedings just beginning to unfold in the Senate chambers.

It was at that moment that the buzzer signaling the roll call sounded. It brought instant response. Senators and their aides poured from doorways and down the hallways. Senate pages, in their neat blue uniforms, began lining up for duty. In less than three minutes, the Senate floor was filled, every eye riveted on the man seated in the black leather chair next to the American flag.

The vice president of the United States leaned forward, let his eyes sweep the chambers slowly. A hundred senators accepted his silent census gravely. Finally he nodded with satisfaction. "All time having been yielded back, the question before us is the bill by Senator Benjamin Hawkes and Senator Howard Larkin. On this question, the yeas and the nays have been ordered. The clerk will call the roll."

The third-floor windows of Bryce Sherwood's office were on the south side of the Richard B. Russell Senate Office Building, providing a stunning panorama of the Capitol. But at the moment, Bryce Sherwood had no eye for the view. The office looked a little like a war zone. The desk was strewn with newspapers, computer printouts, and scribbled vote projections. A half-eaten hamburger and an untouched soft drink were perched precariously on a pile of manila folders. Normally a fastidious

6

dresser, now Bryce had tossed his coat across a chair. His vest was open and the top button of his shirt undone, with the tie pulled loose. Behind him a computer screen waited patiently for data, its cursor blinking with monotonous regularity.

But Bryce Sherwood had no eye for that either. He had the phone jammed up to his ear, his shoulder holding it in place, one hand poised with a pencil. It was that pose, with head cocked to one side, that caused people to compare him to Robert Redford as the crusading journalist in *All the President's Men*. Blue eyes, the color of an early morning sky, and short sandy-blonde hair with just the touch of a natural wave were complemented by cleanly cut features and a mouth that always seemed to be toying with a smile.

He listened intently to the voice drumming into his ear, then broke in. "You're sure of that, Jim?"

The response was unequivocal. "Absolutely! I just left him two minutes ago."

"Great!" Bryce stabbed down on his secretarial call button, then began to scribble furiously on a notepad. "That's terrific, Jim! We owe you."

The door to his office pushed open, and Bryce's secretary poked her head around the corner. He waved her in.

"No, I mean it, Jim. Senator Hawkes won't forget this. You have my word."

Dropping the phone into its cradle, he ripped the sheet off the pad and thrust it at his secretary. "Call a page and get this to Senator Hawkes immediately. Joseph Larson is changing his vote!"

The secretary's eyes widened. "Senator Larson! Wow! That should help."

"Help!" Bryce crowed jubilantly. "That could do it! That could just do it!"

Taking the note, the secretary stepped quickly to the large walnut cabinet on one wall and slid back the doors. She pushed the "power-on" button on the television set built into the cabinet. "They've just started the roll call."

Bryce waved his thanks to her as he swung around in his chair. The screen was filling with the face of the vice-president of the United States. Bryce pulled over a pad already marked in two columns—one titled "yea" and the other "nay"—and poised his pencil.

The camera switched to the legislative clerk, a pleasant looking man in steel-rimmed glasses. He took a deep breath, consulted his list, then called out: "Mr. Anderson."

The junior senator from Nevada, whose privilege it was to be first in every roll call, leaned forward. "Yea," he said loudly.

"Mr. Atwood."

"Yea."

Even with the volume turned low, Bryce heard the murmur that swept through the Senate chambers. Two yea votes did not a victory make, but it was a good omen.

The phone rang and Bryce snatched it up. "Sherwood." He listened for one moment, then yanked the phone toward him so sharply he almost spilled the soft drink. "What!" he shouted.

This time the voice on the line was apologetic, almost whining, which only fueled Bryce's anger.

"I don't care what kind of pressure he's getting, Weatherby gave Senator Hawkes his word."

The whining started again, but Bryce cut it off, smacking his hand down sharply on the desk. "That's not acceptable, Karl, and you know it! Now you get word to that distinguished Senator Weatherby of yours that if he backs down now, Senator Hawkes will not, I repeat *will not*, support his farm bill."

The line was silent.

"He's not bluffing, Karl. You know that. And you know as well as I do, that Senator Hawkes can be a very powerful ally . . . " He let that sink in, then added quietly, "or a potent adversary."

Again there was a pause, then finally over the line came a weary, "Okay, I'll try."

"You'd better do more than try!" Bryce snapped, swinging around again toward the television. "And you're going to have to hurry. They've started the vote." He slammed the phone down, still fuming.

Three blocks farther east, in an older office building beyond the inner circle of government buildings, a group of eight or ten people watched the television with equal avidness. This was a smaller office, more subdued. An old walnut desk in one corner was also covered with papers, but it was arranged in orderly piles. The outer door, standing open, showed a large round plaque with the initials STC in the center. Forming an oval around the letters were the words SAVE THE CONSTITUTION. One wall held a framed replica of the Declaration of Independence, another a large print of Howard Christy's painting "The Signing of the Constitution."

Leslie Adams was the youngest person in the room. Like Bryce Sherwood, she also had a notepad and was tallying the votes as the clerk continued through the roll call. The grandfatherly man who sat next to her leaned over and did a quick count, then shook his head. "Not good. That's forty-five votes so far—thirty yeas and fifteen nays." He let out a discouraged sigh. "Thirty votes is exactly a two-thirds majority so far."

"Mr. Larson," intoned the clerk from the television set.

There was a pause, and a sudden hush settled over the Senate chambers. A heavyset man, with his head down, appeared on the screen. Finally he looked up. "Yea," he said softly.

The hall erupted in a wild burst of noise clearly evident even over the television's speakers. The vice president rapped the gavel sharply. The screen changed abruptly to show the face of one of America's best-known television anchormen. "Ladies and gentlemen," he said breathlessly. "Senator Joseph Larson, senior senator from Michigan, and a man who this morning was considered a solid opponent of the Hawkes/Larkin bill, has just stunned the Senate by voting in the affirmative. That gives the bill an unexpected vote in the yes column."

Leslie looked into the face of the man next to her and just shook her head slowly.

The phone rang again, but Bryce ignored it now. It was too late for any further action at this point. He continued marking the votes as the roll call droned on.

"Mr. Van Orden."

"Yea."

Bryce marked it, counted quickly. If he had not lost track, they were two short of what they needed, with five names to go.

"Mr. Washburn."

"Yea."

One to go!

"Mr. Weatherby."

Senator Roger Weatherby was a vacillator. He was famous for it on the Senate floor. Most knew it was merely a ruse to see what benefits he could pick up for himself if he came down on either side. Bryce suspected that was the reason for the last phone call. Weatherby wanted that farm bill badly. The question was, had anyone else gotten to him with something better?

Bryce leaned forward, suddenly tensing. "Come on, Senator! Don't cave in on us now."

There was no answer, and a sudden tension filled the Senate chambers. The camera cut to a view of the Senate floor, adjusted slightly, then focused on a dark-haired man near the back.

"Mr. Weatherby," the clerk repeated with just a trace of annoyance.

Even through the television, Bryce could feel the electricity in the air as every eye swung to the junior senator from Washington State. Finally his head came up. He looked toward the clerk, ignoring everyone and everything else.

"Yea," he said in a voice that was barely audible.

There was an angry cry from the back of the room from some unseen senator, but Bryce didn't hear it. He leaped to his

10

feet. "All right!" he shouted, punching his fist into the empty air. "All right!"

CHAPTER 2

Bryce was standing at the window, gazing at the Capitol Building. Sixty-eight yeas—one more than they needed—and thirty-eight nays. That represented nearly six months of head-banging, bone-jarring work, planning, and negotiations. In spite of his confident response during the interview earlier, he had not been sure they were going to pull it off. Now it was sweet indeed!

There was a soft knock at the door. He turned, and his secretary was there. "Bryce, Elliot Mannington's chauffeur is here. He says Mr. Mannington would like to see you."

Before Bryce had even reached the gray-and-black limo parked in the underground garage, Elliot Mannington III was out of the car with his hand extended. "Bryce, congratulations! A great victory today!"

A little overwhelmed at the warmth of the greeting, Bryce took his hand, returning the firm grip. "Thank you." He stepped back a little dazzled. Elliot Mannington, scion of one of Boston's wealthiest families, senior partner in Mannington, Carlson, Frederick, and Brown, Boston's most prestigious law firm, and the man who was personal advisor to senators, cabinet members, *and* the president of the United States, was smiling at him like an exuberant fan. Though barely five feet seven, Elliot Mannington was an event. Just over sixty, he was as lean as a marathon runner and every bit as wiry. Dark, thick hair, just now graying at the temples, only added to the youthfulness of the man. The dark eyes were quick, piercing, always alive. One only had to be with him for a few moments before his size was forgotten, for the man wore an unmistakable aura of power and influence.

Mannington laid a hand on his shoulder. "Senator Hawkes is at the White House. The president wants to congratulate him personally, so he asked that I come and get you. We're having a little victory celebration over at my place in Georgetown. Call your secretary on the car phone and tell her I'll have you back about five."

"Well," Bryce said, not trying to hide his pleasure. "Thank you, Mr. Mannington, I—"

"None of this Mr. Mannington, Bryce. It's Elliot, please."

Mannington's condominium was palatial, luxurious, and awash with people. In spite of almost four years in Washington, where one became accustomed to rubbing shoulders with the nationally and internationally famous, Bryce was impressed. He counted over a dozen senators, easily that many members of the House, two cabinet members, several undersecretaries of various agencies, the British and French ambassadors, and more diamond-studded women than one could find at a Cartier's modeling extravaganza. He also noted wryly that as near as he could see, he was the only senator's aide in the entire bunch.

At the moment, the group in which he was standing included Hawkes and his wife, the undersecretary for Middle Eastern Affairs from the State Department, the junior senator from Massachusetts and his wife, and a Supreme Court Justice. Just as Hawkes started one of his famous anecdotes, Bryce looked up. Elliot Mannington was standing nearby. He motioned, almost imperceptibly, with his head. Bryce waited a moment, then excused himself and drifted away. As Bryce moved up next to him, Mannington murmured softly, "Slip away in about ten minutes and come to the condo directly below mine, room eight-oh-seven." He smiled enigmatically at Bryce's surprised look and moved away.

The name on the doorplate read "Sterling Jennings." That surprised Bryce. Jennings, formerly secretary of defense, was now the president of one of the largest of the Fortune Five Hundred companies. Jennings had not been to the party above, of that Bryce was almost certain, for though he had never met the man personally, his face was a familiar one to most of Washington.

Bryce rang the bell, still puzzled by the unexpected invitation. Almost instantly, Mannington was there, smiling broadly.

"Ah, good, Bryce. Come in, come in."

Though not quite as large as Mannington's, this condominium was just as richly furnished. A painting that looked like an original Gaugin hung in the entryway, and an elegant marble bust of a young girl sat on a bronze table in front of a huge mirror.

As they entered the main living room, another man stood. It was Jennings.

"Let me introduce you," Mannington said. "This is Bryce Sherwood, legislative assistant and senior staff member to Senator Hawkes."

Who isn't here! Bryce realized with a sudden start. Hawkes had not been invited! That really set his mind racing.

"And," Mannington was continuing, "this is Sterling Jennings, former secretary of defense."

"Yes, sir. A pleasure to meet you, sir."

Jennings smiled. "The pleasure is mine." He was smoking a cigarette. He stubbed it out quickly, then shook Bryce's hand. Surprisingly, his grip was not particularly firm. But the penetrating gaze more than made up for it. "Great job today, Sherwood. Great job."

"Thank you, sir. I've read a lot about you. It's a pleasure."

"Sit down, Bryce," Mannington offered, pointing to a chair that would put him facing both of them. As they sat down, Jennings motioned toward a well-stocked bar off to one side. "May we get you something to drink, Bryce?"

14

He saw that both of the men had drinks on the table in front of them, but he shook his head. "No, thank you. I'm fine."

That seemed to please Mannington. "We won't hold you too long. Wouldn't want anyone upstairs to miss us." Jennings smiled with him on that. "Besides, we think we can offer you something a little headier than wine tonight."

Mannington cleared his throat. "Bryce, as you know, I'm on the board of directors for a group known as the Committee for Constitutional Reform."

"Yes. The CCR was very helpful in what happened today." Which was more than just back-patting. The Committee for Constitutional Reform was a powerful lobby group made up of two or three hundred of the country's most influential business, political, and professional leaders. They had thrown their considerable support behind the Hawkes/Larkin bill, and there was no doubt that was a major factor in the day's victory.

Again it seemed to have been the right thing to say. Mannington nodded, pleased. "Sterling and I are on the executive committee for the board of directors."

Bryce just nodded, feeling his pulse stirring.

"Today was a major hurdle, Bryce." Mannington was now very sober in his demeanor. "We cleared it successfully, thanks to you."

The former secretary of defense leaned forward as Bryce started to deprecate a little. "Oh, we all know that Senator Hawkes played a major role, but your role was pivotal."

"Today was a tough hurdle," Mannington said, picking up the lead again, but it certainly wasn't the last, or perhaps even the toughest."

That sobered each of them. There were fifty states. Three-fourths had to ratify the amendment before it became law. That meant thirty-seven hurdles to go.

"We need someone," Mannington went on, "someone who'll see to it that we clear those other hurdles as well."

Bryce watched them, eyes attentive, but his mind was tumbling wildly. So that was it! He felt a sudden surge of excitement.

"We think you are that man, Bryce," Jennings said softly.

Bryce felt a chill go through him. "I . . . Well, thank you. I'm deeply flattered. As you know, I believe strongly in this amendment. I want to see it pass."

"This could mean a lot to you," Mannington said, sitting back and sipping his drink.

"Yes, sir. It's a great opportunity."

The former secretary of defense flicked a lighter and touched it to another cigarette. "It's more than that, Bryce," he said soberly. "Senator Hawkes is thinking about retiring after this term."

Bryce's head snapped up.

Jennings puffed deeply, then smiled through the smoke as he blew it out. "That's right. Massachusetts is going to be needing a new senator in four years. You'll be thirty-one then. Minimum age for a senator is thirty."

Bryce looked to Mannington, who was smiling and nodding. "Why not?" he said. "You've got the qualifications—Harvard Law School, courtroom experience, public service. You've got the looks and personality. Your father is a well-known surgeon and medical professor in Boston."

They had him now, and they were working him smoothly, jumping from one stunning comment to another. Jennings took the ball now. "Three or four terms in the Senate and we think you might even have a good shot at the White House."

When Mannington saw the expression on Bryce's face, he laughed right out loud. "I warned you this would be heady wine."

"I . . . " Bryce blew out his breath, shaking his head in wonder. "I don't know what to say."

"You don't have to say anything," Jennings said with a smile. "Just nod your head if you like what you're hearing."

For a long moment, he looked to each of the two men in front of him. Their eyes never faltered. Finally, he smiled tentatively, and nodded his head slowly.

CHAPTER 3

It was just coming dusk, and the temperature in Washington, D.C., had still not dropped below ninety. As Bryce wheeled his red BMW around the corner and up the ramp of the Senate's underground parking garage, he turned the air conditioning up to full and loosened his tie.

Traffic was thinning now, but there was still enough that he decided to just let the sports car roll with the flow. He flipped through his box of cassettes, picked out Prokofiev's "Lieutenant Kije Suite" and pushed it into the tape deck. As the haunting strains of the trumpet solo began, Bryce, for the tenth time, began rehearsing in his mind the meeting with Elliot Mannington and Sterling Jennings. And for the tenth time, he chided himself for the soaring euphoria he was feeling. And yet, on the other hand, somewhere deep inside him he also knew he was not dealing with backyard players. These were the power makers, and if they said it was possible, it was possible! And that left him a little dizzy.

Three blocks later, sitting on the bench at a bus stop, was a familiar figure. He peered through the windshield, then gave a short bark of laughter. It was her! Miss Leslie Adams, with the dark hair, flashing green eyes, and rapier sharp tongue.

On impulse, he buttoned his top button, cinched up his tie again, then shut off the music as he let the BMW pull up smoothly to the curb in front of her. Her head was down, studying a folder of papers. Not until he was directly in front of her did she finally become aware of the car. She looked up, then her eyes widened.

"Hi."

"Hello."

Good start, he thought with a inward smile. The tone of her voice had lowered the outside temperature by no more than five degrees.

"Say, I've been having some pain in my jaw. Any chance for another root canal?"

The temperature dropped five more degrees. "Very funny. Do you do parties?"

"Sorry, I thought a little humor might help."

"Emphasis on the little."

He laughed. "All right, so I'm a politician, not a comedian."

Her head came up slowly. "I didn't know there was a difference."

Bryce shook his head ruefully, deciding that her green eyes were very nice, in spite of the glacial ice in them at the moment. "Are you *sure* you don't work for the *Washington Hatchet?*" he asked.

For the first time there was the slightest hint of softening. "I'm sorry, that was uncalled for."

"Apology accepted, subject dropped."

She seemed to accept that, then promptly dismissed him again by returning to her reading.

"May I give you a lift somewhere? You'll melt in this heat."

She continued reading. "I'm fine, thank you anyway."

"Hey, really. I promise, no more cracks."

She shook her head.

Now the challenge was on him. "What if I promise to focus on the real issues?"

Leslie closed the folder and put it in her lap. He thought he saw the tiniest smile crinkling around her eyes. "I debate only in front of television cameras."

"Let's call it a rehearsal for the next appearance."

"I appreciate your thoughtfulness, but the bus will be here in a minute."

Suddenly his eye caught a figure about fifty feet down the street. A man was leaning against a tree, watching them. In the dimming light, Bryce couldn't see him too well, but he had long hair and was dressed in some kind of strange getup. Bryce seized the opportunity.

"Look," he said, "I don't want to push you, but seriously, Washington is not the place for a single woman at night."

"I'll be fine."

"Maybe. But there's a guy over there who looks like he would like to test that theory."

Leslie turned. The man hadn't moved, but now he was watching them intently. Bryce saw her give an involuntary shudder and knew he had won. There really was something half creepy about the guy.

"Really," he said, his voice softer now, "I only attack the Constitution. Young women are perfectly safe with me."

She looked at him for a long moment, turned back once more to eye the man, then gave in. "I live in Arlington," she said tentatively. "If that's out of your way—"

"It's not." He opened the door. She got in quickly, and Bryce let out the clutch, moving slowly to merge into the traffic. The man had stepped out from beneath the limbs of an overhanging tree and into the light. As they approached, he stared intently at Leslie. She stared back, and just as they passed him, he suddenly smiled at her, eerily, as if he knew her and exactly what she was thinking. She looked away quickly, suppressing another shiver that ran down her back.

"Thank you," she said softly. "My car's in the garage. I don't normally have to do this."

He laughed easily, trying to ease the pain of surrender. "Hey, I don't think *I* would have stayed at that bus stop with him around."

Bryce swung up and around past the Capitol, then turned west on Constitution Avenue. It wasn't the shortest route, but if she noticed, she didn't comment. As they drove slowly past the Ellipse, with the White House glowing brightly on their right, and the gleaming needle of the Washington Monument on their left, he finally spoke. "So, what do you do besides work for the STC, or is that a full-time job?"

"No, it's strictly volunteer work. I teach American History at Arlington High School."

"No kidding?"

"No kidding. Does that surprise you?"

"Yes, I guess it does."

"Why?"

"I thought all high-school teachers wore combat fatigues and carried nightsticks."

For the first time she laughed. He liked it, enough to try to get her to do it again.

He turned left on Twenty-third Street and looped once slowly around the Lincoln Memorial. This was not just for Leslie's benefit. Bryce had been in Washington for over four years. He loved the city—its pulse and continuing drama. He loved the pressure and the challenge of pitting his own ingenuity and resourcefulness against it. But every now and then, after a harried week or a particularly brutal battle, he would come home this way, past the monuments—the Washington, the Jefferson, the Lincoln, the Kennedy Center, the somber black marble of the Viet Nam Memorial. Often he would get out and walk around, or sit on the grass, or linger in the shadows of the massive pillars. He called these times—which not even Senator Hawkes knew about—his way of keeping in touch with the things that really mattered.

He was pleased to see that Leslie's eyes were also drawn to the Lincoln Memorial and that she too seemed moved by it. Suddenly, without turning to him, she spoke.

"Do you believe in God?"

That startled him. Finally he shrugged. "Yes."

21

"Do you believe he takes a hand in the affairs of men?" She finally turned to watch him.

He let out his breath slowly. He had hardly expected this turn in the conversation. "I don't know. Sometimes I think he's got more important things to do than watch over a slightly wobbly, terribly out-of-tune world, but other times . . . " His voice trailed off.

"Other times what?"

"Well, believe it or not, I minored in history in college. And there are some times when it certainly makes you wonder if he didn't take a hand in things."

She nodded, then with the same unexpected swiftness as before, totally changed tacks. "Your accent isn't Bostonian."

It wasn't a question. He smiled. "No, Californian. We moved to Boston when I was ten."

"Oh."

He laughed. "Do you do this with your students?"

"What?"

"Keep throwing them conversational hand grenades?"

That won him his second laugh, deep and throaty. "It drives my father crazy," she said, nodding.

He pressed her further. "You know that I was raised in Boston, and earlier today you knew I graduated from Harvard Law School. How is it you happen to know so much about me?"

She flushed slightly and dropped her eyes. He waited, a little amused that he had her bobbling the hot potato now.

"I looked you up in *Who's Who in the East.*"

"I'm flattered."

"You don't need to be, not when you've made *Who's Who* before you're thirty."

He gave her a quizzical look. "Is that a compliment or a cut?"

She smiled faintly. "A statement of fact. Just because I totally disagree with you philosophically doesn't mean I don't respect what you have accomplished with your life."

"Oh." Though that pleased him, he decided not to pursue it any further and lapsed into silence, asking only for directions as they moved onto the Arlington Memorial Bridge and crossed the Potomac.

Three minutes later she tossed him another one. "How well do you know Elliot Mannington?"

That brought Bryce around sharply to stare at her, and then she really blushed. "On the news this afternoon your name was mentioned as being at the victory celebration. I wasn't spying on you."

He nodded, only partially mollified. Nothing in Washington went unnoticed.

"Well?"

"Well what?"

"How well do you know him?"

"He and my father belong to the same club in Boston. His firm hired me as a law clerk while I was in law school. I joined his law firm when I graduated. He's also a longtime friend of Senator Hawkes."

"Are you a member of the Committee for Constitutional Reform?"

"No." At least not yet, he added to himself.

"Oh."

"What?" he drawled. "Not even a 'Praise the Lord' or a 'Hallelujah' or two?"

"Mr. Sherwood," she snapped, her voice suddenly cold again, "I know you believe that our governmental system needs reform. I happen to disagree, but I understand how you could feel that way. But the CCR has openly stated that their goal is to completely overhaul the Constitution."

He kept his voice light. "So maybe it needs some overhauling."

"Just like that," she retorted, the tartness in her voice raising it a notch in volume. "Two hundred years of the finest government the world has ever seen and now you're going to fix it."

23

"Ah, just the point. Two hundred years! You said your car is in the garage? How come?"

She saw it coming but was honest enough to answer him anyway. "The mechanic says the valves are gone."

"How many miles does it have on it?"

"Eighty-nine thousand."

"The Constitution has two hundred years. I'd make that just about equivalent to eighty-nine thousand miles, wouldn't you?"

She took a deep breath, then shook her head quickly. "Turn left here," was all she said.

For the next five minutes the cool silence in the car prevailed except for her occasional directions. They were moving through a residential section, modern apartment buildings and some single family dwellings.

"It's not far now," Leslie said. "Just turn right at the next intersection; then it's only a few blocks."

Bryce, feeling a little guilty about his final barb, decided to try to save the ride from ending in total disaster.

"So where do you come from originally?"

She smiled faintly. "I'm a real woman of the world. I was born and raised here in Arlington."

"No kidding?"

"All right, let's hear it."

"Let's hear what?"

"The last time you said, 'No kidding,' there was some kind of crack about combat fatigues and nightsticks. So what have you got to say about natives of Arlington?"

"I envy them," Bryce said soberly.

She glanced at him sharply.

"I mean it. I love Boston; it reeks of history. But Washington! This is the center of everything. To have lived here your whole life—that must give you more perspective than traveling around the world a dozen times."

She was watching him closely, to see if he was teasing her again. When she realized he was completely serious, she nodded. "Thank you."

24

"You probably know about places to see I haven't even heard of. I—"

Bryce stopped, staring out the window. They were just passing a streetlight. Standing beneath it, thumb out, was a man—long haired, strangely dressed. Bryce felt a chill. It was the same man at the—

He shook his head and blinked twice. It couldn't be! He jerked around as they passed. The man was staring directly at him with exactly the same eerie smile he had given Leslie.

"What's the matter?" Leslie was staring at him, startled by the look on his face.

"That hitchhiker."

She turned and looked out the window. "What hitchhiker?"

Bryce whirled, but a line of trees now blocked his view.

"I don't see anyone."

"Back there. I could have sworn . . . "

"What?"

"It . . . It looked like the same guy as the one at the bus stop."

Her eyes widened. "How could that be?"

"That's just it, it couldn't. But he looked right at me."

"Well," she said slowly, "I suppose it's possible. We didn't take the shortest route through the city."

He shook his head. "The chances of him taking exactly the same route are astronomical." He glanced once more in the rearview mirror, then shook his head again. "No, it couldn't be. It must have just been a look-alike."

She shrugged. "All these weirdos look the same to me—creepy!"

"True." He let out his breath slowly, trying to get his pulse to stop pounding as if he had just run a marathon.

Two minutes later, Bryce pulled up in front of an older home with a well-kept yard and turned off the engine and the lights.

Almost immediately Leslie opened the door. "Thank you for the ride. I'm sorry I was so difficult about it. I really do appreciate it."

"You're welcome." He gave her an apologetic smile. "I really hadn't planned to carry on the debate we started on the Capitol steps."

The corners of her mouth curved up slightly. "Me neither. I apologize for the hand grenades."

"Wouldn't have missed it for the world."

She got out.

"Listen," Bryce said suddenly, "I . . . "

She turned back, her eyes curious.

"I'd like a chance to cross swords again sometime. How about dinner Friday night?"

He was pleased to see that caught her completely by surprise and momentarily flustered her. Most of the girls he went out with had been manuevering toward another date the whole night.

"Who knows," he added quickly, "maybe you can show me the error of my ways." He paused, then smiled. "Or vice versa."

"I . . . That's very nice, but I think I'd better not."

"What?" he asked in amazement. "Can this be the same Leslie Adams I met in battle today in front of national television? Surely your faith is sufficiently strong to face the infidel."

She looked at him steadily for a long moment, then slowly a smile crept into her eyes. "Do you really think a device as transparent as that can work on someone who deals with a hundred and seventy teenagers every day?"

He pulled a face. "It was the best I could think of on the spur of the moment. Perhaps I should have slapped you on both cheeks with my glove."

The smile stole downward to soften her mouth. "It would probably suit my nature better."

He grinned. "Well, then, let's call it a duel. What do you say?"

"All right, you're on."

"Great! Pick you up at seven-thirty?"

26

"Fine. See you then. And thanks again for the ride."

He watched her run lightly up the walk and into the house. As the door shut behind her, Bryce started the engine and flipped on the lights. He reached down and turned on the tape deck. As the music from "Lieutenant Kije" enveloped him again, he smacked the steering wheel once with the flat of his hand. "And how about that?" he asked no one in particular.

CHAPTER 4

As Bryce pulled back onto one of the main streets of Arlington, he decided to swing over and pick up the Capital Beltway that looped all the way around the metropolitan area. He was in no particular hurry to get home, and on the Beltway he could give the BMW its head and let his mind savor the events of the day.

From the time he was ten, Bryce Sherwood knew he did not want to follow in his father's footsteps and pursue a medical career. This was a severe disappointment to his mother, but, surprisingly, not to his father. Theodore B. Sherwood was a pragmatic man, and rather than trying to push his son in a predetermined direction, he began to lay opportunities before Bryce like some kind of experiential smorgasbord. As a nationally famous heart surgeon, there were few financial limitations to what he could offer; and being on the faculty at the Harvard Medical School only added to the broad base of social contacts and growth opportunities Bryce was given. Boston, with its rich historical and cultural heritage, provided a fertile seedbed for a bright and inquisitive mind, and summers spent yachting and fishing in Cape Cod also added to his formational experiences.

By the time Bryce entered an exclusive prep school, he knew he was going into law and then into a public career. Nothing deflected him from that point on, and his father saw to it that the proper connections were made on the way up. His mother had not really completely forgiven him until Elliot Mannington had come to the house some four years ago and told them that Senator Benjamin Hawkes was looking for a legislative aide. At first she had balked. "Aide" hardly fit her concept of a move upward, but when Mannington, with some amusement, explained what this would mean for Bryce, she, from that moment on, became a fierce advocate and total supporter of his life's career.

Bryce laughed quietly to himself. His mother—so slight and diminutive, so elegant in every respect, so Boston, even though she was not a native—would be absolutely beside herself with joy when she learned what the CCR had offered her son today.

Bryce took his foot off the accelerator and let the BMW slow. He was approaching a major intersection and could see the signs directing him to the Beltway. Then suddenly he stiffened. Leaning casually against a light pole was a hitchhiker. Bryce blinked, trying to clear his vision. It couldn't be! But this time his car was moving slowly, and the man was directly under a streetlight. There were the same round features, the same shoulder-length hair, the same long jacket that looked like it had come fresh off the racks at Goodwill Industries. And most unmistakably, it was the same haunting, mysterious smile that sent chills coursing up and down Bryce's spine.

Stunned, Bryce just stared as the car rolled slowly past the man. Instinctively, his eyes lifted to the rearview mirror as he passed. For a second or two he tried to make his eyes adjust, then he yelled and slammed on the brakes, whirling around to stare out the back window. The lamp pole was still there, the street brightly lit. But the sidewalk was empty!

A woman in a van swung out around him, laying on the horn. There was a clipped burst of obscenity. But Bryce neither heard nor saw. There was no one there!

Bryce put a hand to his forehead. What was happening to him? Once more he peered down the empty sidewalk. Feeling like an idiot, and yet fighting a sudden trembling in his hands, he turned off the tape deck, then hit the power door-lock button.

With the hair on the back of his neck prickling, he released the clutch and slowly moved away.

Getting onto the beltway was completely forgotten now. Barely conscious of where he was going, he moved deeper into a quiet residential neighborhood, his mind searching for some logical explanation, feeling a sense of madness creeping up on him.

Suddenly he started. The hamburger! Of course! His secretary had gotten him a hamburger for lunch. He had taken two bites, then left it until he had returned from the Mannington party. Without thinking, he had finished it and the lukewarm soft drink over the last of his paperwork. That meant the meat had been sitting out for several hours!

Bryce slapped the steering wheel and laughed out loud. That was it! He had gotten some bad hamburger. Relief flooded over him like a wave. Shaking his head at his own foolishness, he slowed the car, pulled a U-turn, and headed back the way he had come, fighting the temptation to open the windows and sing something ridiculous.

And then he turned the corner.

This time the man was standing directly in the center of the road, once again in the circle of light from a streetlamp. Both hands were up, and he was smiling pleasantly into Bryce's horrified stare.

"No!" Bryce punched his foot down on the accelerator, swung the wheel hard, and rocketed out and around the man, engine howling. He went through the next intersection at close to fifty, not even seeing the stop sign. There was a white blur off to his right, a squeal of brakes, a blare of a horn. Bryce jerked his foot off the accelerator, his eyes snapping up to the rearview mirror.

A Volkswagen convertible with a teenage boy and girl was stopped in the middle of the intersection. He had missed them by no more than inches.

Shaking violently, Bryce let the BMW roll to a stop. He shut off the engine, forcibly loosened his grip on the steering wheel, took a deep breath, then another, then cautiously lifted his eyes to the rearview mirror.

He hoped to see a man standing in the street. Mentally, he was prepared to see nothing. But nothing could have prepared him for the face that filled the mirror, grinning at him happily!

Bryce screamed, then jumped so sharply he nearly ripped the shoulder belt out of its mount. He whirled, his mouth agape, then screamed again. The man was sitting in the back seat, smiling pleasantly back at him!

"Good evening!"

At that moment Bryce's instincts took over. He clawed wildly at the seat belt. As he felt the catch snap and the belt release him, he lunged for the door, yanking hard on the handle. It wouldn't open. Terror drove him like a madman. *The power door lock!* Something in the far recesses of his mind screamed the words at him. He stabbed at the button so hard he broke a fingernail. There was no corresponding click. He hit it again and again.

Out of the corner of his eye, Bryce saw the man lean forward over the seat. "Lands a mighty, Boy!" said the deep voice. "Settle down! I'm not going to hurt you."

Bryce raised one shoulder and heaved with his full strength against the door. Nothing! He began to hammer at the window with his fist. Somewhere in the wild haze gripping him, Bryce heard the man speak again, half to himself. "Bad choice on my part, I guess."

Suddenly the man was standing outside the car, in the full glare of the headlights. Bryce jerked up short, staring, not comprehending. He spun around. The back seat was empty!

He whirled back around, too stunned to move. The man had one foot propped up on the bumper, hands in his coat pockets. "There, is that any better?" he said.

But Bryce had passed into one mode and one mode only, and that was escape. He cranked the ignition. Nothing! He hammered the wheel with his fists, tried it again. The engine was grinding, but there was no answering roar of power. Desperate now, he swung his feet up and started hammering at the passenger door.

"Sherwood!" the man barked sharply, "get hold of yourself!"

Bryce blinked as that registered, and his feet came to a stop.

The man peered at him through the windshield. "Good heavens, Boy. I expected surprise, but not stark terror."

"You know my name?" Bryce whispered, barely audible.

"Of course I know your name. You think I just pop in on anyone like that?"

"Who are you?" he asked in a hoarse whisper.

"Nathaniel Gorham." The man waited, expectantly, then his face fell. "You don't recognize it?"

Bryce could do no more than shake his head.

"Figures. If I'd said George Washington or Benjamin Franklin then you would have perked up. But Nathaniel Gorham? No."

Bryce was still staring, the words only half registering.

"But my name's right there next to theirs."

"Right where?" Bryce echoed, still too stupefied to make sense of what the man was saying.

"At the bottom of the Constitution. Big as life, just like Ben's and General Washington's."

Gorham watched him for a moment, then shook his head sadly. "Well, I can see this isn't the time to try to talk this out. Look, Son, I'll see you tomorrow." And with that he lifted one hand and instantly disappeared!

Bryce looked around wildly. There was nothing. Not outside, not in. He jerked around to check the back seat. Nothing! Tentatively he reached for the keys, still looking around trying to find the man. But he was gone.

The engine caught on the first try and roared into life. But as Bryce reached for the gear lever, hand trembling violently, the power window on the driver's side suddenly started downward. He jerked his hand away, but no part of his body was even near the switches.

"One other thing," Gorham said into his ear.

Once again Bryce jumped sharply enough to crack his head on the ceiling. Gorham was at his window, his face not two inches from Bryce's.

"At least you had the good sense to take that young lady home."

"Leslie?" Bryce echoed numbly.

He nodded. "Now there's an intelligent young woman. Has her head on straight, as you moderns would say. She's an Adams, you know. Fifth great-granddaughter of John Quincy. He has a right to be proud."

He noticed the look on Bryce's face.

"Blood always tells, I say."

And once again he was gone, leaving Bryce to stare at nothing but empty air.

It was past ten when Bryce climbed the stairs to his apartment. But instead of stopping at his door, he went up one additional flight and knocked hard on the door of apartment 5-B. He heard a muffled voice, so he hammered again. Finally the door opened a crack, hitting the chain.

"Mr. Chapman?"

"Bryce? What the . . . ?" The door shut again, there was a brief rattle, then it opened widely to show a middle-aged, balding man in a rumpled bathrobe.

"Roy, look, I'm sorry to bother you this late. But I need to borrow an encyclopedia."

"*What?*" He was staring at Bryce, not believing what he had just heard.

"An encyclopedia. You know, like the *Britannica* or something. Don't you have one?"

"Of course, but . . . " His eyes narrowed. "Have you been drinking?"

"I don't drink," Bryce said curtly. "Please may I borrow the encyclopedia?"

Chapman took a breath, shaking his head. "I suppose. Which one?"

"Which one?"

"Yes, which one? Or do you want to borrow the whole set?"

33

"Oh. No, I . . . C. I need the C volume."

Chapman nodded, shuffled away, and was back in a moment. "You can keep it until tomorrow." He rolled his eyes.

"Thanks. Thank you very much."

In his apartment, Bryce didn't even sit down, just dropped his briefcase and his suit coat and started thumbing rapidly. "Constantine, Constantinople," he murmured. "Ah, Constitution, U.S." He skimmed quickly through the article, then suddenly stared. There it was, the list of delegates from each of the colonies. He started slowly down the list, finger pointing, hardly daring to breathe. Then very slowly he sat down, his eyes reading the names of the two delegates from Massachusetts—Rufus King and Nathaniel Gorham.

Chapman had obviously gotten back in bed, and Bryce had to bang on his door louder than before. The door opened, and there was an instant groan. "I thought I told you to—"

"I'm really sorry, Roy. But I need G, too. Could I borrow the G volume?"

And it was in there as well. Not more than a paragraph, but it was there! "Nathaniel Gorham (1738–1796). One of the original signers of the United States Constitution. Served in the Massachusetts legislature during the Revolutionary War from 1771 to 1775. Also served several terms in the Continental Congress, including a term as president of that group in 1775. Supporting a strong central government, Gorham chaired an important committee in the Constitutional Convention in Philadelphia and was one of the instrumental figures in the drafting of that document."

For several minutes Bryce just stared, reading it over and over, his mind whirling. Then suddenly he shut the book and walked swiftly to the desk. He found the phone book that covered Arlington County, Virginia, and turned to the A's and started looking for the name of her street.

"Hello?"

"Leslie?" Thank heavens *she* had answered and not one of her parents. "This is Bryce Sherwood."

"Bryce?" Any sleepiness in her voice was instantly dispelled.

"Yes. I'm really sorry to bother you, but—"

"What?"

Any guilt was swallowed up in the urgency of his quest. "Leslie, this is going to sound stupid, but I need to ask you something."

There was a long pause, then a very tentative "All right."

"You wouldn't happen to be . . . " Suddenly the absurdity of what he was doing hit him, and he let out his breath in a little self-deprecating laugh. "You're really going to think this is strange."

"I'm listening. Go ahead."

"Well," he said lamely, "I was thinking about your name on the way home. You wouldn't happen to be a descendant of John Quincy Adams, would you?"

If the first pause was a long one, this one went on for what seemed like the rest of the summer. "Yes," she said, finally. "Why?"

"Do you happen to know what the relationship is?"

"Yes, he is my fifth great-grandfather. But why?"

"Well," he said, feeling suddenly very cold again. "I just suddenly got to wondering about it. I . . . Thank you very much, Leslie. Sorry I bothered you."

"Is that all?" There was no mistaking the perplexed tone.

"Uh . . . yeah. See you Friday night." He hung up the phone gently and turned to stare at the encyclopedia opened up on the couch in front of him.

CHAPTER 5

Bryce made one last swipe with the razor, ignoring the blood-shot eyes that stared back at him from the mirror, then glanced at his watch. It was already a minute past seven o'clock. He grabbed a towel and moved quickly into the living room of his apartment and turned on the television. The pleasant voice of the host of "Good Morning, America" came on immediately. Bryce watched for a moment, wiping the last of the shaving cream off his face, then moved back into his bedroom and finished dressing. The brief news summary carried a one-line item on the passage of the Hawkes/Larkin bill, but he only half listened to the other news, the weather, and the stock-market reports.

Several times his face pulled into a frown as his mind jumped back to the bizarre happenings of the previous night, but each time he thrust the thoughts away quickly. He would try to sort out that experience when he had some quiet moments.

He walked into the kitchen as the show's host began to intro-duce their first special guest, the star of a controversial television series. He screened out the inane chatter as he got a glass of orange juice, a bowl of "Total," and a piece of toast.

As they took another commercial break, Bryce rose and took his dishes to the sink. He stopped long enough to jot a note or two on a pad. The senator had a speech to give to the Washing-ton Press Club tomorrow, and he was mulling some phrases over in his head. By the time the advertisements had finished and the voice of the host came back on, Bryce was in brushing his teeth in the bathroom, only half listening again now, his mind already practicing some of the phrases to see how they felt. He reached for a glass and turned on the water.

"Ladies and gentlemen," the affable host of the show was saying, "in our news summary, we heard about yesterday's significant Senate victory on the Hawkes/Larkin bill."

Bryce shut off the tap, took a swallow of water from the glass and began to rinse out his mouth.

"Our next guest will have to do with that Senate action yesterday."

Curious, Bryce stopped, cocking one ear.

"Ladies and gentlemen, please welcome to our studio a very special guest. Here by special permission of the Council of Founding Fathers is Mr. Nathaniel Gorham, one of the original signers of the Constitution of the United States."

The glass slipped from Bryce's fingers and hit the washbasin with a crash, spraying the front of his shirt and pants with water and glass.

Bryce crossed his bed in two great leaps, lost his balance as he hit the floor, and slid into the chest of drawers, cracking his shin hard against the corner. With a yelp of pain, he grabbed his leg and half hopping, half hobbling made it into the living room. He stopped, staring, then slowly sank down onto the couch. The nightmare was starting all over again.

There on the screen, sitting in the same chair the movie starlet had occupied a few minutes previously, was Nathaniel Gorham. And the host of "Good Morning, America" sat across from him, relaxed and smiling, as though having someone from eighteenth-century colonial America was not in the least bit out of the ordinary.

"Mr. Gorham, welcome to our show. It is indeed a privilege for us to have you here."

"Thank you." Gorham looked around. "So this is how they do this television thing? Amazing, just amazing!"

There was no mistaking it. It was the same deep voice, the same thin face and sharp angular features, the same piercing

dark eyes that had confronted Bryce last night. And the costume—it looked totally authentic. His shirt was ruffled at the
throat and sleeves, the coat black and long enough that if he
were standing it would come to mid thigh. His pants, also black,
ended at the knee. White stockings and buckle shoes completed
the outfit. The only difference was the hair. Last night it had
been loose and shoulder length. Now it was pulled back tightly
from his face and fastened in a bun at the nape of his neck.

Once again Bryce's mind was tumbling like a rubber ball
down a coal chute. There had to be an explanation. He clenched
his fists, feeling the edge of madness pressing in on him again.
He forced his mind away from it, concentrating on the television set before him.

"Tell us more about this Council of the Founding Fathers,"
the host was saying.

Gorham readjusted himself slightly, then nodded thoughtfully. "Well, all of us who were privileged to have had a part in
the forming of this great country still get together on a regular
basis."

"In the world of spirits?" the host broke in.

"Well, I suppose you could call it that. We prefer to think of
it as the adjoining sphere."

"Could you name some of those on the council?"

"Well, there are all of the names you would recognize—Washington, Jefferson, Franklin, Tom Paine, Paul Revere. There are
over three hundred of us, actually. I wish all were as well known
to this generation as the others. Every one played a part—along
with thousands of others whose names are not in any history
books."

The host of "Good Morning, America" nodded thoughtfully. "We are most interested in hearing more about what this
great council of yours does, Mr. Gorham. But first let's take a
commercial break." He looked straight into the camera. "Stay
right with us, we'll be back in a moment."

Bryce leaped to his feet as an idea struck him. Last night, in
the encyclopedia, as he had been looking for Gorham's name,

there had been a full-color picture of the signing of the Constitution, the famous one—he couldn't think of the artist—that hung in the Capitol building. He looked around, saw the book on the desk where he had dropped it the night before, and limped over to get it. He turned quickly, found the heading for the Constitution, then turned more slowly. There it was. Painted by Howard Chandler Christy. And below it, as he had remembered, was the little sketch that gave the key to the forty or so figures in the painting.

Bryce ran his finger down the names quickly, passing over George Washington's and Ben Franklin's. Then he saw it. Number twenty-two! Nathaniel Gorham. It was the man on the far left, nearly out of the picture. With his pulse suddenly pounding, he forced his eyes up to the copy of the painting. There was a involuntary gasp, then Bryce let the book down slowly until it sat on the desk.

One could dress in costume, and a television studio could bring on an actor posing as one of the founding fathers as a gimmick. But could they make him into the same man as the picture in the encyclopedia?

Suddenly he had another idea. He moved quickly to the television, turned on the video recorder, and checked to see if it had a tape in it. If there was some evidence, something to show to others, then he could validate his sanity. He punched the buttons and started the tape rolling, just as the host's cheerful face reappeared on the screen.

"Once again, ladies and gentlemen, we have in the studio with us, Mr. Nathaniel Gorham, one of the original delegates to the Constitutional Convention held in 1787. Mr. Gorham, tell us why this group you call the Council of the Founding Fathers has sent you to visit the twentieth century."

Bryce leaned forward, listening intently.

Gorham grew very serious. "Well, the primary reason is that we are still very much interested in what you people are doing with the nation we gave you."

"And is the council pleased?"

"With some things, most definitely. You have come to greatness in so many ways."

"But in other things . . . ?" he prompted.

"We see some things that are deeply alarming."

"Such as?"

"Well, just let me give you one example. When we drafted the Constitution, we went to great lengths to provide a set of checks and balances between the three branches of government. That was the only way we saw to create a strong central government and yet still keep it from becoming a tyranny. Yet today, you have created numerous so-called government agencies that violate this system of checks and balances."

"In what way?"

"You've given some of these agencies not only the power to make laws, but also to adjudicate and enforce them. In other words, some of these agencies now have administrative power, judicial power, and legislative power all under one head."

Gorham's voice was rising in intensity. "And what is worse, these agencies are under the direction of people who are *appointed* officials. They are not elected by the people!"

The horror was so evident on his face that the host smiled. "Well, there are certainly plenty of people who would agree with you on that. And this new amendment that passed the Senate yesterday? A lot of people are saying that this will return government back to the people. How do you feel about that?"

Gorham smashed his fist down against the arm of his chair, startling even the host. "That is a damnable bill!" he roared. "Damnable! It cannot be passed. It threatens the very heart of the freedoms we fought for. You may as well gut the whole Constitution, for it breaks down the check-and-balance system almost completely. How can you have a strong president if he can be tossed out of office at every whim? And how can the Congress function without set terms of office? Already your senators and congressmen are so worried about winning the next election, they can hardly function. This amendment will put that completely in shambles!"

40

The camera had moved in tight on Gorham now. He leaned forward and peered into the lens. Bryce felt a sudden chill, as though Gorham were looking directly at him. "We gave the best blood of our generation to win liberty for ourselves and our posterity. Would you throw it away so cheaply? And with the very instrument we gave you to protect it? How can you be so blind?"

"Okay, Bryce, what is it you want me to see?" Senator Hawkes settled into the chair across from Bryce's desk.

Bryce got up and walked to the cabinet and opened it up. He turned on both the television and the video recorder. "It's only about a three-minute clip."

He hit the play button then returned to his seat. The recorder clicked and whirred; then settled into a low hum, but the television screen was filled with snowy whiteness.

Bryce waited a moment or two, then got up and returned to the cabinet. He pressed the fast-forward button. He could hear the recorder respond, but still no picture appeared. "Hmmm. I thought it was right there." He hit the stop button, then ejected the cassette. It was at the beginning, exactly as he had rewound it before he had left his apartment. He put it back in and fast-forwarded it for a moment, then hit the play button again. But still there was nothing but a blank screen.

"Maybe it's further in," the senator suggested helpfully.

Grimly, Bryce leaned on the fast-forward button again, a sense of foreboding coming over him. Suddenly the screen filled with images, and he let off the button, stepping back.

The tape slowed to show a sleek Mercedes Benz sports coupe racing through the Swiss Alps. Bryce stabbed at the buttons and the tape stopped.

Bryce turned slowly, somehow not really surprised. "I guess I lost it."

"Well, at least you got the commercial," Hawkes said with a laugh. Then sensing Bryce's disappointment, he added, more kindly, "What was it?"

"An interview on 'Good Morning, America'."

"You mean Michaelson?"

Bryce blinked. "Who?"

"Michaelson."

Bryce was still uncomprehending, and Hawkes gave him an odd look.

"Representative Michaelson, Republican Representative Howard Michaelson, from Oregon. Our most vocal opponent in the House."

"Oh, *that* Michaelson." Bryce was groping wildly.

"Yes, they did a quick interview with him on the show this morning. Didn't you see it?"

"I . . . I must have bumped channels or something. I didn't see Michaelson. I must have recorded something else."

"What?"

Bryce let out his breath slowly, shaking his head, feeling as though the ground were swirling around him. "I don't know exactly who it was. Somebody talking about the Constitution."

"And?"

"And . . . well, he made a point or two that could harm us. I . . . I wanted you to see it," Bryce finished lamely. "See what you thought."

"Hmmm. Too bad you lost it." For a moment, Hawkes gave him that shrewd, appraising look that Bryce knew so well, then finally shook his head and moved to the door. "Why don't you write me a summary of what it was?"

As the senator shut the door, Bryce once again walked to the cabinet and started the recorder. He rewound it to the beginning then stared at the blank screen as the whole thing replayed through to the point where the commercial appeared. Then he sat down slowly and stared out the window at the nation's capitol.

CHAPTER 6

Bryce leaned forward in his chair, rubbing the back of his neck slowly as he stared at the computer screen, rereading the concluding lines of the speech he had just written. He nodded in satisfaction. It was good. Good enough to give to the senator for his review in the morning.

In fact, it had been a good three hours—not only because he was pleased with the product, but also because it had kept his mind occupied with something besides Nathaniel Gorham. He raised his hands to the keyboard again, typed in the commands for filing the document, shut the computer off, and stood up. The building was quiet now. It was nearly six, and the rest of the staff had left over an hour ago. He liked this time of night best. No phones, no constituents dropping in with this or that request, no media people pressing for information.

At that moment the phone in his secretary's office started to ring. He grabbed his phone and pushed the line that was blinking. "Senator Hawkes's office."

"Yes, is Mr. Sherwood there?"

It was a feminine voice, pleasant, with just a trace of huskiness to it. His mind raced, trying to place it. "This is Mr. Sherwood."

"Oh, hello. This is Leslie Adams."

Of course. He smiled. "Well, hello. This is a surprise."

Slight hesitation. "I didn't know if you'd still be in the office or not."

"Just finishing up."

"I see. Well, I . . . "

There was a short pause, and he sensed what was coming.

"I'm sorry, but a problem has come up with Friday night."

"Oh?"

"There's been a meeting called. I have to be there. I really am sorry."

"I see."

"Perhaps some other time."

It had been a long and frustrating day. And playing games had long ago ceased to interest him. He took a breath. "Look, Leslie, I'll tell you what. We've both been out of high school for a while now, so let me ask you straight out. Do you really mean that about some other time, or is that just a polite way of saying, 'I'd really rather skip it'?"

There was a soft intake of breath, a pause, then finally she laughed. "That is the straightest talk I have ever heard from a politician."

He smiled back, softening a little. "And that non-answer makes you as good as any politician I've ever heard."

"No evasion, I was just a little bit taken aback by your question."

"So?" he pressed.

"Well, I would have to admit that I am a little nervous about the coming duel, as you call it, but no, this is not a polite brush-off. I really do have a meeting that's just been called, and I really do have to be there." There was a brief pause. "And I really would like to do it some other time."

"How about tonight?" he asked bluntly.

Silence.

He relented a little, feeling a twinge of guilt for his abruptness. "Look, I'm sorry. It's been kind of a crazy day here. Why don't I just call you sometime."

"Could you give me an hour?"

Now he was the one caught by surprise. "What?" he finally managed to say.

"I promised Frank—the president of our group—that I'd finish a project for him, but I can be finished in an hour."

"You're serious?" he asked, more pleased than he had expected to be.

"Why not? You keep slamming these stinging serves into my court. So I'm returning one. Did you really mean it about tonight, or was that just an attempt to call my bluff?"

"I really meant it."

"Then I accept."

"Great! Do you like Chinese, Mexican, or Italian food?"

"Mexican," she said without hesitation.

"Wow!"

"Wow what?"

"Thank you for not saying, 'It doesn't really matter to me, Bryce, whatever *you* like.' That is refreshing honesty for a change."

"Ah, the heavy burdens of the single male." There was just the tiniest trace of tartness in her voice.

"Sorry, I was trying to compliment your honesty."

"And I'm sorry. I tend to bristle too easily."

"Probably a good characteristic in a duel."

She laughed.

"So, seven o'clock then?"

"Fine. Do you know where the Cooper Building is on Third Street?"

"Yes."

"I'll be out front."

"Great, I'll see you then."

Bryce watched the six o'clock news and was relieved that there were no surprises. No weird stuff. And in fact, the reports on the passage of the proposed amendment were overall very favorable. Several polls were showing a 65 percent approval rate from the people.

Just as the news was finishing, the phone rang again, this time on his private line.

"This is Bryce."

"Bryce, Elliot Mannington."

"Oh, hello."

"Listen, I've just got a minute. I'm glad I caught you. The full board met this morning. Your appointment is finalized."

"Great!"

"I talked to Senator Hawkes a few minutes ago and gave him the news."

"Oh." Bryce felt a stab of disappointment. Senator Hawkes had been very good to Bryce Sherwood, and he had wanted to tell him personally, break it as gently as he could.

"He was disappointed, of course, but he's pleased for you. Can we meet sometime tomorrow, start working out the details of the transfer?"

"Sure."

"Shall we say three-thirty at my office?"

"I'll be there."

"Good. See you then." And he hung up.

It was a quarter to seven when Bryce straightened the papers on his desk, stood, and put on his coat. He checked to make sure everything was off, then started out. He made it to the doorway of the outer office when he suddenly froze in midstride. He turned back slowly, feeling the hair on the back of his neck start to rise. The sharp click from inside his office had been unmistakable. Now he jumped, his eyes widening as a new set of sounds came clearly from his doorway. There was no mistaking what it was. The combination of buzzes, beeps, and hums was as familiar to him as the sounds of his BMW. It was his computer booting up!

In one instant he grabbed an umbrella that hung on a coat rack behind the secretary's desk, and lunged toward the door, the umbrella poised to strike. There was a sharp crash as the door flew back and hit the wall, then Bryce pulled up short, dumbfounded.

The office was empty! It was still full daylight, and Bryce's chair and computer were fully bathed in the last rays of the sun. No one was there!

He whirled around, jerked the door back, and looked behind it. Nothing!

Then suddenly he jumped, nearly dropping the umbrella. The keyboard started to click! Someone was typing, slowly, almost hesitantly. In one leap he was on the other side of the desk, his umbrella-sword pointed at the space beneath his desk—the only place left where a person could escape detection. Nothing!

Bryce lowered the umbrella slowly, chills racing up and down his back, his breath coming heavily as he stared at the computer terminal. The cursor was blinking steadily on a new line. Directly above it were the words, HELLO, BRYCE SHERWOOD.

Then, even as he stared, there was a distinct click, and on the screen the letter "T" appeared.

Bryce clutched at the umbrella, raising it like a ball bat, and took one step toward the computer. Then the "H" key clicked down and up. He stopped, too shocked to move further, and watched as slowly but inexorably one key after another clicked and the letters appeared on the screen.

T-H-I-S B-E-A-T-S A Q-U-I-L-L A-N-D A-N I-N-K-W-E-L-L-!

No! It couldn't be! He tossed the umbrella on the desk and leaned over the keyboard, his mouth tight. He was a competent typist and his fingers fairly flew.

W-H-O A-R-E Y-O-U-?

There was a two- or three-second pause and then a key clicked. Once again, slowly, as though each key had to be sought for, the next line began to fill.

W-E-L-L-, I-T I-S-N-'-T B-E-N F-R-A-N-K-L-I-N-.

Bryce stared, then fell back two steps. There over the keyboard, looking almost like flecks of dust in the sunlight at first, but gradually forming, appeared two hands. At first totally transparent, they quickly took on form and shape. They were big and well worn, the knuckles gnarled and scarred. The fingers

47

were searching back and forth, then suddenly stabbed at a key, then another. Now wrists began to materialize, then black sleeves and white ruffles protruded from them, and finally the rest of the body formed rapidly—the broad shoulders, the finely cut head with the nose sharp and aquiline in profile.

Bryce sank slowly into a side chair as Nathaniel Gorham finished typing and peered at the screen. He gave an audible grunt of satisfaction, then turned to look for Bryce. When he saw the look on Bryce's face, his eyes widened.

"Oh," he said, a bit startled. He looked at his hands, then down at his feet, which were just becoming fully visible now. Finally, he turned back to Bryce. "Well, judging from your expression, I guess you can see me now, huh?"

It didn't register. Bryce just continued to gape at him, his jaw slack.

Gorham's heavy eyebrows narrowed. "Look, I know this all comes a little hard for you, but the sooner you start accepting what your eyes are telling you, the sooner we can get on with this."

"On with what?" Bryce finally managed.

"With getting this amendment thing put to rest."

"The amendment?" Bryce echoed.

"Of course. You think I came down just to play with your writing machine?"

"Are you . . . Are you really Nathaniel Gorham?"

"Of course. You think I'd make up a name like that?"

"And . . . " Bryce let his breath out slowly, still fighting off the dreamlike quality of what was happening. "And you really are from . . . the seventeen hundreds?"

"Absolutely." He peered at Bryce closely. "So now what? Are you ready to talk?"

Bryce rubbed his eyes, still dazed. "Am I really supposed to just sit here and accept the fact that I'm talking with a ghost?"

Gorham winced. "Please! Not *ghost*. I mean, really, that word has such ridiculous connotations."

"Then what?" Bryce burst out, the frustration suddenly boiling over. "Spirit? Specter? Spook?" He laughed, a bit more wildly than he had intended.

"Are you about through?" Gorham said dryly.

"Or, how about goblin? Or . . . or boogeyman?"

"How about human being?" Gorham asked quietly.

That brought Bryce up short, and the twisted smile slowly disappeared.

"I'm no different than you," Gorham went on softly, "except for the fact that you still inhabit your mortal body and mine lies in a churchyard in Massachusetts."

Once again Bryce felt the rush of madness rising. "Why *are* you here?" he finally whispered.

"The Council of the Founding Fathers sent me. I was chosen because you're from Massachusetts, and I was a delegate from that state."

"But why? Why *me*?"

"I told you. The Council of Founding Fathers is deeply concerned about this amendment you and the senator rammed through the Senate yesterday."

Gorham began to pace, obviously getting agitated. "It's foolish business, Boy, foolish! We couldn't just stand by and let you throw away all we worked for."

"You haven't answered my question."

That caught the older man in midstride. He turned back, puzzled. "What question?"

"Why me? If this is really happening, why did you come to me? Why not to Senator Hawkes, or the president of the United States for that matter?" He shook his head. "Or if you really wanted to change things, why not appear during a full session of the Senate?"

Gorham nodded. "Good question. There are two reasons, actually. The first is simple. The Council of Founding Fathers is not allowed to interfere directly in the events of your world. To appear directly to the president or to try scare the Senate into a different vote is much too direct."

Bryce threw up his hands. "And this isn't!" he cried.

"Not in the same way. But the second reason is as important as the first."

"What?"

Gorham suddenly reached into a vest pocket and pulled out a pocket watch. "But I believe you've got to be meeting Miss Adams for dinner. I—"

Bryce started. For some obscure reason, his date with Leslie had completely slipped his mind. He glanced at his watch. It was eight minutes to seven.

"I'll see you tomorrow," Gorham said, putting his watch away. "Then we can really talk."

He started to fade rapidly, to the point that Bryce could see things starting to appear through him.

"Wait!" he cried.

The fading halted, and Gorham's quizzical look was barely discernible in the dimming light of the office.

"What is the second reason?"

"You are more important than you think in this whole thing," Gorham said quietly. "The council sent me to see if I could change your mind."

Bryce gave a bark of derisive laughter. "You came to a senator's aide to try to change the course of American history?" Bryce laughed again, a hollow sound without mirth. "Boy, do I have some bad news for you."

Gorham didn't smile. "Don't underestimate yourself, Son. Even though they were just trying to flatter you last night, what Mannington and Jennings said was true. You do have great potential."

Bryce's head came up sharply. "You know about that?"

"Of course. That's what finally convinced us we had to do something." He smiled faintly at the dazed look on Bryce's face. "But in spite of their motives for doing so, what they were telling you was the Lord's truth, Lad. You're at a pivotal spot."

When Bryce just stared back at him—or through him—he smiled again. "Well, don't you keep Miss Adams waiting. She doesn't know it, but she's on my side. Listen to her. She's got some good common horse sense. And we'll talk some more tomorrow.''

And with that Gorham was gone, leaving Bryce to stare into the empty air where he had been just moments before.

CHAPTER 7

Still churning from his encounter with Nathaniel Gorham, Bryce swung over to Third Street and found Leslie waiting for him at the curb. She was wearing a dress of soft floral pastels and a pale pink linen blazer. Bryce caught an envious look from a passing male as he helped her into the car.

She seemed genuinely pleased to see him, and as they drove south out of the city and along the Potomac, they kept the conversation easy and filled with lighthearted banter. Bryce felt the tension slowly melting away, and he realized that he was finding the company of this crusading young volunteer very pleasant medicine.

The Casa del Sol was a small Mexican restaurant tucked off one of the main streets of Alexandria, Virginia. It wasn't long on decor, but the two olive-skinned brothers from Guatemala played authentic Central American music, and the food beat anything Bryce had found between D.C. and Boston.

Dinner was pleasant, and Leslie seemed to enjoy both the music and the food. Now as Bryce watched her, he noted how the pale pink of her blazer set off the tanned skin and wide, green eyes. That, added to the dark hair that framed her face, made the overall effect very nice indeed. Washington had a considerable number of lovely women, and at twenty-seven, Bryce had dated his share of them. But while there were some who might outdo Leslie in sheer beauty, Bryce couldn't remember one that had drawn his approval quite so readily. There was an openness, a frank earnestness about her that he found even more attractive than her physical beauty.

She looked up suddenly, catching him, and cocked her head, her eyebrows rising quizzically.

"Would you like some fried ice cream?" he said quickly, to cover himself.

"*Fried* ice cream?" she echoed, pulling a face.

He nodded. "Don't knock it if you haven't tried it. It's great stuff. What they do is take a ball of ice cream, dip it in a caramel sauce, roll it in some kind of crunchy stuff, then put it in a deep-fried pastry shell. It really is good."

She hesitated only for a moment. "All right, I'll take your word for it."

Bryce beckoned for the waitress, chalking up another point in Leslie's favor. One of the things that irked him most about women he dated was when they went to great lengths to let him know they had offered all on the altar to the great God of Slenderness. Nothing deterred these worshippers—not social etiquette, not the risk of offending a hostess who had labored for hours preparing a meal. They shrank in horror from anything with more than three and a half calories per ton, and watched him with sad, mournful eyes, daring *him* to be so insensitive as to eat as if there were no Bathroom Scales awaiting him at the judgment. When Leslie had hesitated, he had expected more of the same, and it pleased him greatly that she had surprised him.

Again he suddenly realized she had caught him watching her and was returning his gaze with questioning eyes. He smiled and looked away, then looked back in time to see a smile start to play around the corner of her eyes. "Is all this being nice to me an initial feint to throw me off guard before the duel begins?"

"Absolutely," he said in mock seriousness. "Want to eat your fried ice cream before I unsheathe the swords?"

She laughed lightly. "The condemned is given a hearty meal, right?"

"Exactly!"

At that moment, the waitress reappeared with their order. He fell silent until she left, then nodded toward the ball of ice cream. "You first."

Picking up her spoon, she took a bite, then smiled. "Ummm. That really is good."

"Great, another convert." He picked up his spoon and they ate in silence for a few moments. He finally spoke without looking up. "So how did you ever come to be a high-school teacher?"

"My father teaches history at George Washington University. From the time we were little, he took us to every major historical site along the eastern seaboard. I grew up loving history."

"And is high school just a stepping stone to a college professorship some day?"

Her eyes widened slightly at his perceptiveness. "Well, at first that was my plan. I was sure I would hate dealing with teenagers—I mean all the horror stories you hear about what goes on in the classroom."

"I heard that's where the nuclear arms race first started."

She smiled. "I guess that's true of some of the inner-city schools, but not at Arlington."

"And now? Have you changed your mind?"

She shrugged. "I don't know. I'm just finishing a master's degree at Georgetown. I'd like to go on for a doctorate. Right now I find the high-school age exciting. Their minds are so pliable."

"So's Play Doh," Bryce remarked dryly.

She tossed back her head and laughed. "Are you really that cynical about today's youth? It isn't *that* long ago that you were one of them."

He pulled a face. "Actually, I had to speak at a high school once not long ago. Covered an assignment for Senator Hawkes. I found the kids as a whole loud, obnoxious, overdressed, growing up too fast with too much. And yet they were also bright, articulate, full of so much potential. Somehow it was exhilarating and depressing all at once."

She nodded soberly. "The permissiveness of this generation is creating numerous tragedies, but I find it more exhilarating than depressing to think that I might shape and mold those minds."

For some reason, at that moment, the image of Nathaniel Gorham popped into Bryce's mind. He frowned slightly, playing absently with his ice cream. "And so, do you teach those pliable young minds that the Constitution is the answer to all of our national dilemmas?"

She rocked back slightly, taken by surprise. Finally she forced a small smile. "Did I just detect the launch of the first strike?"

He pulled a face, cursing himself. He had spent the night steering the conversation safely through the mine fields; then, without thinking, he had opened up with a broadside salvo when she was least expecting it.

He tried to cover it with a smile. "Sorry, I lost my head there for a moment."

But there was no answering smile. She was silent for several seconds, then nodded. "Yes, as a matter of fact that is what I try to teach them. Guilty as charged."

Mentally kicking himself, Bryce searched for a way to rectify the damage, but she wasn't about to sit dead in the water waiting for him to fire again.

"I guess it is a little disconcerting," she said evenly, "for you and the Committee on Constitutional Reform to have young people who value this country and who understand what made it strong. That will certainly make your task more difficult."

Bryce gave her a long searching look, knowing that there was little choice left now but to answer. "And you don't see any danger in that? I mean, treating the Constitution with this sense of reverential awe?"

"No," she replied, with just a touch of barb in her own voice. "I think the danger lies with those who view their own wisdom with reverential awe."

"Look," he said, trying to keep his voice light, "I have as much respect for the Founding Fathers as you do, but I don't think we honor them by blindly accepting the Constitution as though it were the Ark of the Covenant or the tablets from Sinai."

Bryce had cut his teeth on debate, and in spite of his previous resolve he found himself being drawn into it. "Leslie," he said, "we're no longer talking about a collection of small, rural colonies that were protected by two oceans. We're part of a worldwide community that is interdependent economically, socially, and militarily. The farmer in Montana or the steel worker in Pittsburgh can be as profoundly affected by Japan's economic policies as they can by a decision of Congress."

"Not nearly as profoundly as they will be if they lose their Constitutional freedoms!"

"We are not talking about losing Constitutional freedoms!" he burst out. "All we are trying to do is make a very large and unwieldy government more responsive to the voice of the people."

"Now you sound like a recording of Elliot Mannington the Third," she said quietly.

It hit home and he instantly bristled. "Why is it all you pulpit thumpers insist that you're the only ones who love the Constitution? I love America as deeply as you do." Nathaniel Gorham's face flashed before him again. "And I think I love it every bit as much as the Founding Fathers."

He sat back, a little surprised at his own intensity. Leslie's eyes had dropped, and she studied her hands carefully. Finally, she set down her spoon. "It's been a lovely evening," she said, voice low. "I guess it's time to go."

Bryce took a deep breath, then let it out slowly. "Leslie, look, I . . ."

She looked up at him, her eyes unreadable.

"I apologize. That remark about pulpit thumpers was totally out of line."

"It was no more out of line than my comment about Elliot Mannington. I'm sorry too."

He forced a smile. "What say we put away the swords and sign a truce, at least for tonight?"

56

She smiled faintly. "Where's the pen?"

But the damage had been done. They finished their dessert pretty much in silence, and though the ride home was pleasant enough, the earlier warmth was gone, and the barriers were clearly back in place.

When he let her off at her house his nerve failed him, and his previous determination to try to set another date with her faltered. He drove home slowly, his mind alternating between self-recriminations for blowing it with Leslie and the depressing realization that tomorrow he had to face additional visits from one Nathaniel Gorham, whose body lay somewhere in a graveyard in Massachusetts.

CHAPTER 8

Even though it was barely 7:00 A.M., someone was already at the bank using the automatic teller machine, so Bryce shut off the BMW's engine, stepped out of the car, and leaned back against the fender. It was going to be another scorcher in the nation's capital—it was already getting uncomfortably warm, and the humidity was rapidly becoming oppressive.

The woman at the machine, a slender, well-dressed young brunette, finished her transaction and returned to her car. Bryce watched her, absently comparing her to Leslie. He shook his head in sudden irritation and moved to the machine. What was it about Leslie that he couldn't shake her out of his thoughts?

He inserted his card and punched in the code number without thinking. Suddenly he started. Out of the corner of his eye he saw that a man in a business suit had come up behind him. Bryce moved his body slightly so the man couldn't watch the screen, a little annoyed. ATM etiquette called for standing back a polite distance while another completed a transaction.

Punching in the amount on the keypad, he asked for a hundred dollars, then waited. There was a soft whir, then the machine started clicking out the five twenties.

"Well I'll be a two-legged stool!"

Bryce whirled, then groaned.

"How'd you do that?" Gorham demanded, staring at the money.

"Gorham?" Bryce blurted, unable to believe his eyes. "Is that really you?" The face was unmistakable, with the sharp, angular features, the hooked nose. But what a transformation! Three-piece gray pinstripe business suit, maroon handkerchief in the pocket, gray and maroon tie, gleaming black wing-tipped shoes, hair short and neatly trimmed, expensive-looking steel-rimmed bifocals. He could have walked through any corporate board-room in America and never raised an eyebrow.

He looked down at himself, then smiled primly. "Judging from the expression on your face, I guess I look okay."

Bryce just nodded slowly, still eyeing him up and down.

Gorham stepped forward and peered at the machine, leaned over, tried to see where the money had come from, all the time shaking his head. "Incredible," he mumbled softly. "Absolutely incredible."

Suddenly Bryce's irritation was back. "Can't you just leave me alone? Why don't you go haunt the IRS or something?"

The gray eyes narrowed slightly as Gorham straightened. "You know, Sherwood, sometimes you can be an insolent pup. My patience is starting to wear a little thin."

"*Your* patience is wearing thin! What about mine?"

"I'm not here to keep your patience intact!" he shot back. "I've tried the gradual approach, tried to let you get used to the idea of me. And all you do is moan and complain." His eyes narrowed. "But I'm through, Lad. This is serious business I've come on, and it's time we talk."

Bryce looked around quickly. Then he turned back, his voice a low growl. "I don't want to talk to you. Especially not here."

"Fine," Gorham snapped. "I'll see you at the office." He raised a hand, one finger up, as though he were hailing a taxi. Then he was gone.

"Wait!" Bryce looked around wildly, suddenly picturing the results of having Gorham show up in Senator Hawkes's office. "Come back!"

"What?"

He jerked around. Gorham was sitting in the passenger seat of the car, arm resting comfortably out the window.

Bryce sighed. "All right. You win."

"Good. I'll ride as far as the Capitol with you."

Muttering angrily, Bryce collected his money, stabbed at the keypad, waited for his receipt, then stalked to the car.

"That would sure make life a whole lot easier," Gorham said slowly as Bryce got in beside him.

"What?"

"Having your own money machine."

Bryce stared at him, then suddenly roared with laughter.

Gorham looked surprised, then instantly his mouth tightened. "What's so funny?"

"Nothing," Bryce said, trying to hold it in. "Just welcome to the twentieth century."

"Well, so much for the twentieth century."

Bryce looked over at his traveling companion to see what had drawn the comment. They were moving slowly, one of the tens of thousands of cars carrying the army of federal workers to their battle stations in the central city. There was an occasional honk, and now and then someone would spurt forward, cutting in and out, trying to pick up a space or two in the traffic jam, but for the most part the drivers were docile and patiently inched forward at a stop-and-go pace.

"What's that supposed to mean?" he asked.

Gorham swung his head to look back on the long lines of cars. "I could drive my wagon from Boston to New York faster than this."

"It's only like this at rush hours."

Gorham snorted. "I've seen your so-called freeways. What an ironic name that is! I don't know what hell is like, but I would think that New York City at five o'clock is enough to make any sinner totally repentant."

Bryce chuckled. "Except for about eight million New Yorkers."

"You think the twentieth century is so hot?" Gorham pushed on, obviously still smarting from Bryce's comment fifteen minutes earlier. "Well, you can have all your fancy little gadgets and your money machines. You're the instant-on, instant-off generation. Everything's got to be fast for you people." He lifted his hand in disgust, waving at the sea of cars around them. "I guess it's only right that this is where it all gets you."

There were several seconds of silence as Bryce, sobered, considered that. Then his curiosity got the better of him. "So you watch us?"

There was no response, and he decided to push it a little. "What *do* you do up there?"

"What makes you think it's *up*?"

That startled him. "You mean it's not?"

"You'll find out for yourself, soon as not."

Bryce's head snapped up. Gorham ignored his questioning look, but Bryce wasn't about to let that pass. "Do you know how soon . . . I mean, do you know when I'm coming up—uh, . . . or over, or whatever it is?"

There was a faint smile. "Don't know when. But you are, sometime, sure as Molly's cow gives white milk."

Bryce relaxed, feeling a little ridiculous for the sudden rush of fear that had grabbed him.

"Now," Gorham said, "let's get on with what I'm here to talk about."

"The amendment," Bryce said flatly, feeling any enthusiasm go out of him.

"That's right. Why is it you can't see the long-range implications of what you're about?"

"I guess for the same reason you can't see that the document you drafted, good as it was for your time, needs some revision."

"Ah, yes," Gorham drawled sarcastically. "My time. Tell me again how wonderfully advanced you people are, how far you've come since we simple folk inhabited the earth."

61

Bryce flushed a little. "I'm not saying you were simple, but can you really sit there and tell me that the age of the musket and the bayonet is the same as the age of thermonuclear weapons and the B-1 bomber?"

"Now you're being asinine. You know I'm not saying that."

"Well, then. Our society faces a set of challenges that are much different than the ones your generation faced."

"No question about that," Gorham said tartly. "I mean, all we had to do was try to keep people free and happy, see that they had good honest work to do, tame a continent, fight off a big superpower that was trying to colonize the world. Nothing really unique like your generation faces."

"All right, all right!" Bryce cut in. "I get the point."

"Do you?" Gorham retorted, peering at him. "Every generation has tended to look on the past with an air of condescension. I call it historical snobbery, and your generation is smitten with one of the worst cases ever."

Bryce had no answer for that.

Gorham stopped, shaking his head. "Good land, Boy, are you really that naive? Can't you see that the real question isn't whether it's bombs versus muskets or wagons versus automobiles? It still comes down to more basic things like people's right to life, to liberty, and to peacefully enjoy the fruits of their labor."

They were moving into the city now, and Bryce slowed to a stop as the light turned red and pedestrians streamed across the walk in front of them. He glanced at them, then at Gorham, then solemnly put his hand over his heart. "Amen, Brother!"

Gorham's mouth tightened into a hard line.

"Well," Bryce said, as the light changed and the sports car accelerated smoothly again, "isn't that what I'm supposed to do when I hear the words, 'life, liberty, and the pursuit of happiness'? Come on, Gorham! You know this amendment does not take away those basic human rights. Not in the least."

62

Gorham gave him a long, searching look, then finally said quietly, "And that is where you are wrong, my young and very foolish friend."

"No!" Bryce retorted sharply, suddenly tired of it all. "That's where you're wrong. Regular elections and a congress and president hammering out national policy were fine when there were thirteen colonies and a population of less than five million. You haven't seen the docks of Boston lined up with acres of Toyotas and Hondas. You haven't walked through the empty steel mills of Pittsburgh."

He threw up his hands. "You accuse me of being narrow minded. Well, maybe it's time you opened your eyes, Mr. Colonial America. Maybe it's time this tired old democracy you created got a new shot of adrenalin."

"We didn't create a democracy," Gorham said softly.

That cut Bryce's next sentence off before he even started it. His mouth opened, then clamped tight again.

Gorham just shook his head, sadly and with infinite weariness. "You still can't see it, can you?"

"All right, so you created a republic and not a democracy. It still is supposed to represent the voice of the people."

"Do you really understand the difference between a republic and a democracy?"

"Yes," Bryce snapped right back. "First class in law school, thank you." He lifted his voice, as though reciting. "In a democracy, authority is derived directly from the masses, through mass meetings or other forms of 'direct' expression of will. In a republic, authority is derived from elected representatives who best represent the people they serve."

Gorham snorted in disgust. "Yes, that sounds about like the depth that your modern universities are teaching it. Land a mighty, Boy! Can't you look any deeper than that?"

Bryce opened his mouth to fire off a sharp retort, but Gorham's eyes were suddenly snapping fire. "Don't you know why you've got a national debt big enough to build every man, woman, and child in the solar system a solid-gold outhouse?

63

And why half the world is on the verge of bankruptcy? Don't you see the basic flaw in a true democracy?"

There was no response from the driver of the BMW.

"A democracy cannot exist as a permanent form of government because sooner or later the people come to realize that they can vote themselves direct benefits out of the public treasury. From that moment on the majority always votes for the candidate or the program promising the greatest benefits from the public treasury. That's what killed Rome. Even the emperors couldn't keep up with the constant demand for bread and circuses. Sooner or later the government goes bankrupt. Democracy always collapses over a loose fiscal policy, and inevitably, no matter how long it may take, it will always be followed by a dictatorship."

Bryce's mouth had opened again, but now it shut slowly. Gorham sat back, staring out the windshield into space, breathing hard. "And all this talk about giving more say to the people. That's what's happening here. In the last few years the primary function of the United States government has become the redistribution of wealth—taking money through taxation from one segment of society and giving it to another. And all of those who keep wailing about giving more power back to the people— men like Mannington and Sterling Jennings, men like Senator Hawkes and the other bubbleheads up there on Capitol Hill— they think they can stay in power by continually gratifying—" his voice grew heavy with sarcasm, "—the will of the people."

Finally, he turned and looked at Bryce, his eyes grave. "Let me tell you something, Sherwood, and if I can't get one other thing through your head, you let this one stick. The real movers behind this amendment, the ones who drive those long black cars and live in the luxurious apartments in Georgetown, don't give a tinker's dam about the voice of the people. They're after power, pure and simple. The Constitution stands in their way, and their sole purpose is to remove that and every other stumbling block that prevents them from reaching their goal."

Bryce blinked. "That's a little strong, don't you think?"

"You think you're in some game of mumblety-peg here?" he roared. "They're users, Sherwood! You can help them achieve their ends, and so they'll use you. Oh, they'll reward you handsomely in the process—until your usefulness ends. Then they'll cast you aside, just as they're doing to Senator Hawkes."

That snapped Bryce's head up sharply.

Gorham gave a short, bitter laugh. "Your myopia is something to behold, Boy. You think Senator Hawkes *wants* to retire next term?"

"He's . . . he's almost seventy."

"And how many senators do you know who are currently over seventy and still serving well?"

Again Bryce started at that. There were at least a half a dozen, maybe more. And with their seniority, they were some of the Senate's most powerful voices.

Gorham just shook his head. "You know what your problem is, Sherwood? The other day Elliot Mannington stuck stars in your britches and you haven't been able to sit down comfortably ever since."

Bryce felt like he was standing at the bottom of Niagara Falls, trying to look up. Gorham's words cascaded over him one burst after another.

Gorham took a deep breath and finally turned to Bryce. When he spoke again, his own voice was low and tinged with sadness. "It's bread and circuses all over again, Lad. And your amendment is one more step on the long road to so-called democracy. If you can't see that, and get others to see it, then may God help you, Son. God help you all."

CHAPTER 9

As Bryce drove up to the Marriott Hotel and gave the BMW to the parking attendant, his mind turned to Nathaniel Gorham. Since their confrontation in the car the previous morning, Gorham hadn't reappeared. Bryce was on his way in now to listen to Elliot Mannington give a speech on the proposed amendment to the League of Women Voters, and what Gorham had said about Mannington kept running through his mind. "After power pure and simple. He's put stars in your britches. They'll cast you aside once they've used you."

He shook it off angrily as he walked into the hotel, realizing that this was exactly what Gorham had meant to do—sow seeds of doubt. True, the old man had made some good points. His analysis of the weakness of a democracy had been sobering, and Bryce was still weighing it in his mind. But the attack on Mannington showed that Gorham still ignored the hard realities of the day. He had never gone through a session of Congress and watched the paralyzing crawl at which it moved. He hadn't lived through the "imperial presidencies" of a Johnson or a Nixon.

Bryce entered the banquet hall and scanned it quickly. There were several empty places at tables up nearer the front, but before he could start for one, a waiter approached. "Good evening, sir."

"Good evening." Bryce handed him the ticket Mannington had sent over.

"Just a moment, sir. The tables are preassigned. I'll get your number from the maitre d'."

"Fine." Bryce had known he would likely end up at a table with someone he didn't know. He really didn't look forward to that, but he could hardly miss a major speech by his future boss.

Suddenly he started. The waiter had gone to a small desk where a man in black tie and tails was sitting with a book open in front of him. Several other waiters were also there, waiting to get their assignments. But it was not the waiters that Bryce was staring at. It was the maitre d', who looked very much like Nathaniel Gorham. Someone stepped in front of him, blocking Bryce's view. Unable to believe what he thought he had seen, he started toward the desk, but suddenly his waiter was back. "This way, sir."

Bryce glanced once more over his shoulder, but there were too many people now, and he finally shrugged it off. They threaded their way through the elegantly dressed crowd, drawing some curious looks as they went, but Bryce saw no one he recognized. As the waiter approached a table with two empty seats, Bryce stopped in midstride. A couple was already seated. The man, in his late twenties, was laughing at something his partner was saying. Bryce had never seen him before. But the woman sitting next to him was Leslie Adams.

The man looked up and smiled in tentative greeting. Leslie started to do the same, then her jaw dropped as she saw who it was.

"Here you go, sir," the waiter said, pulling out a chair.

Bryce swung around. "Uh . . . " he said in a low voice. "Don't you have something a little closer to the front?"

"Sorry, sir. All the places are assigned." He bowed and departed hastily.

Bryce turned around, sighed, then smiled wanly. "Hello, Leslie."

By the time they were starting on the salad, Bryce had dreamed up and then rejected nearly a hundred reasons for excusing himself from the table. The fact that Daniel Fowler was the associate editor for the *American Conservative*, a well-known and prestigious national magazine; and the fact that Leslie was there as his partner; and the fact that he was not only very good looking, but a very likable guy; and the fact that when she watched him, her eyes followed his every expression—none of that added greatly to Bryce's comfort. And he could hardly wait until Mannington started his speech. That would really relax things.

Suddenly the waiter was back. "Mr. Fowler?"

Fowler looked up. "Yes."

"You have a telephone call. There's a phone in the cloakroom."

Fowler excused himself and then walked away. Leslie turned back and began toying with her salad. Bryce took a breath and plunged. "Look, Leslie, I'm really sorry about this. I had no idea you were here. And then to end up at the same table. I can't believe it." He thought of the maitre d' again, and was pretty sure he had his answer now.

She smiled faintly. "It's all right. Daniel's a good friend. He doesn't mind."

Good friend, Bryce thought, enviously. Was that what it took to get those eyes to look at you like that?

Leslie said, "I guess if I had thought about it, I should have expected you'd be here."

Bryce gave her a rueful grin. "Well, I did think about it, and the last place I ever expected to see you was at a speech given by Elliot Mannington."

She laughed softly. "Daniel's magazine wanted him to cover this and gave him two tickets. When he invited me, I thought, 'Why not?' "

"It's always good to take the measure of the opposition, right?"

She nodded, then dropped her eyes to concentrate on her salad.

Bryce watched her for several seconds, working up his nerve. "Leslie?"

Her eyes came up, wide pools of emerald, watching him carefully.

"Look, this is going to sound crazy, but remember what I said the other day about not playing high-school games?"

"Yes."

"Well, I don't know what it is about you . . . " He stopped. Was that stupid enough? He took a quick breath, and tried another tack. "These last few days, well, we've hardly gotten off to the best start."

Though her face was sober, her eyes were flecked with little sparks of amusement. "And here I was trying so hard to impress you."

He laughed. "Yeah, me too."

For a moment both were lost in thoughts of their previous encounters, then Bryce cleared his throat. "Look, this is really tacky. I mean, here you are with Daniel and all, and soon as he leaves I make this pitch."

"Oh?" Her face was sober, but her eyes were teasing him. "Just what pitch are you making?"

"I'd like a chance to try again." He held up his hands quickly. "I promise, no philosophical discussions, no politics. I'd just like a chance to get to know you better."

She took a deep breath, not meeting his gaze, and Bryce felt his heart sink. "I . . . All right, I'll be honest too. I would like that. I really enjoyed dinner the other night." His hopes leaped, but then she pulled a face. "Up to a certain point." Down they went again.

She hesitated, obviously groping for the right words. Then suddenly she looked up and past him. Bryce turned and saw that Fowler was coming back toward the table.

She spoke more quickly now, and softly. "I'm not sure we can leave the other out of it, Bryce."

"I know, but I'd like to try."

69

Fowler was nearly on them. She looked away. "Let me think about it," she murmured. Then she looked up and smiled, a radiant smile meant only for Fowler. "Anything the matter?" she asked.

He shrugged. "We had a bad connection. Whoever it was finally hung up."

The waiters were just clearing the salads away when a deep voice behind Bryce spoke. "This is your table here, sir."

Bryce looked up, then nearly dropped his fork. It was the same waiter that had escorted him, but this time the man with him was banker Gorham—three-piece business suit and all. The steel-rimmed glasses were back, and the hair was considerably more gray than maitre d' Gorham's.

Bryce opened his mouth to protest, then clamped it shut again as Gorham sat down and smiled at each of them and Fowler made the introductions. He sat back, face grim. As if it hadn't been bad enough before.

All of a sudden Gorham snapped his fingers, pointing to Leslie. "Didn't I see you on television the other day?"

Bryce groaned inwardly. That Gorham was up to some mischief, there was no doubt, but Bryce had at least expected a decent interval before he launched into it.

Leslie seemed pleased as she nodded. Gorham snapped his fingers again. "Let's see, you're a volunteer worker with that organization, uh . . . tell me the name of it again."

"The STC. Save the Constitution."

"Yes, that's it. It's a great work you are doing, young lady. I'm sure the Founding Fathers would be proud of you."

Bryce rolled his eyes, then went immediately stone faced as Leslie glanced in his direction. She smiled. "Mr. Sherwood was my opponent in the debate that day."

Gorham glanced at him, nodded briefly. "Oh, yes. I remember." Then instantly he turned to Fowler. "And you, Mr. Fowler. Why does your name ring a bell with me?"

Leslie answered for him, telling what Daniel did.

"Of course," Gorham crowed, "the *American Conservative.* I've read several of your articles. In fact, I thought your recent series on the effect the Constitution has had on other world governments was superb. Just superb."

And so it went for the next ten or fifteen minutes. Gorham charmed both Leslie and Fowler, neatly steered the conversation away from himself, and all but virtually ignored Bryce. For the most part Bryce sat quietly and listened, contributing only a polite nod or a strained smile at the appropriate places.

Finally, the bridgehead had been laid, and Gorham got down to what he was there for, which was, of course, to get in a few more licks at the senior aide to Senator Benjamin Hawkes. He turned the discussion to the subject of Mannington's upcoming speech and proceeded to batter away at the foolishness of the whole concept of the amendment. Leslie kept glancing in Bryce's direction, sensing his growing irritation.

Finally Bryce had had enough. "Just out of curiosity, Mr. Gorham," he broke in, "your name rings a bell with me. Wasn't there a man by that same name during the Revolutionary War?"

Gorham shot him a warning look, which Bryce fielded with bland innocence. "A British spy or something?"

"I beg your pardon," Gorham said archly. Then instantly his eyes narrowed as understanding dawned.

Bryce just put on a more thoughtful look. "I know there was somebody by that name," he mused. He turned. "Leslie, you're the American history major; does that name sound familiar to you?"

She thought for a moment. "No, I don't think so."

Bryce bit back a smile as he saw the look Gorham flashed her. A couple of more shots like that and Bryce figured he'd be even with Gorham for sending him to this table.

Gorham drew himself up to full height. "There *was* a man by that name," he said archly, "but he was not British. He was a delegate to the Constitutional Convention from Massachusetts."

71

"Really?" Leslie asked in surprise.

"Yes, really," Gorham responded, just a bit tartly. "In fact, he's one of the original signers of the Constitution. His signature is right there on the document."

"Along with George Washington's and Benjamin Franklin's?" Bryce breathed in wide-eyed wonder. "And are you related to him in any way, Mr. Gorham?"

To watch Gorham wiggle out of that one would have been sweet indeed, but unfortunately, at that moment the president of the National League of Women Voters stood up and rapped the microphone sharply. "Ladies and gentlemen, may I have your attention please?"

Though Bryce had been around Elliot Mannington quite a bit, he had never heard him speak. He had expected to be impressed. In actuality, he was totally dazzled. No wonder he was a confidant of presidents. Mannington was poised, witty, extremely articulate, and thoroughly charming. If he had prepared notes, he had memorized them completely. There was no reading, no lecturing. This was a master orator in tune with his subject, and more importantly, completely in touch with his audience. By fifteen minutes into the speech, the crowd had interrupted him five times with warm and enthusiastic applause.

"I'll grant you this," Gorham murmured in an aside to Bryce during a new spate of applause, "he's good. Too good."

Bryce merely nodded. Mannington was a lot more than good. He was superb. The other three at the table became increasingly more grim as the speech continued, and it became painfully obvious that Mannington had the vast majority of the crowd with him.

After another burst of applause, Bryce leaned slightly to his left. "You think the new amendment is out of touch with the will of people?" he said into Gorham's ear. "Well, you just take a look at that, Mr. Gorham!"

Gorham didn't even look at him, just stared straight ahead.

Ten minutes later as Mannington finished with a ringing call for change in government, the audience shot to their feet, and the applause was deafening. Bryce came up too, clapping enthusiastically. Slowly, Leslie and Fowler stood too, but Gorham sat stubbornly in his seat, ignoring the angry glances he was getting from those around them.

When the president of the League of Women Voters had effusively thanked their speaker and all for coming, Gorham excused himself quickly and walked away, face grim. Fowler pushed back his chair, then turned to Bryce. "Is it true that you've been asked to chair the national committee for ratification of the amendment?"

Leslie's head snapped around like it was on a rubber band. "Yes."

Fowler stood up. "Congratulations," he said, his face expressionless.

Leslie stood quickly.

Bryce stood too, watching only her. "Leslie, I . . . "

She shook her head quickly. "You know that thing we were talking about earlier?"

He felt his heart sink. "Yes."

"All things considered, I don't think it would be a good idea."

He nodded, hardly surprised. "I understand," he said softly.

Bryce waited for nearly five minutes, then finally decided there was going to be no chance to get with Mannington tonight. He was still mobbed with some of Washington's finest. Bryce maneuvered to the point where he could catch his eye. When he looked up, Bryce mouthed, "I'll call you tomorrow."

Flushed with triumph, and obviously enjoying every moment of the results of it, Mannington waved his assent, then turned back to a woman who was heavy with diamonds.

As Bryce moved into the main lobby of the Marriott, he pulled up in surprise. Most of the crowd had gone now, but

Leslie was standing on the far side of the lobby, alone. He changed direction in midstride and came up on her blind side.

"Hello."

She turned around in surprise. "Oh, hello."

"I thought you had gone."

Nodding toward the cloakroom, she shook her head. "That call for Daniel came through again."

Bryce nodded, and for a moment considered trying just one more time to pick up the pieces. Then as quickly as the thought had crossed his mind, he dismissed it. The damage from the dinner seemed total. So he just smiled briefly and lifted a hand in farewell. "It was good to see you again, Leslie. Good night."

"Good night."

He got about five steps, then, "Bryce?"

He turned back.

Her voice was soft. "I'm sorry for being so rude in there. Congratulations on the new assignment." She took a breath. "Even though I deeply disagree with what you're doing, I have to admit they've chosen the best person to head up the campaign for ratification."

Why did she do that! Here he was, ready to walk away; then she turned those deep green eyes on him and melted every resolve he had made to put her behind him once and for all. He nodded his thanks. "Coming from you, that means a lot." Pause. Ideas for prolonging the conversation popped into his head, but Fowler was still just a few feet away on the phone. "Good night, Leslie."

"Good night, Bryce."

Just as Bryce turned and started away, there was the sharp sound of a phone being slammed into its cradle. Fowler's voice burst out, angry and frustrated.

Not wanting to eavesdrop, but still curious, Bryce moved across the lobby and took up station near a pillar where he could watch. Fowler was in front of her, obviously upset. Leslie kept nodding sympathetically. Then, to Bryce's surprise, Fowler thrust something into her hand, turned and walked swiftly out of the hotel. Leslie watched him for a moment, then moved toward the desk of the bell captain. Bryce leaped into action. He headed directly for the desk.

"Leslie?"

She turned, surprised to hear his voice again.

"I just saw Daniel go hurrying out. Is everything all right?"

She sighed, looking toward the door. "There's some kind of problem at the press that does his magazine. He had to go right over."

Bryce shook his head, managing to look appropriately stricken. He hesitated for an appropriate moment, then gave her a tentative smile. "Listen, if you need a ride, I know the way to Arlington."

She searched his face, then finally shook her head. "Thank you, but he gave me money for a cab."

He grinned. "Washington, D.C., at night is not a safe place for a single young woman."

Again those green eyes probed his, unreadable. Then slowly they softened. "That's what I've been told."

They were standing at the front entrance to the hotel, in the softness of the night, not talking, content to look at the lights of the city. The red BMW pulled around and stopped directly in front of them. "Here it is," Bryce said, as the parking attendant started to get out. Bryce leaned down and opened the door for Leslie. She slid in, and as he shut the door, the attendant came around behind him.

Fishing a dollar from his pocket, Bryce turned. "Thank you very—" He stopped, his eyes widening.

"Thank you, Sir!" Nathaniel Gorham said, taking the dollar and dropping the keys into his hand. He was now in coveralls and baseball cap and smiling sardonically at him. Gorham glanced at Leslie in the car, and the smile broadened. "Too bad about the young lady's escort."

Bryce gave him a sharp look. "Yes, isn't it."

"Good night, sir." There was a soft chuckle. "And good luck."

On the ride home Bryce drove leisurely. This time he wasn't about to make the same mistake he had made before. He skirted widely around any talk of the amendment or the Constitution or Elliot Mannington or anything that stood one chance in a million of somehow leading them back into the quicksand again. At first, Leslie was quiet, almost reserved, but when he started telling her some of his experiences in law school, she started to come out of it, and soon they were swapping horror stories about graduate school and she was laughing softly along with him.

And even more heartening, when he pulled up in front of her house, she wasn't out the door and into the house before he could shut off the ignition. That was definite progress.

She leaned her head back and closed her eyes. He watched her for a minute, then asked, "When do you start school?"

"The week before Labor Day."

"Do you look forward to that?"

She turned her head and nodded. "I know it sounds crazy, but yes, I do. I really do."

"I don't think it sounds crazy at all."

"And what about you? You always hear about the Labor Day recess in Congress. Do Senate aides get a recess too?"

"For the most part." He chuckled. "Not quite as long as the senators do, but yes. I'm going home to Boston, as a matter of fact. Then down to Cape Cod with my folks."

"Really?"

"Yes. I haven't been home since Christmas. Mom's threatening to shut down the government if I don't come."

"Cape Cod," Leslie said dreamily. "You always read about that. Is it as wonderful as they say?"

"It's delightful. We've been going up there since I was a kid. I love it."

76

She turned back, watching out the window as the leaves rustled with a soft breeze. Finally she straightened. "Well, this seems to be getting to be a habit, but thank you once again for the ride home."

"Two times does not a habit make. But you're welcome."

She reached for the door handle.

"Look, Leslie, I—" He stopped, not sure where to go from there as she turned back to face him.

"What?"

"All right, look," he said, suddenly determined. "I'm going to give this one last shot. Then, I promise, I'm out of your life. No more rides from the bus stop. No more horning in on you and Daniel at dinner."

She gave him a mock scowl. "That's the second time you've mentioned Daniel this evening. I told you, he's a good friend. That's all." She let him digest that, then, "And what if I told you that I'm not sure that's what I want?" she said softly.

"What?"

"To have you out of my life."

He looked at her closely, his hopes leaping. "Then let's give it a chance. Let me show you that underneath this bumbling, stick-the-foot-in-the-mouth exterior, there actually lives a half-decent guy."

She smiled, almost shyly. "I've known that since that first day on the Capitol steps."

Bam! Two in a row. He was really soaring now. But the corners of her mouth pulled down slightly, and he instantly felt that familiar sinking feeling.

"But that doesn't change things between us."

"So what if we do have a few philosophical differences—"

She hooted at that.

"All right, so I'm on Alpha Centauri and you're on Betelgeuse. I accept that, but I can't just walk away without giving it one more try."

"I don't want you to just walk away either, and yet—"

Bryce exploded. "There you go again. 'And yet,' 'but,' 'if only.' I know all of those are there, but I don't care. I'd like to see what it is that's clicking between us. Or else let it die once and for all."

"But—" She caught herself at his look and laughed, holding up her hands. "Okay, I see what you mean."

"All right, Miss Adams, here's my deal. It's the sixth of August. Let's give this thing until the first of September. Until then, no duels. As far as this amendment thing goes, I'll listen to every argument you can throw at me. I really will listen."

She started to answer, but he held up his hand. "I'm not even asking for equal time. I'll listen to you, that's all. We'll start with Saturday night. The New York Philharmonic is in town giving an all-Beethoven concert at the Kennedy Center. Then you can choose the next activity. I'd love to have you take me to some of the historical sites around here. Then I'd like to take you to a great little pizza place up in Chevy Chase, and then—" He stopped, a little breathless. "And then, come the first of September, if we find we're still cruising in different star systems, I'll say thank you very much, it's been wonderful, and I really will bow out of your life."

There was silence in the car for several long seconds, then finally she laughed quietly, but her head was half turned and he couldn't read the emotion behind it.

"What?" he asked, holding his breath.

"No wonder the Hawkes/Larkin bill passed the Senate."

He grinned in relief. "That bad, huh?"

Her hand came over and touched his arm. "Bryce, if I tell you I want to think about it, are you going to throw a hammerlock on me and insist I decide this minute?"

"*Is* that what you're going to tell me?" he shot right back.

"No hammerlocks?" His expression was so rueful that she laughed aloud. "Promise?"

"All right, I promise."

"Okay, then my answer is yes, I want to think about it."

He sighed, so deeply that she laughed and shook her head helplessly. Then she opened the door. "Thank you, Bryce. For the ride." She paused, her lips softening. "And for not giving up."

"On that you *do* have my promise."

Forty-five minutes later, Bryce unlocked the door to his apartment, tossed his suit coat on the couch, and went straight to the phone.

"Leslie?" he said, when she answered on the other end.

"Yes?"

"This is Bryce. Have you thought about it?"

She laughed, and it was the same delightful sound he was coming to love. "You promised."

"It's been almost an hour. Work on a problem much longer than that and your brain cells turn to rubber."

"I can't believe you!" He could picture her shaking her head.

"Would you like me to talk to your parents or something? Give references? Send my blood type?"

Now he really had her laughing. "Thank you, no."

"Well," he said sadly, "I thought it was at least worth a try."

"I've already talked to my parents."

"Good. Listen, I really wasn't going to bother you tonight. I'll call—" He stopped. "You what?"

"I already talked to my parents."

"*Really?*"

"Really." Now she was laughing at him. "I told them I really liked Beethoven."

Bryce sat back slowly. "I thought you said you wanted to think about it."

"I did think about it. All the way up to the front door."

"Are you kidding me?" he asked suspiciously.

"No, Bryce, I'm not kidding you." Then suddenly her voice became serious. "But there's one condition."

"What?"

"I don't want it to be all one sided. I don't want you to hold back what you are thinking and feeling."

79

He thought about that. "All right, but I really am willing to listen to your side."

"How willing?"

He sensed a trap but didn't care. She had said yes. That was enough. "Willing willing. Why?"

"Would you like to come to dinner Sunday?"

That really threw him, but he had the answer processed in milliseconds. "I'd be delighted. But what has that got to do with being willing to listen?"

"You think I'm an avid constitutionalist?" she said, her voice suddenly teasing. "Just wait until you meet my father."

CHAPTER 10

In some ways, the next two weeks were like a cross-country flight—for the most part smooth, but with occasional patches of turbulence.

The concert at the Kennedy Center went without a hitch, and Bryce was delighted to find that Leslie had the same deep love for classical music he did. Dinner at the Adams home the following day turned out to be a more pleasant experience than he had expected. Leslie was the eldest of three children, and Bryce was an instant hit with Kellie, a sixteen-year-old younger version of Leslie, and Keith, a mischievous and yet delightfully bright twelve-year-old. The conversation had barely touched on the amendment, and so Leslie's solemn prediction about her father had gone unfulfilled. The one time Paul Adams turned the conversation in that direction, his wife shot him such a look that Bryce had to bite back a smile. What he would have liked to have known was, who had given the warning—Leslie or her mother.

On Monday he picked Leslie up after work. They went to Old Georgetown, leisurely strolled through the shops, had dinner, then walked for almost an hour through the posh residences. When they returned to her home, her parents were in the living room, her father reading, her mother doing counted cross-stitch. It was that night that Bryce came to realize why Nathaniel Gorham had gone to such trouble to set things up between him and Leslie at the Marriott Hotel. Between Leslie and her father,

Bryce was suddenly getting all the pro-Constitution arguments he could handle.

They had dinner twice more at the Adams home, and now any restrictions on Paul Adams had been lifted. Dessert was barely over before the kids were off to do other things and the debate picked up where it left off the time before.

Paul Adams, a tall, wiry fifty-year-old, taught history and political philosophy at Georgetown University. He was articulate, had a quick wit, and was brilliant in debate. It was not hard to see where Leslie got her rapier tongue and deep, passionate patriotism.

Vera Adams, a gentle woman of immense graciousness, reminded Bryce of his own mother. For the most part, she would sit back, content to watch her husband and daughter lead out in the conversation. But when she spoke, she almost always made a telling point. Occasionally, when the debate became too fierce, she would even jump in on Bryce's side, much to his gratitude.

But that in no way meant Bryce was going down to defeat. In some ways, it was just the opposite. He found that the debates forced him to crystalize and articulate his own thoughts and feelings. It was excellent preparation for the coming battle over ratification. Though officially Bryce would stay with Senator Hawkes until the day after Labor Day, he and Elliot Mannington were meeting regularly now to plan strategy and set up the national network for the campaign. Often Bryce would serve as the devil's advocate and throw Paul Adams's logic at the chairman of the Committee for Constitutional Reform, telling Mannington they needed to sharpen their response to the opposition. And Mannington was no mean opponent. He seemed to relish the challenge and would tackle Bryce's arguments head-on, providing some excellent rebuttals. Then Bryce would take that and his own thoughts back to the next session at Leslie's home. It was a roller-coaster ride, but he loved it.

And yet some days, he and Leslie seemed content, almost glad, to set the whole subject aside and let the relationship have its head. One Saturday they spent a lazy afternoon playing in the surf of the Atlantic. Another, they spent all day wandering through the numerous buildings of the Smithsonian.

That night, after a visit to the little pizza restaurant Bryce had told her about, they came back into the city and walked slowly along the Mall, past the Reflecting Pool, talking quietly of trivial things, sometimes not talking at all. They ended inside the Lincoln Memorial, and there, beneath Lincoln's brooding gaze, he kissed her for the first time. She pulled back, looking up into his face, her eyes troubled. But finally she just sighed and laid her head against his shoulder, letting him hold her.

The following Saturday they went on what Bryce called his "Civil War orientation tour." They visited a couple of national battlefield monuments; stopped at Richmond, capital of the Confederacy; swung over to Appomattox, where General Lee signed the surrender document that ended the Civil War; then ended at the elegant and serene Monticello, home of Thomas Jefferson. It was dark by the time Bryce pulled the car up outside her house and turned off the engine.

Leslie laid back with a contented sigh and closed her eyes. "Thank you, Bryce. That was a delightful day."

"Thank *you.*" Then he laughed softly. "You know how inadequate you make me feel?"

She opened her eyes in surprise. "Inadequate? Why?"

"I minored in American History at Harvard. And yet I learned as much today as I did in my whole undergraduate career."

She smiled, closing her eyes again. "Is wild exaggeration a typical Sherwood family trait?"

"No, I mean it. You made those places come alive. I've studied about those battles, but you can tell me exactly what happened and their overall importance to the Civil War. You know every monument, every item in the museums and why they're significant. I was impressed."

She turned and laid her head against him, snuggling in as he put his arms around her. "Well, even if it is a shameless lie," she murmured contentedly, "I love it. Keep it up."

83

He laid his cheek against her hair, his mind returning to something that had happened that afternoon. They had been walking across the great sweep of lawn that fell away from the graceful mansion at Monticello. They were holding hands and Leslie's head was half turned, looking at the view below them. And suddenly, at that instant, it had hit Bryce with a jolt how much this dark-haired, emerald-eyed woman was coming to mean to him. It was sobering, for he wasn't sure that Leslie felt the same. That she cared for him was clear enough. But at that moment he realized that he was thinking more and more in terms of long-range commitments, something he had never done before.

She turned her head to look up at him. "Tell me what you are thinking."

He looked into her eyes for several moments, almost sinking into their depths, then leaned down and kissed her softly. "I was thinking," he said, when he pulled back, "that this was a great day. Thank you."

"Ummm," she murmured. "It was for me too." She reached up, touching his cheek. "One of the best yet." Then she straightened and kissed him back, a warm, soft acceptance of his thanks.

When she finally pulled away, her eyes were shining.

"Leslie, I—"

Her hand flew up, and she pressed one finger to his lips. "No. Not tonight, Bryce."

His eyes widened in surprise. Had she known what he was going to say?

"We'll come back to reality tomorrow. But let's not spoil today."

"Okay." He sighed, wishing something could somehow just wipe away the differences that lay between them.

"Speaking of tomorrow, Mom wants to know if you would like to come to dinner."

He shook his head. "You know I always enjoy that, but I'm starting to feel guilty about how much I'm over here."

"Look, Mr. Sherwood," she said with a laugh. "My mother is a quiet woman, but underneath it all she's every bit as strong minded as my father."

"And her older daughter," he said with mock gravity.

She smiled. "That too. But when Mom says ask Bryce to dinner, I ask you to dinner, and you'll just have to live with your guilt, Mr. Sherwood."

Leslie's mother shooed Bryce and her husband out of the kitchen with gentle but insistent firmness. Leslie smiled at Bryce, and he finally surrendered. He tossed Leslie the dish towel and went out into the living room where her father was waiting. Evidently, Bryce had left him smarting a little after their last session, and he had barely sat down before Paul picked up the discussion exactly where it had left off. Bryce smiled to himself. No wonder Gorham hadn't appeared to him for the last week or so. There was no need. He couldn't have a better advocate for his position than Paul Adams.

But on this Sunday afternoon, somehow the mood imperceptibly changed. Paul said something about the logical fallacies of "Bryce's amendment," and Bryce retorted a little more sharply than he had intended. Paul fired right back, and suddenly the usual amiability was gone. They were head to head, impassioned, intense, their voices rising.

Leslie was suddenly at the doorway, bringing them both to silence. She didn't meet the gaze of either of them, just looked out the window. "Bryce and I are going to walk down to the park for a while."

Her mother was suddenly beside her. "Good idea." She gave her husband a sharp look.

Bryce stood, puzzled, and yet glad for the reprieve. "Thanks again for the dinner, Mrs. Adams. It was great as usual."

"You're welcome." She looked at Leslie. "You go on now. We'll have some pie in an hour or so."

"Leslie?"

She looked up from where she had been pulling up blades of grass and making a little pile in her lap.

"What's the matter?"

She shook her head, suddenly fighting tears.

Bryce moved over and put his arm around her. "What is it?"

Again she shook her head, turning away so he couldn't see her.

He took his arm off her shoulder, and leaned back, debating whether to venture a guess. Then he had a better idea. He raised his hand, and with his finger began tracing letters on her back. I L-O-V-

"Please, Bryce, don't."

He took her firmly by the shoulders and turned her around. "I do," he said softly. "Don't ask me how it happened, but I do love you."

"I told you it would come to this." She brushed away the grass from her skirt, not looking up.

"To what?"

"There in the living room, with Dad."

"What?"

"He was saying nothing more than what I believe."

"I know that."

"But suddenly I was angry with him."

"With your father?" he echoed in surprise. "Why?"

"For what he was doing to you."

Bryce just stared at her, not sure he understood.

"It's tearing me apart. I'm so sure that he's right and you're wrong. But suddenly I find myself saying that I don't care whether you're wrong or not. I don't want him hurting you."

He reached out and touched her cheek, moved by what he saw in her eyes. "He's not hurting me. That was our deal. I told you I wanted to hear your side of things. We just got a little warmer than usual today."

"I know, but it's more than that. Nothing has changed. Has it?"

86

He thought about that, searching his own feelings. "Perhaps. I don't know what to think sometimes. You and your father have some reasoning that's pretty hard to answer."

"And so do you." Her head came up in challenge. "Are you ready to turn in your resignation to Elliot Mannington?"

That caught him off guard. "I . . . No, not really."

"Exactly my point. And so we just keep making it more and more difficult."

He straightened. "That may be. I'm not sure of all my philosophical feelings any more, but this much I do know. I know how I feel about you."

She forced a smile through the tears. "You think that makes it easier?"

"It would if I knew you felt the same way."

The tears welled up again and spilled over. "Don't you know?" she whispered. "Do you have to ask?"

He nodded. "I'm pretty dense. I don't read nonverbal cues very well."

She threw her arms around him and buried her head against his shoulder. "I love you, Bryce Sherwood. Darn it all, I love you too."

Bryce laughed right out loud. "That's the most tender confession I've ever heard."

She sniffed, laughing now too, in spite of herself. "It's not funny. I don't want to love you."

He took her into his arms and kissed her gently. "Well, force yourself."

He held her that way for a long time, both of them silent; then Bryce sat bolt upright.

"What?"

He was staring at her, his mind racing.

She sat up now too. "What?"

"Oh, wow," he said, shaking his head. "This is going to sound crazy."

She laughed. "More crazy than what I just said?"

"Yes." He took a breath. "Leslie, I . . . "

She waited, watching him closely, sensing his sudden excitement.

"You start teaching tomorrow?"

"Yes, why?"

"How early could you be through on Friday?"

"Probably by two or two-thirty. Why?"

"Why don't you come to Boston with me? No, wait," he rushed on, when her mouth dropped open. "You'll love Cape Cod. And our summer home up there is big enough. You'd have your own bedroom. There's only my eighteen-year-old sister at home now. My brother's in medical school at Stanford. Mom and Dad would love to have you. We'll leave right from school and come back Labor Day evening."

She was staring at him incredulously. Finally she shook her head in wonder. "And this is supposed to be a solution to our problem?"

"I know. I told you it would sound crazy, but just listen. This will give us a chance to really talk things out. No more debates. No more arguments. We'll just talk about us. What we're feeling. Where we're going. Sort the whole thing out."

She was looking dubious and so he rushed on. "You haven't lived until you've spent some time in Cape Cod. We'll go sailing. Lay on the beach and burn. Explore the little villages."

"Wait!" she said, throwing up her hands. "I feel like I just tangled with the Massachusetts Chamber of Commerce."

He grinned. "Sorry."

"That won't solve our basic problem, Bryce," she started, then quickly put her hand over his mouth when he started to protest. "No, you listen. This will only make it harder."

He nodded, moving her hand away gently. "I know what you're saying, and I understand. But we'll talk it out, just you and me. There'll be no Elliot Mannington. No Senator Hawkes." He grinned. "No Paul Adams. Just you and me."

"And what if we can't?" she said sadly. "What if we can't work it out?"

He took a deep breath, not wanting to consider that possibility. "Then I'll do whatever you think is right."

"Oh, no. That's not fair."

He grinned. "Okay, then you'll do whatever I think is right."

She poked him hard in the ribs.

"Leslie," he said, sobering, "I don't know what we'll do. But I want to give it every chance, do whatever it takes. Okay?"

Suddenly she was smiling. "Is your father going to badger me like mine does you?"

"Oh, no," he responded. "My worry is my mother."

"Your mother?"

"Yes. I have never taken a girl home with me before. She is going to go absolutely bananas."

CHAPTER 11

One thing you had to say for Elliot Mannington. He never did anything halfway. Not even lunch. The Ristorante Mediterranean, a long brick building with a red tile roof, sat on the brow of a low hill, not far below the Arlington National Cemetery. It wasn't much of a rise, but still the city, shimmering in the summer heat, stretched out below them. As they waited to order, Bryce let his eyes run over the familiar landmarks—the Washington Monument, the Jefferson and Lincoln Memorials, and, almost lost in the haze, the dome of the Capitol.

With Leslie starting school, Bryce hadn't seen her since Sunday, but they had a date for tomorrow night. It would be here, he decided. At night the view must be spectacular. Then Friday, it was off for Cape Cod. He was looking forward to that with more anticipation than he had anything for some time.

Mannington took a sip of water, letting his gaze roam over the scene as well. "Quite a town, isn't it? If we get this amendment passed, and we will," his arm swept out in the direction of the city below them, "then you can write your own ticket down there."

Suddenly Bryce remembered what Gorham had said about Senator Hawkes in the car that morning. On impulse, Bryce picked up his spoon and starting drawing patterns on the napkin. "What if Senator Hawkes decides not to retire next term?" he asked casually.

Mannington shot him a quick look, then laughed. "Don't you worry about that. Ben won't be a problem. We'll get him an ambassadorship or something."

We? Bryce thought. It was rumored that Mannington had almost open access to the White House, but . . . Suddenly the feelings of uncertainty began to well up again.

Mannington seemed not to sense the change in his mood. As they finished dessert, he leaned back comfortably, took out a gold case, and extracted a cigarette. He tapped it lightly on the table, watching Bryce. "Are you going home for the recess?"

"Yes. I leave Friday. You know Mom. If I'm not there by dark, Senator Hawkes will have a delegation of the National Guard on his doorstep."

Mannington smiled, then reached again into his coat and took out a matching gold cigarette lighter and flicked it into flame. "I suppose your family's going down to the Cape."

"Yes. It wouldn't be Labor Day if we stayed in the city."

"Good. Look, we're going to be in Hyannis Port. There are some people I'd like you to meet. Why don't you come over for dinner Saturday night?"

Bryce was startled. No Mannington, he had vowed solemnly to Leslie. Just you and me. He could picture her face if he suggested dinner with him! Finally he shook his head. "I'd like that, but I'm going to have a guest with me."

"Fine, bring him along." He caught the expression on Bryce's face and chuckled. "Or is it bring *her* along?"

Bryce flushed a little. "Well . . . I'd feel a little funny doing that."

"Nonsense! I'd like to meet this lucky young lady. Anyone I know?"

Bryce shook his head quickly. "No, just a friend."

Mannington winked knowingly. "Okay, then bring your friend. Let's say Saturday then. Seven o'clock?"

It was like saying no to a D-9 Caterpillar. "Really," Bryce started, "I think another time—"

91

Mannington's smile hardened just the slightest trace. "These are important people, Bryce. They'll play an important role in our national strategy."

Bryce sighed. He could always leave Leslie with his folks. "Fine."

"You know where we live, don't you? Just down from the Kennedy compound."

"Yes."

"Good."

Bryce let out his breath, feeling as if Mannington had taken his elbow and was steering him down a crowded street.

For the next half an hour, and then all the way back into the city, they talked about the ratification drive—which personnel to recruit, where to set up various state headquarters, which states to target first. Bryce nodded, made appropriate sounds at the right time, and tried to put away a growing sense of uneasiness. Senator Hawkes gave Bryce a lot of head, and Bryce liked that. It was how he operated best. Was Mannington going to be this intimately involved every step of the campaign? Bryce tried to shake off his growing sense of dismay.

As the chauffeur pulled up in front of the Senate Office Building, Bryce opened the door and started to get out. "Thanks for lunch."

"Oh, by the way."

Bryce turned back.

Mannington smiled briefly. "Word on the street is that you've been seeing one of the volunteer workers from the Save the Constitution group."

That startled Bryce enough that the expression on his face gave Mannington his answer.

"Is it the same one who challenged you during that television interview that day?"

"Yes." Bryce kept his voice even, even as he cursed the town in which he lived. The proverbial glass house had nothing on Washington, D.C. A man could miss one day of washing his socks and find it plastered on the front pages of every newspaper in the city the next morning.

Mannington smiled again, but there was no mistaking what was in his eyes. "I'd think about that carefully, Bryce."

Bryce nodded, keeping his own face impassive.

"People could misconstrue that, you dating someone from the opposition."

"I suppose they could."

"Not only could, but would," Mannington said pointedly. "Well, think it over. And we'll see you Saturday."

He shut the door, and the limo moved smoothly out into the traffic. For a long moment, Bryce stood at the curb, barely aware of the stifling heat as he thought with growing resentment about the neat little box into which Mannington had just shoved him.

"Leslie?"

She looked up.

It was her principal. "Telephone."

Surprised, she hurried to the office and picked it up. "This is Leslie."

"Hello, Miss Adams. I don't know if you know me or not, but my name is Elliot Mannington."

"Yes," she said, feeling a sudden catch in her throat. Had something happened to Bryce?

"Look, Miss Adams, I don't normally interfere in other people's affairs, but . . . "

Five minutes later as Leslie came out of the office, her mouth set in a tight line, she had her second surprise. An older man was waiting in the hall. He straightened when he saw her. "Miss Adams?"

"Yes."

"I don't know if you remember me. The other night at the Marriott?"

"Oh, yes, of course. Mr. Gorham."

His eyes showed pleasure for a moment but then instantly sobered again. "I happen to know what that phone call you just got was all about. Would you mind if we talked?"

Bryce was at his computer, working hard to finish the draft of the farm bill that Senator Hawkes was co-sponsoring in return for Senator Weatherby's swing vote on the Hawkes/Larkin bill. His buzzer rang.

"Yes."

"Mr. Sherwood, it's a Leslie Adams on line one."

"Good." He punched the button. "Hi, Leslie."

"Hello, Bryce."

Her tone was even, almost cool. He didn't notice. "I tried to call you earlier, but I didn't want to get you out of class."

"Yes, I got your message."

"Good. Listen, I talked to Mom and Dad last night. Everything's set. They're really excited about your coming." He laughed. "It took me almost half an hour to calm my mother down."

There was no response, and Bryce felt the first stirring of a warning bell. "I told them we'd arrive around seven or eight on Friday. We'll just meet them at Cape Cod."

"And what about Saturday?" Leslie asked quietly.

"On the beach and in the sailboat," he said exuberantly.

"I meant what about Saturday night?"

There was a long pause as Bryce felt the bottom dropping out from under him. "Saturday night?"

"Yes. I believe the time is seven o'clock somewhere in Hyannis Port."

Bryce just stared at his desk, stunned. He had barely left Mannington an hour and a half before. He had said nothing to anyone . . .

"I appreciate getting the invitation directly from him. It gives it so much more meaning that way."

"Mannington called you?" Bryce said in disbelief.

"Yes." Her voice was hard with bitterness. "Of course the invitation came only after a very broad hint that it would really be better for your career if I didn't accompany you to Cape Cod, but if I insisted, he would really love to meet the girl who finally has Bryce Sherwood on the hook."

Bryce sat back slowly, cursing Mannington. Where did the man get off taking a hand in Bryce's private life? "Leslie, I—"

"But the phone call wasn't nearly as interesting as the visit I just had with another friend of yours."

Feeling battered, Bryce barely managed a quiet "Who?" but he was not sure he wanted to hear.

"Oh, it's been quite the afternoon."

"Who?"

"Nathaniel Gorham."

Bryce felt the breath go out of him.

"What? no innocent protestations that you don't know the man? You put up such a good show the other night at dinner."

"Look, Leslie, yes, I do know Gorham. He's . . . " His voice trailed off as he thought about how to finish that sentence.

"Why did you pretend you didn't know him?"

"That is a long story. But I give you my word, it had nothing to do with trying to deceive you."

"Is it true Mannington has offered you a shot at Senator Hawkes's job next election?"

That caught him completely off guard, and he didn't answer.

"And that they're talking about the eventual possibility of the White House?"

"Leslie, I—"

"No wonder Mannington suggested I could hurt your career."

"Leslie, listen to me. I don't know what Gorham has been telling you—"

"Well, I'll tell you one more thing he said."

Bryce sighed, cursing the old man from Boston, cursing Mannington, cursing the fact that all this had blown up in his face before he had had a chance to talk with her. "What?"

"He said that Mannington has already suggested to you that it would be better if you stopped seeing me. Is that true?"

"Yes, but—"

"And what did you say to him when he said that?"

Somehow Bryce should have been surprised, but he wasn't. Gorham was too efficient to let an opportunity like this pass. "I . . . He caught me totally by surprise. I guess I just stared at him."

"How courageous."

Bryce flared at that. "That's not fair, Leslie. If you really think I'm going to let Mannington tell me what to do with my private life, that doesn't say much about your opinion of me."

She was silent for several seconds, then sighed. "Bryce, it doesn't really matter what I think, or what you think. This whole thing just makes it clear that we have our heads in the sand. It's not going to work."

He took a breath, not wanting to ask, but knowing he had to. "So no Cape Cod?"

Her voice was suddenly low and husky. "I'm sorry, Bryce, but I can't take any more of this."

"Leslie, I can explain everything. Just give me a chance."

"Bryce, I . . . You really do have a wonderful career ahead of you. I wouldn't want slow you down."

"Leslie," he cried, pleading now.

"Good-bye, Bryce. Thank you for everything."

And with that there was a soft click, and Bryce was left to stare at the dead phone.

CHAPTER 12

Bryce worked until nearly midnight that night, finishing up the last of his work for the senator and cleaning out his office. He kept telling himself that he wasn't sure he would move his things into the office Mannington had leased for him, but underneath he knew it was a bluff. In spite of his anger at Mannington for calling Leslie, he knew he still wanted a shot at the ratification campaign. Besides, it was Gorham that was the primary target for his fury.

By eight o'clock the next morning, Bryce was packed and ready to leave for Boston. He threw the last of his luggage in the trunk and got in. As he made his way through traffic to the Capital Beltway and took the northbound on-ramp, he thrust away the thought that if it weren't for Nathaniel Gorham, he would be turning south for Arlington. But now, Leslie Adams was a dead issue. This time there would be not resurrecting it, and the sooner he accepted that the better. He selected a Beethoven symphony from his box of cassettes, put it in the tape deck, laid the speedometer on sixty-five, set the cruise control, and settled back in his seat. There would be lovely women by the ton dotting the beaches of Cape Cod, any dozen of which would be thrilled to get an attentive look from a senior senator's senior aide.

He shook his head, knowing that when he reached the point of trying to lie to himself, he was in bad shape. He cranked up the volume on the stereo and hunched down in the seat, scowling out at the world.

He crossed over into Connecticut shortly before noon and stopped for gas at Norwalk. As he got back in the car, on impulse he got out the map. He had followed Interstate 95 all the way up through Maryland, New Jersey, and New York. Tired of the urban corridor, he decided he was running enough ahead of schedule to try a little of New England's back country. If he took U.S. 7 north, he could pick up Interstate 84 at Danbury and follow it all the way to Boston. It would take him through Hartford, but that was the only large city he would have to go through.

What had started to be a cloudless day had now socked in with a solid overcast, and as he finished lunch at a small diner next to the gas station, a warm drizzle started to fall. He drove more leisurely now, letting the strains of a Mozart piano concerto and the rich green countryside massage him until the tension slowly began to slough off. The rain had increased now, and the steady swipe of the windshield wipers seemed to almost match the tempo of the music.

Half an hour out of Norwalk, the weather really settled in, and Bryce had to turn the wipers up to full speed. The clouds were dark and low to the ground, and flashes of sheet lightning rippled occasionally in the gray mass above him, followed immediately by the deep rumble of the thunder. He had driven smack into the middle of a good old-fashioned New England summer thunderstorm. Not that he minded. He had loved thunderstorms from the time he was a kid. He turned off the tape deck so as to hear the thunder better.

Five miles north of a little town called Cannondale, he came around a gentle curve where the road followed the line of the Norwalk River. The rain was coming down hard enough that he had let his speed drop to under fifty. As he crossed over a narrow bridge, a dark figure suddenly loomed up in front of him, standing right on the edge of the pavement. Bryce gasped, instinctively jerking the wheel to the left even as he stabbed at the brake. The BMW had a superb suspension system, or he might have thrown it into a broadside spin on the rain-slick pavement.

"You idiot!" he shouted as he straightened the car out, the surge of adrenaline instantly putting his heart into a thudding drumbeat. Then suddenly he slammed on the brakes and brought the car to a sliding halt. The details of the figure who had loomed up out of the storm finally registered in his brain. He yanked at the door and leaped out, staring back the way he had come.

The dark figure was trudging steadily toward him—long dark coat, knee-length trousers, white socks, head erect. Bryce groaned.

He got back in the car and slammed the door. In a moment the other door opened and Gorham slid in beside him. There wasn't a drop of water on him. "Much obliged," he said.

"What are you doing here?"

Gorham smiled briefly. "Heard you were going to Boston. Thought I'd see what my hometown looks like nowadays."

"Just like that, huh?"

Gorham scowled right back at him. "Just like what?"

"After that little trick you pulled with Leslie that's all you've got to say?" He waited, but Gorham didn't answer. Finally, in disgust, he put the car in gear and started out again. "I asked you a question."

Gorham swung around, his mouth tight. "I thought I was doing that young lady a favor by getting you two together. But when I saw what you were doing to her, I knew I had made a mistake."

"What!" Bryce yelled. "What was I doing to her? You know that dinner appointment with Mannington was not my idea. I tried to get out of it."

"Yeah, you really stood up to him."

"You meddling old fool! You think I'd let Mannington tell me what to do with Leslie? No way, man. This was just your way of getting back at me because you can't convince me you're right."

Gorham was silent, but there was a pained expression on his face as he stared out through the windshield and the rain. Finally, when he spoke, it was not directly to Bryce. "It's not surprising really," he mused. "You grew up in a wealthy home, never wanting for anything, having everything done for you. Socially sheltered, gently reared—it's no wonder you've lost the capacity to feel any commitment to something besides yourself."

"Oh, brother!" Bryce exploded. "Shall we have a little funeral music while you lament my passing?"

The old man finally turned to Bryce, eyes filled with sadness. He reached inside his jacket pocket and pulled out a sheaf of papers. "You familiar with this document?" he asked.

"What document?"

He started reading. " 'When in the course of human events, it becomes necessary for one people to dissolve the political bands . . .' " His eyes dropped further down. " 'We hold these truths to be self-evident, that all men are created equal, that they are endowed by their Creator with certain unalienable rights—' "

"Come on, Gorham," Bryce cut in rudely. "I know what the Declaration of Independence is."

"Do you know how it ends?" the old man asked softly.

Bryce's mouth opened, then shut again. His mind was racing, but he couldn't remember.

"Well," he said wearily, "let me read it to you. Perhaps you can learn something." He turned a page, skimmed quickly, found the place. " 'And for the support of this declaration, with a firm reliance on the protection of divine Providence, we mutually pledge to each other our lives, our fortunes, and our sacred honor.' "

Finally he looked up at Bryce. "You think that was an empty boast, a little grand theatrics with which to conclude the document?"

"No, I—"

"Five of those whose signatures are at the bottom of that paper were captured by the British, tortured as traitors until they died. Twelve had their homes ransacked and burned. Two lost sons in the war. Carter Braxton of Virginia was a wealthy planter and trader. He saw his ships swept from the seas by the

100

British Navy. He had to sell everything to pay his debts, and he died a pauper.

"At the Battle of Yorktown, Thomas Nelson learned that General Cornwallis had taken over his home for his headquarters. He quietly urged General Washington to open fire anyway. The home was destroyed. Nelson died bankrupt.

"John Hart . . ." Gorham's voice suddenly faltered. He took a breath, then went on, a huskiness deepening the tone noticeably. "John Hart was driven from his wife's bedside as she lay dying. Their thirteen children had to flee for their lives as well. For over a year he lived in caves and in the forest. After the surrender, he returned to find his wife dead, his children gone. *Thirteen children*, and every one of them vanished! He died a few weeks later of a broken heart."

Bryce let our his breath slowly, moved in spite of himself. "All right. I've never said that those men were—"

"No!" Gorham suddenly roared. "Don't you say it! Don't you even speak of those men. They gave their lives! They gave their blood! And here you are, pouting like a child because a young lady finally saw you for what you are."

Surprised by the sudden intensity in Gorham, Bryce did not respond, just drove on silently, moodily.

"And what about the amendment?"

Bryce snapped around, incredulous. "The amendment?"

"Yes. What are you going to do about it?"

He slammed his fist against the steering wheel. "You can't give it up, can you?"

Gorham just looked at him steadily, his eyes dark pools that could not be fathomed.

"Well," Bryce said, breathing heavily, "I'll tell you what I'm going to do about the amendment. When I return to Washington the day after Labor Day, I start work for one Mr. Elliot Mannington. And we're going to put together an organization that will roll through the states of this Union like a thunderclap through the Appalachians. You think I was committed before? Well, you watch me now!"

Gorham again made no response, just stared morosely out into the blackness of the storm. Bryce watched him out of the corner of his eye, his chest heaving with anger.

But Gorham's next words caught him completely off guard. They were spoken so softly that Bryce had to lean over slightly to pick them up. They were also spoken with a sadness so deep, it left him staring at the man. "Is there no way I can change your mind, Lad?"

"About the amendment? Absolutely not!"

Gorham sighed, a sound of deep pain. "I truly regret to hear you say that. You leave us no other choice."

Bryce snorted in disgust, and shook his head. "Oh, wonderful! Now come the dark threats, right? Shall we dance around the witch's cauldron?"

But at that instant, lightning struck about a hundred yards off to the right of the road, directly in line with Bryce's vision. He jumped sharply as the flash and shattering crack of thunder came simultaneously, rattling the car.

"Man!" he cried, "That was close!" He turned to see Gorham's reaction, then his mouth dropped open. Nathaniel Gorham had disappeared!

Any thoughts of Gorham were instantly blotted out as another deafening crack slammed off to his right. He slowed the car, momentarily blinded by the intensity of the flash. He was coming around a curve, and the rain was coming down in sheets, making everything a blur. Suddenly he yelled. A blinding whiteness was coming at him, like the high beams of some gigantic vehicle in the dead of night. He slammed on the brakes, felt the back end of the car swing sideways, then screamed as it went into a slide and slammed into the wall of whiteness at close to thirty miles an hour.

There was no shattering crash, no splintering collision. There was one brief burst of whiteness so intense that it seemed to burn his retinas, then instant, all-consuming blackness.

The first thing Bryce was conscious of was the cold wetness along the whole back side of his body. The next was the incredible glitter of stars that filled his vision. He blinked once, then again. Somewhere in the back of his mind it registered that it had stopped raining and the sky had cleared. Gradually other things began to impinge upon his consciousness—the steady, rhythmic droning of crickets; then, in deeper harmony, the raspy seesaw of frogs further away; then, finally, the fact that he was flat on his back in deep, rain-soaked grass. Slowly he pulled himself up to a sitting position, the memory of the storm and Gorham and the blinding whiteness returning.

There was a sound behind him, faint but growing rapidly in volume. He turned toward it, saw a flickering, ghostly light flashing through a stand of trees. Then the headlights of a car came from behind the trees and whipped past him, the hiss of tires on wet pavement rising, then falling in time with the sound of the engine. He ran his hands through his hair, looking around wildly, seeing little because of the temporary night blindness caused by the headlights.

Half dazed, he stumbled toward the highway, instantly soaking his pants up to the knees in the rain-soaked grass. By the time he reached the road, his night vision was returning. There was only a quarter moon, low in the sky, but it was enough to show him, as he looked back and forth in dismay, that his BMW was nowhere to be seen. What had happened? He remembered blacking out as he hit the wall . . . That brought him up short. It had been somewhere around one thirty or two o'clock in the afternoon when he had stopped for Gorham. Now it was . . . He lifted his hand, turned his wrist until the face of his watch picked up the moonlight. He drew in a quick breath. It was nine thirty-six! He had been laying there for seven or eight hours!

Alarmed now, he tipped his head back and studied the heavens above him until he spotted the North Star. To the left was north, the way he had been driving. He remembered the small town he passed just before seeing Gorham. With sudden determination he turned to the right and headed south.

He had only gone about ten yards when he saw a flash of white on the ground in front of him. He changed directions slightly, leaned down, and picked up the sheaf of papers slowly. They were barely damp. He brought them up close to his face. The light was faint, but it was bright enough that he could discern the typewritten title: "Declaration of Independence."

For a long moment he stared. This was the sheaf of papers Gorham had taken from his pocket, the papers from which he had read to Bryce. He looked around now, searching the empty roadside. There was nothing else. No car, no luggage, no other sign of Bryce's having been here except for the papers Nathaniel Gorham had somehow left behind.

Bryce folded them slowly, stuck them in his back pocket, then turned and trudged southward again.

CHAPTER 13

The town was small, no more than half a mile in length from outskirts to outskirts, and there was no highway marker to identify it. The houses were also small and older frame structures. For the most part they were dark. He passed one or two with lights and nearly stopped, but up ahead, near what must be the center of town, he could see a blue neon light blinking on and off. Dimly he thought he could make out the word *motel*.

It was a motel, and a small cafe, now closed, which together carried the rather questionable title of "Dew Drop Inn." Beneath that, the offerings of the place were listed in peeling paint—"T.V. in every room. Telephone." Singular, Bryce noted. Not "telephones," just "telephone." He shook his head and checked his watch as the neon flashed on again. It was a few minutes before eleven.

Walking to the door that had an "office" sign over it, Bryce paused. At first he thought he was going to have to roust someone out of bed, because the office was dark. But now he could see a faint light coming from a back room. From the bluish glare and the way it varied in intensity, he decided someone was still watching television. He raised his fist and knocked sharply.

He waited a moment, then knocked again, more firmly. A light came on, blinding him momentarily. Then he glimpsed a figure of an older woman who came into the office. There was the click of a lock, and the door opened slightly.

"Yes?"

"Hello. May I use your phone?"

She looked him up and down carefully, then peered past him. She was in her late fifties, perhaps early sixties. The face was narrow, the cheeks hollow, almost gaunt, the eyes quick but holding a promise of pleasantness. She was obviously suspicious but didn't seem frightened. She finished the check behind him and looked back at him.

"My car's been stolen."

Her eyes widened slightly.

"Is there a police station in town?"

She shook her head.

"I was afraid of that. Then may I use your phone?"

"I'm sorry, but state law requires that you be a guest to use the phone."

"*What?*" Bryce had heard sick excuses before, but that was the most transparent ploy for business he'd ever run into.

Her eyes were troubled, not wanting to meet his. "I'm really sorry. But I could lose my business permit."

Bryce opened his mouth to fire off a hot retort, then shut it suddenly. Unexplainably, he believed she was telling him the truth. "Is there a public phone in town so I could—"

Again she was shaking her head.

"Then could you call the police for me? Tell them my car has been stolen."

She took a breath, fumbled nervously with the doorknob, not meeting his eyes. "I can, but the nearest ISD station is Norwalk."

"ISD?"

She nodded, not reading the question in his voice. "They likely won't come this late, unless it's really serious."

"My car has been stolen! What do they want, a dead body across the hood?"

"It would be better if you waited until morning."

"All right," he said, throwing up his hands. "Do you have a room? Then I'll call them myself."

106

"Yes, I have a room." Suddenly her eyes were pleading. "But please believe me when I tell you that you are making a serious mistake if you call them tonight."

Bryce scanned her face, trying to fathom what it was that he saw there. But finally he gave up. The weariness was on him like a blanket. He didn't give one whit at this stage if there were some fat, backwoods sheriff who was going to be in a foul mood for being yanked out of bed, but he wasn't going to fight this woman over that. Once he was checked in, he would call whomever he wanted. "Just give me a room," he said tiredly.

She nodded and stepped back, opening the door wider. Bryce entered, following her as she went to the small counter. The television was playing softly, a man's voice speaking. Bryce listened absently as she fussed behind the counter. It was some kind of documentary on farming.

"Here," she said, pushing a registration card and ball-point pen at him.

He took them, noting the heading on the card: "Dew Drop Inn, Bollingbroke, Connecticut. New England Confederation." He looked again at the last three words. New England Confederation. Maybe it was the motel chain. He gave a short laugh. A chain of two, maybe. And for that matter, Bollingbroke wasn't the name of the town as he remembered it. But at this point the tiredness was seeping deeply into him, and he didn't trust his memory in the least.

He filled out the card in quick bold strokes. As he looked up, he caught her looking curiously at his clothes. Suddenly he remembered that he was still quite damp from his trip through the meadow.

He looked at himself, then laughed briefly. "I had to cut through the field. I got a little wet."

She nodded, knowing he had caught her in her open appraisal, but not seeming to care. She took the card, read the name and address, then slowly looked up at him again, one eyebrow arching upward. But all she said was, "That'll be eight dollars."

107

Bryce reached for his wallet. Eight dollars? Was that just for the room or did he get a bed with that? He took out a ten and slid it across to her.

She glanced at the bill, then shook her head, and slid it back toward him. "Sorry."

That caught Bryce completely off guard. "What?"

"I can only accept local currency."

"*What?*"

"Local currency only."

"Local currency only?" He fought to keep from screaming at her. "What is that supposed to mean?"

"There's a bank in the general store. You can exchange it in the morning."

Bryce just stared at her, trying to make that register. Shaking his head, he took out his American Express card and tossed it onto the counter. Again she picked it up. Again there was a curious look on her face. She turned it over slowly, examined the back, turned it again, examined the front.

Bryce took a breath and bit his lip to keep hold of his temper. "Don't tell me you don't take American Express either."

"What is it?"

He rolled his eyes heavenward, pleading for help. "How about VISA? Or Diners Club?"

There was no change in her expression, just the same look of blankness. He picked up the ten-dollar bill again and shoved it in front of her. "And you're telling me you won't take cash?"

She started to shake her head, then her eyes dropped to the bill. Suddenly she snatched it up and stared at it. She moved slightly so the light fell on it. She read something on the front of it, then her eyes lifted to stare at him, now for the first time frightened. "You're from the United States of America?" she asked in half a whisper.

Now it was Bryce's jaw that dropped.

She dropped the bill back on the counter as though it were suddenly hot. "You can pay in the morning," she said hurriedly, pushing a key at him. "Room one-oh-six. Around the side, then down the hall."

"What was that crack about the United States supposed to mean?"

"Nothing. I . . . I was just curious. The bathroom's at the far end of the same hall. So's the telephone."

Bryce stifled a groan. Bathroom, singular. Telephone, singular. What kind of burg had he fallen into? "Thank you," he said wearily, taking his key. He couldn't resist one parting shot. "They don't shut off the telephones at night, do they?"

She shook her head, ignoring his tone. "There will be a charge of five cents added to your bill for each call."

"Five cents?" Then he laughed, on the verge of wildness. "How did Ma Bell ever miss *this* place?"

She just watched him, eyes veiled.

"Five cents is fine. Thank you very much."

The room was tiny but neat and comfortable. Baseboard electric heaters ran beneath the window. There was a framed photograph of a man in a military uniform with lots of ribbons and medals whom Bryce did not recognize. It hung above the single, narrow bed that was covered with a plaid bedspread. The television was as tiny as the room. Half curious, Bryce clicked it on. It was black and white. A head shot of a man in a suit appeared, and as Bryce turned up the volume, he realized it was the same voice he had heard in the office. The man was droning on about farm production, and Bryce turned the channel. Nothing. He clicked it again. Then again. Nothing. Really surprised now, he went all the way around the thirteen slots. Only the farm report. Shaking his head as much in disbelief as in disgust, he turned it off again, made sure he had his key, then stepped out into the hall and went to the phone.

By the time Bryce had gone through his third operator, his head was pounding. "Look," he said, trying with every ounce of willpower left in him to hold his patience, "all I want to do is call Boston. I have given the operator the number, I have given *you* the number. I know the number is correct. It has been the

109

same number for the past seventeen years. It's my home, for crying out loud!" He took a deep breath, then spoke more pleasantly. "Did you get the area code correct?"

"What is an area code?"

"What is an area code?" he yelled. "Tell me you're joking!"

There was no response, just the sound of her steady breathing.

He tried again. "Boston's Area Code is six one seven, then five five five, three two—"

"I am sorry, Sir," came the curt reply.

This was definitely the voice of a night supervisor. And if she looked like her voice sounded, Bryce pictured her as broad shouldered, barrel chested, and big enough to eat hay and pull a wagon.

"I don't know if this is some kind of joke," the curt voice continued, "but there is no number like that in the Boston area. There is no number even close to that. Now if there is anything else we can do for you, please let me know."

Bryce threw up his hands. "All right. Let's try something else. Can you connect me to Maryland. The area code is—"

"Maryland?" The voice deepened with a sudden note of suspicion.

"Yes, you know Maryland? Mary. Land. Just north of Virginia."

"I know where it is," the voice answered him coldly.

"Okay, then, I want to call Maryland. The number is—"

"Give me the number of your permit please."

That stopped Bryce cold. "My what?"

"Your permit."

"You mean my credit card?"

"No, your permit. You must have a government permit to place a call out of the country. I need the number of the permit."

"Out of the country?" Bryce shouted. "Maryland?"

There was a long pause, and he pressed one hand against his forehead. "Okay, okay. Let's go very slowly. I know it's late. Perhaps you've had a long day. How about connecting me with the police station in Norwalk."

"The police?"

Bryce gritted his teeth. "Or the county sheriff, or whatever they happen to call themselves in this part of the country."

"You mean the ISD station?"

There it was again. "What is the ISD?"

This time the pause was positively deafening.

"I asked you what ISD stands for."

"Internal Security Division."

"Is that the state police?"

"Sir, what is your name?"

"My name?" Bryce repeated in exasperation. "Why do you need my name?"

"Just give me your name if you will."

"Bryce Sherwood."

"And where are you calling from?"

He blew out his breath, then lost the battle with his patience. "I am calling from a narrow hallway just outside the public bathroom in a little motel called—yes, ladies and gentlemen, called—believe it or not—the Dew Drop Inn. Not the 'Do Drop In.' No, that's D-E-W D-R-O-P I-N-N. It is not one of the world's finer hotels, but it will do for the night. And so, Ms. Supervisor, whoever you are, if you could simply place a call for me, I am no longer fussy about which call it is. I will take any call. Boston, Maryland, or even this ISD station if you will. Then I will go back to my small and totally inadequate bed, snuggle in for the night, and try to get some sleep."

"Which room are you in?"

"Room one-oh-six. What! You want to come and see it for yourself?"

"I will call the ISD station in Norwalk for you. If you return to your room I will call you when I have them on the line."

111

And with that there was a sharp click and the line went dead. For several seconds, Bryce just stared at the phone in disbelief, then slammed it back onto the receiver and stalked back into his room. Fifteen minutes later, when the phone had still not rung, he kicked off his shoes and lay back. Three minutes later he was sound asleep.

Just as Bryce managed to lather himself up with a foul-smelling bar of dark-brown soap, he discovered that the capacity of the Dew Drop Inn's water heater was somewhere around three quarts. The water went from hot to warm to cold in a little under a minute, leaving him gasping as he tried to rinse off.

That didn't add a lot to the dark mood that had been building for the last twelve hours. He had finally awakened again about 2:00 A.M., gotten undressed, and climbed under the sheet. The bed was so narrow that even when he folded his arms both elbows hung over the side. He slept fitfully until the sunshine coming in through his window finally awakened him about six. Then came the cold shower and the remembrance that his shaving kit was stolen with his car. Growing more foul by the minute, he combed his hair as best he could with his hands, then brushed his teeth using a finger and cold water. By the time he came back into the hall to use the phone, his mood had darkened to a full-blown thunderhead.

Ready for battle, he dialed "O" and waited. There was no response. He clicked the receiver hook sharply and lifted his finger to dial again, but it stopped in midair. He had half turned, and a small bulletin board on the wall caught his eye. In the dim light of the previous night, he hadn't seen it. Now in the full light of day he simply stared.

There was a cheap brochure advertising the wonders of the Dew Drop Inn, a colored photo of someone holding a string of fish. But that was not what he was staring at. It was the full-color map that covered two-thirds of the board.

Stunned, Bryce stepped closer. "THE CONFEDERATED STATES OF NORTH AMERICA." The title was boldly placed across the top in inch-high letters. North America it certainly was. There were the Great Lakes, the familiar lines of the east and west coasts, the huge blue gouge of the Hudson Bay in Canada. Correction. Not Canada. What should have been the eastern third of Canada was colored a light purple and labeled "The Confederation of Canadian States." Everything west of the province of Manitoba was colored orange and labeled "Republic of Canada."

Bryce's eyes ran over the map slowly, not comprehending. Instead of the familiar outlines of forty-eight contiguous states, everything east of the Mississippi was covered by three divisions. In addition to the Confederation of Canadian States, there was a small section of pink-colored area labeled "The New England Confederation." That caused him to start. That was what he had seen on the registration card last night. The pink section included everything from Maine to the southern border of New York State and westward to Lake Ontario. The rest of the eastern section of the U.S. stretching all the way down into Florida was a pale lavender color. Across the whole expanse was emblazoned the words "Atlantic States Alliance."

The western half of the continent was even more shocking. Everything west of the Mississippi River was in a dull beige color, with hardly any more detail than the line of a few rivers and the blue splash of the Great Salt Lake. It too had three main divisions marked off. As he had already seen, the top was called "The Republic of Canada." As he looked closer, he saw someone had penciled in below it the words "Free Canada." The central section, which went down only as far as what would have been the northern borders of New Mexico, Arizona, and Nevada, was labeled "The United States of America." Below that, the area continuing into Mexico and off the map, was labeled "The Republic of Latin American States."

He leaned closer. A bright-red two-inch-wide band separated the eastern third of the continent from the beige portion of the map, running from top to bottom, most of it following the line of the Mississippi River. Bryce leaned closer, then gave a soft cry. In three or four different places the red band was labeled "Demilitarized Zone."

He stepped back, feeling the hair on the back of his head start to prickle. Had the map been hand drawn, he might have put it down as someone's sick joke. But this was printed, professionally done. He felt his head whirl and the strange sensation that reality was moving away from him, retreating into the mists.

There was a soft noise behind him, and Bryce turned. A large man was just coming out of his room, clutching some papers. He saw Bryce, looked startled, then spun and started swiftly down the hall in the opposite direction.

"Hey!" Bryce yelled.

The man broke into a run and disappeared around the corner. Bryce dropped the towel he was carrying over his shoulder and sprinted down the hall. The door to his room was open. His mouth opened and then shut as he saw inside. On the night table, his loose change was still there but his wallet was gone! He heard a door slam somewhere behind him.

Bryce swung around and dashed down the short hallway to where it turned and opened into a small alcove. Empty! He took stock quickly. There were two doors, the one he had come through last night from the outside, another marked "Private." He was out the first in two strides. The sun was up, and a beautiful late summer morning was breaking on the world. He scanned quickly in every direction but no one was in sight.

Ready for battle now, he ran back inside, stepped to the second door. Bam! Bam! Bam! The door rattled with the fury of his pounding. Nothing! He hit it again! Five times. Six. Still no sound. He grabbed the doorknob, twisted it hard. Locked. Jaw tight, he straight-armed the outside door, and with growing fury ran around to the front office, stopping only long enough to grab a solid piece of spruce from a stack of firewood piled against the building.

CHAPTER 14

Through the window of the motel office he could see the woman working behind the counter. Twice she glanced around nervously. He turned the knob on the door slowly, then gave the door a hard shove. It slammed against the wall with a crash, and she visibly jumped, knocking over a can full of pencils.

"Oh!" She fumbled quickly, trying to pick them up.

"All right, lady!" he said, stepping up to her and thrusting his face right next to hers. "Where is he?"

She shook her head, almost imperceptibly, eyes darting sideways. For one instant Bryce had the distinct impression of being warned, but detecting subtleties was not his strong suit at the moment, and he reached across the counter and clamped one hand over her arm. "Somebody just broke into my room and stole my wallet. He went in that back door that leads straight into your apartment."

She just stared at him, eyes now full of fright. And sadness! Somewhere in the far back of his mind that registered. There was a deep sadness.

He shook her arm. "I know he's in there! Get him out here! Now!"

"This what you're looking for?"

Bryce dropped her arm and spun around, the club coming up instinctively. The man who had stepped out of the doorway was of medium height and build, fair skinned, but with narrow, darting eyes. He wore a black suit—slightly rumpled—and a narrow tie. He held Bryce's wallet up in his left hand. But it wasn't the wallet that Bryce was gaping at. It was the small-bore, snub-nosed automatic that pointed directly at his stomach.

"Drop the club!" he demanded.

Bryce lowered his arm slowly and let the piece of firewood clatter to the floor. A second man stepped out. Everything about this man was big—his hands, his shoulders, his neck and head, his brutal features. It also registered in Bryce's mind that this was the same man who had come out of his room.

The shorter man inclined his head slightly, and the other sprang into action. He moved to Bryce, kicked the wood aside, then frisked him—quickly and very thoroughly. Then he stepped back.

"Mr. Sherwood, I presume?" the first man said pleasantly.

Bryce licked his lips, feeling the blood pounding in his head.

"Oh, come, Mr. Sherwood, let's not be bashful. Certainly not now." He shot the woman a hard glance. "We'll be talking to Mr. Sherwood in his room. We are not to be disturbed. Do you understand that, Mrs. Lambert?"

She met his gaze, then finally nodded. To his surprise, Bryce saw her eyes smoldering with hatred. She wasn't in on it, and that was why she had tried to warn him.

"You're already in serious trouble for not reporting this last night," the smaller man said to her. "Don't add to your problems."

"I understand, Captain," she said quietly. Again Bryce noted the bitterness, but, strangely, no fear. His heart was pounding like a jackhammer, but this middle-aged woman showed no fear.

The man stepped forward and jammed the gun into Bryce's ribs. "All right, move!"

At first the interrogation totally baffled him. They sat him down on the bed, and then the captain, as the woman had called him, started firing questions at him. Where are you from? Is this address in Maryland correct? This, as he jammed Bryce's driver's license under his nose. Where did you get this driver's license? How did you get here? What route did you take?

Suddenly, Bryce realized, with a rush of relief so strong it was almost palpable, that the men confronting him were policemen.

"You're police?" he blurted, incredulously.

The other's eyes narrowed suspiciously. "Who did you think we were?"

"Why didn't you say so?" Bryce blurted. "I tried to call you last night. My car was stolen. I hit something. There was a storm. When I woke up my car was gone. I—"

"A car?"

"Yes, a red BMW. About five miles north of here. I—"

"BMW?" He had a small notebook and pencil and was making notes now, the pistol back in his jacket pocket. "What is a BMW?"

Bryce gaped at him, then bit back a sharp comment. "It's made by the Bavarian Motor Works—BMW."

"You say you tried to call us last night?"

"Yes. The operator said she would call back, but—"

"You also tried to call Boston and to make a call to Maryland without a permit. Who were you trying to call in Boston?"

"My parents. They were expecting me and . . . " He stopped as the man's words registered. "The operator? She told you all this?"

He ignored that. "We also have no record of your crossing the border, Mr. Sherwood."

"Border? What border?"

The ferret eyes narrowed. "You wish to play stupid, Mr. Sherwood? I assure you this does not make things better for you."

"Hey, look," Bryce started, beginning to feel like the only one at a party who couldn't speak the language, "I don't know what you guys are up to, but this has gone far enough. Let's talk about my car and how it was stolen."

"First, I would like to hear how you crossed into our state without passport or identity card and driving a car I have never heard of."

"Passport?" Bryce laughed nervously. "You need a passport now to get into Connecticut? I heard you weren't wild about tourism, but this is ridiculous."

The man stepped forward menacingly, his mouth twisting into an ugly gash in his face. "You think traveling without a passport and identity card is amusing?"

At that point, Bryce's patience gave out. Jerkwater policeman or not, this had gone far enough. "I'd like to make a phone call," he said evenly.

The big man tipped his head back and laughed. The captain only smiled grimly. "And where will you call, Mr. Sherwood, to some nonexistent number in Boston?"

Bryce felt his head starting to whirl. Something was terribly wrong. The operator had called these men last night. And yet . . . He looked up. "I don't appreciate being treated like a common criminal. My car was stolen. I demand you take some action to find it."

"You demand?" the man said incredulously.

"Yes, I demand. I'm a lawyer. I know my rights. If you want to avoid the biggest lawsuit Connecticut has ever seen, I suggest you stop the television tough-guy act and find my car."

What Bryce saw in the other man's eyes was suddenly very frightening. He had known one other man like this—short in stature and shorter on self-esteem, who made up for it with a wicked, sadistic streak when anyone pricked at his enormously inflated ego. At that moment Bryce realized he had made a serious mistake.

The big man leaped forward, grabbed Bryce's shirt, and yanked him to his feet. "How did you get into this country?" he screamed into his face.

The whiff of bad breath tinged with alcohol was so strong that Bryce wrinkled his nose. "You know," he said, trying to keep his voice conversational, "I think I walked into the state looney bin last night. You, the operator, the motel lady—you're all crazy." Then his own self-control snapped. He put his hands against the big man's chest and shoved free of him. "Look, buster," he shouted, "I don't know where you went to police academy, but you lay another hand on me and the governor will hear about this one."

The man smiled, a thin, mirthless smile that looked more like a grimace. Then suddenly he doubled his fist and drove it with the full force of his body into Bryce's stomach. Bryce gasped and dropped to his knees like he had been poleaxed. Both men watched him impassively as he retched frantically, trying to get air.

Dimly Bryce felt the huge hands sweep down and grab him by his shirt. Buttons ripped as he was yanked to his feet. Bryce saw the blur of the massive fist. He jerked his head, but not fast enough. It caught him a glancing blow along the jaw. Lights exploded in his head and he catapulted backwards, unconscious before he even hit the bed.

Bryce groaned and rolled over. His eyes opened slowly, trying to focus on the bulk towering over him. There was the warm, salty taste of blood inside his mouth. The big man stepped back, and Bryce pulled himself into a sitting position, grunting as the pain in his stomach nearly doubled him over again. The captain was leaning against the door, looking bored.

He watched absently until Bryce swung his feet off the bed. "Now, Mr. Sherwood. I think we've really had quite enough of your being cute." The captain glanced at the big man. "Sergeant, call Captain Rodale in Hartford. I want a complete run-down on this man."

The big man gave him a questioning look, but the other frowned quickly. "I'll be fine. Get out there and call him!"

He exited quickly.

"While he's at it, he'd better call you guys a lawyer," Bryce said hoarsely, still trying to recover his breath. "This is still the

United States of America, and you're in more trouble than you've ever dreamed of."

There was an instant narrowing of those dangerous eyes, and he stepped forward. "The United States of America?"

"You'd better believe it!"

"So that is why you carry U.S. currency? Are you from the USA?"

Bryce just gaped at him.

"Why then do you carry papers from the ASA?"

"The ASA. I don't know anything about any ASA."

"The Atlantic States Alliance."

"Never heard of it." Then suddenly Bryce's head came up. On the map. Stretching from Florida to Pennsylvania. The fear abruptly returned, sending chills coursing up and down his back.

The man reached in the inside coat of his jacket and withdrew a sheaf of papers folded longways down the middle. He opened them, looked at them, then looked at Bryce over the top of them. "The United States of America. But of course. That would explain everything."

"What are you talking about?" Bryce said slowly, trying to maintain some semblance of defiance but feeling only a growing sense of baffled horror.

His inquisitor suddenly thrust the papers under his nose. The top page was titled "The Declaration of Independence." Bryce knew what they were instantly. The documents from Nathaniel Gorham.

"Where did you get this document?"

Bryce leaned back against the headboard, fighting for calm. "I refuse to answer any further questions until I have an attorney present."

In one swift movement, the captain's hand whipped to his coat, then out. In an instant the barrel of the pistol was jammed up hard against Bryce's face, grinding the flesh against his cheekbone. "Now let me tell you something," the captain hissed softly into his ear. "This document has been outlawed in the Confederation of North American States for over a hundred years. The penalty for having it in your possession is death."

Bryce didn't dare move, but his eyes flew open with the shock of the man's words.

"I can shoot you on sight as a spy from the United States government and no one will bat an eye here. Do you understand me?"

He twisted the muzzle hard, and Bryce yelped with the pain.

"Now I'm going to ask you one more time, Mr. Sherwood. Where did you get this document?"

Bryce hardly heard the last question. Death! For the Declaration of Independence. Something snapped inside of him, and he laughed wildly, unable to control himself. "A ghost gave it to me."

The laugh died in his throat as the captain stepped back, the pistol coming up slowly to point directly at Bryce's head. The man's hand was trembling, but Bryce, his clarity sharpened by the sudden horror of the moment, saw the man's finger start to tighten on the trigger.

There was a heavy clump against the door. The noise seemed to cause something in the captain's head to click, and suddenly he was rational again. "It's open," he snapped over his shoulder. The wave of relief hit Bryce like a blast of water from a fire hose. He had come within a fraction of an inch of having his head blown off.

"I said it's open," the captain snarled, jerking around to grab the doorknob. He yanked the door open, then jumped back as the sergeant's body tumbled into the room. A man was standing in the doorway, deer rifle covering the small room. The captain leaped back, his pistol whipping upward. Both weapons fired simultaneously, and the blast in the small room was deafening.

The captain's shot hit high, burying itself in the plaster just to the left of the man's head, but he was slammed backwards as the heavy-grained bullet from the rifle caught him square in the chest. Eyes bulging in horror, Bryce stared as the man slid slowly downward to a sitting position, leaving a red smear on the wall-paper, then toppled forward onto the body of the sergeant.

The man with the rifle was young, dressed in overalls and a long-sleeved shirt. He stared at the two bodies for a moment, breathing hard, then finally lifted his eyes to Bryce. There was a soft sound, and the woman, Mrs. Lambert, was at the door, eyes wide and filled with fright. She motioned quickly to Bryce. He didn't move, just stared at her, still in shock.

"Come!" she hissed. "We must move quickly!"

Still he just stood there. She came to him, gently took his arm as the boy leaned over the two men, checking quickly for vital signs. "Please!" she pleaded, pulling him toward the door. "We don't know how soon there will be others."

Bryce followed her dumbly, like a child in a stupor. The man with the rifle stood. "Go!" he commanded. "Get him out of here!"

The events that followed became the rapid blur of a night-mare for Bryce. The woman half dragged and half shoved him out a back door and to a beat-up old pickup truck hidden in a stand of trees. "Get under the tarp," she commanded, pointing to the back of the truck. "You mustn't even stick your head out until we stop again."

Still dazed, Bryce obeyed, feeling her tuck the canvas around him. The engine coughed into life, died once, then started again. There was a lurch, the crunch of the tires on gravel, then they turned onto pavement. They drove at a sedate speed along the highway for only five or six minutes, then turned left onto a rough dirt road. Now she really put the pedal to the floor, and for the next fifteen minutes Bryce's body was battered and bruised as the truck bounced and careened wildly over a road that could not have been much more than a deer track. Several times he was tempted to peek out, then his mind would flash back to the image of the captain's body slamming against the wall and the bright red smear he had left as he slid to the floor. That was enough to keep him under cover.

Finally the truck careened to a stop in a spray of gravel. The truck's door opened, there was a soft step, then the canvas was pulled back. Bryce sat up slowly, blinking at the light.

"Hurry!" she urged. "You mustn't be seen."

He climbed stiffly out of the truck. They were in front of a one-room cabin, roughly built, half hidden in a heavy stand of birch and white pine. Thirty yards in any direction and one would be lost to sight in the thick trees.

She motioned with her head. "This way."

They went only ten or fifteen yards, and for a moment Bryce thought she was going to hide him in the forest, for they had stopped in front of a thick clump of mountain laurel. But then she reached down and pulled. Bryce was startled to see a door open. It was a root cellar, dug right into the hillside, with its door still covered with soil and grass. His estimation of the woman went up yet another notch. One could walk into that clump of brush with a magnifying glass and pass right over the door.

The cellar was small, no more than ten by ten, and had a dirt floor. The air was musty and smelled of rotten potatoes. Inside was a small wooden bin filled with sawdust, a beat-up old army cot, and a wooden crate turned upside down. On the crate sat the lid of a jar with a small candle stuck vertically in its own wax.

She lit the candle with a match retrieved from somewhere. "I'll bring you some food tonight." She pointed to the sawdust bin. "There are a few carrots in there."

Bryce nodded, sensing her urgency, but also feeling his own grasping need for some answers. "Who were those men? Why are you doing this for me?"

She looked surprised, then quickly shook her head. "I've got to get back and help my son." She moved back to the door. "I'll be back after dark. Keep the door closed. Don't go out for any reason."

123

He fought back the urge to grab her and shake the answer out of her, but again he just nodded numbly.

Satisfied, she opened the door, slipped out, and pushed it shut again. Bryce stared at it, watching his shadow flicker and dance in the dim light of the candle.

CHAPTER 15

Bryce was half dozing in the darkness, trying to ignore the discomfort of the narrow cot and wondering why after seven or eight hours his nose had still not grown completely accustomed to the smell of rotting potatoes. The door above his head scraped softly. He was up instantly and crouched in the corner.

"It's me." It was her voice, and he saw a dark shape framed against the starlight as the door to the root cellar opened, then closed again almost immediately. "Just a moment," she said.

There was a loud scratch, a match flared, and she raised the glass on a kerosene lantern and touched the match to the wick. As the light filled the cellar, she set it on the upturned crate, then turned and smiled. "There. Is that better?"

Bryce nodded gratefully. He had never been claustrophobic, but the candle had burned out after a couple of hours, and after six or seven more hours in total darkness, he better understood the feeling.

She turned. Next to the door was a small cardboard box which she lifted and put next to the lamp. Bryce stepped forward, catching the sudden whiff of something wonderful. Fried chicken. Sandwiches. A bottle of milk. Some peaches. After his eighth or ninth carrot, he had finally lost his ability to get another one down and had tried to ignore the gnawing hunger.

"Eat," she commanded, pulling the cot over close enough to serve as a chair.

Bryce obeyed without hesitation, biting into a chicken breast eagerly.

"I'm sorry it took so long." She looked away. "There was much to do."

Bryce stopped chewing, feeling a sudden lurch in his stomach. "Are they dead?"

"Only the one." She saw the look on his face, and frowned. "We had no choice."

"I know," he said, slumping back. He had been interrogated like a common criminal, slugged in the stomach, and smashed in the jaw. He had seen the rock-steady muzzle of a pistol poised at his head. But in spite of all that, he had hoped that he was not party to a killing—especially the killing of a policeman. And yet, in reality, there had been no hope. The horror of the captain smashed backwards by the bullet would never again leave him.

He sighed, wearily. "What about the big man?"

"He's in another cellar, not far from here. We'll send him north to Boston, ship him out on a freighter headed for Africa or India. They won't hear from him for at least three months."

Bryce nodded, grateful that they hadn't killed the second man too. On the other hand, he knew he owed a great debt to this woman and the man who was her son. If they hadn't opened the door when they did . . . He stopped, remembering. Would the captain have pulled the trigger? He wasn't sure. The man's rage had been enormous. Bryce shuddered, pushing the thought away. "Who were they, anyway?" he asked woodenly.

She shrugged, her face forlorn. "ISD." At his blank look, she added, "Internal Security Division."

Internal Security? There it was again. "What is this Internal Security Division?"

That surprised her. "From the Ministry of Internal Affairs. They're the secret police. That makes it very, very serious for us." She gave him a reproving look. "Why didn't you listen to me? I warned you not to call them."

"Secret police?" There it was again, the whirling sense of surrealism, like being part of a conversation, understanding every word, but not comprehending a thing.

He set the piece of chicken down slowly. "Secret police? In the state of Connecticut?"

"The *province* of Connecticut," she corrected. "But no, the ISD is the national police, for all of CONAS."

"CONAS? What is that?"

She gave him a sharp look. "The Confederation of North American States."

The vision of the map on the bulletin board swam before his eyes. "What is happening?" he asked of the empty air. "One moment I'm in the United States of America, and the next, I'm in some wild, insane nightmare."

That brought her head up slowly. "So you *are* from the United States?"

"Of course, I—"

She grabbed his arm. "When?"

"When what?"

"When did you come from there?"

He rubbed his hand across his eyes, fighting for some semblance of sanity. "Yesterday."

She leaned back, eyes glowing. "When I saw your currency, I couldn't believe it. The United States!"

"Look, lady—Mrs. Lambert, I—"

"Please, my name is Jessie."

He grabbed her arm, swallowed hard, took a deep breath. "Look, Jessie, I am very, very confused. Something is terribly wrong here, and I want to know what. Let's start right at the beginning. See if I can sort this out."

"First, I must ask two questions."

He sighed. "Okay, what?"

"Could you lead us back to the United States of America?"

He just stared at her.

"I mean if we get the necessary papers? We'll need new passports, identity cards—"

"But we *are* in the United States of America!" he said, fighting not to scream it at her.

Now it was her turn to stare. "Is that what you think?"

"Of course that's what I think. Where do *you* think we are?"

"In the Confederation of North American States," she said slowly, "and more specifically, the New England Confederation." She was looking at him strangely.

He rubbed his hand across his eyes. "The map," he mumbled. "That's what it said on the map."

"What map?"

"The one on the bulletin board in the motel."

"Yes, what about it?"

"Is that . . . " He swallowed. "Is that accurate?"

She gave him a long look. "Yes, of course."

He felt like the sergeant had slugged him in the stomach again. He dropped his head into his hands, staring at nothing.

Jessie stood, went to the box she had brought and fished out a thin sheaf of papers from the bottom, then turned back and thrust them at him. "Here's my second question."

He didn't really need to look. He already knew what it was as he took the papers from her. He glanced down to confirm, saw the title, then started slightly. There was a dark red stain in the upper corner, next to where it read "Declaration of Independence." Bryce felt his stomach turn. The captain had been holding these papers when the gun battle began.

"Is this authentic?" Jessie asked softly.

He handed the papers back to her. "Yes, it's just a copy, but it is authentic."

Jessie sat down slowly on the cot, her hands trembling. She caressed the paper reverently with her fingertips, and Bryce was stunned to see sudden tears well up and trickle down her cheeks.

"We always heard it was real," she whispered, "but we couldn't be sure."

The penalty for possession was death. That's what the captain had shouted at him. The penalty for possession of this document is death. It has been outlawed for a hundred years. Now as he watched this middle-aged woman weeping over it, Bryce suddenly knew that everything here was very, very real. He didn't understand it. He couldn't comprehend how it had happened. But of this he was sure: this was no dream, no nightmare, no temporary flight into insanity. He was right smack in the middle of something very horrible and very, very real.

He straightened slowly. "Jessie, we have got to talk."

The next morning, just before dawn, Jessie returned. She brought Bryce more food and a can of kerosene for the lantern. She looked drawn and haggard but brushed aside his solicitations. They had to leave by tonight, and there was still much to be done in preparation. She had brought a small box camera, and they went out into the daylight long enough for him to stand in front of a makeshift background made from a blanket and have three pictures taken.

"Jessie?" he asked a few minutes later, watching her hands as she took the food from the box and put it on the crate.

She looked up, brown eyes dark and tired.

"Do you believe what I told you last night?"

Straightening, she looked away for several seconds, then met his gaze. "It seems so crazy, so impossible."

"I know," he said forlornly.

"And yet." She took a breath, then sighed. "And yet, it is the only explanation that makes sense of everything—the United States currency, the foolishness of your phone calls, your driver's license with the Maryland address." There was a long pause, then, "Yes, I believe you."

Bryce opened his mouth, then shut it again, surprised at the sudden burning in his eyes and catch in his throat. For the last twenty-four hours he had been skirting a mental breakdown. To have this woman, who exuded such New England practicality and common sense, say she believed him meant more to him than he could express. Finally, he got control. "What ever prompted you to intervene in my behalf?"

129

There was a short hoot of disgust. "You heard the captain. I was in serious trouble for not calling in and reporting you when you first showed up."

He shook his head. "Trouble, yes. But not anything like you're in now."

Her eyes were suddenly glistening, and she turned, so he couldn't see her face. Bryce took a step closer to hear as she continued softly, "Eight years ago my husband went south, into the Atlantic States Alliance, to buy some things for the motel. His papers were not in order, or so they said."

She turned back to him slowly, and Bryce saw the lines around her eyes deepen and her mouth tighten. "He was arrested." She swallowed, fighting for control. "No one helped *him*."

"Is he still in prison?" Bryce asked softly.

She shook her head. "He died of tuberculosis three years ago."

"I understand. Thank you."

Her head came up. "But it was more than that."

"What?"

"When I saw your money, I couldn't believe it. We hear rumors about the USA. But no one is allowed to travel there, and no one from there has ever come here. I thought it was some kind of test by the secret police or something. I almost called them, but I kept thinking, 'What if he is really from the United States?' Then, after the big man searched your room, I heard the captain talk about the document they had found." She finally met Bryce's gaze, steadily and proudly. "That's when I decided I would help you, no matter what the cost."

CHAPTER 16

Bryce lay on the cot, staring at the roof of the root cellar. He had turned the lantern down until the wick barely glowed. Suddenly he jerked up, aware that he was not alone. In the dim light he saw the figure of a man perched on the orange crate.

"You!" he shouted.

"Hello, Laddie."

Bryce leaped to his feet. "Gorham! Man, am I glad to see you. The most incredible thing has happened."

Gorham didn't move, but suddenly the wick of the lantern flared higher, filling the cellar with light.

Bryce rushed on, not even noticing. "You're not going to believe this, but I've been dropped right in the middle of the most bizarre nightmare. The United States is gone. Well, not really gone, but it's not here anymore. It's out west. Here it's . . . it's—there's secret police, different currency. I was arrested, nearly shot. A captain of the secret police was killed. I'm implicated in the murder and now . . . "

His voice trailed off as he peered at the old man. "You already know all this."

Gorham nodded slowly.

"My car? The motel? Jessie? You know it all, don't you?" The thoughts were coming faster now. "The Declaration of Independence? That's why you gave it to me, wasn't it. For Jessie?"

Gorham just watched him steadily, face expressionless.

Bryce turned and started to pace angrily; then suddenly he spun back around. "You did this!" He stepped forward, understanding coming in a rush now. "You did it! You brought me here!" His voice was hoarse with shock as he stared at Gorham. "You tried to warn me. There in the car, just before I hit that wall of whiteness."

"Yes," Gorham sighed. "I tried to warn you."

Bryce's eyes were blazing now. "Then take me back! Get me out of here!"

There was no response.

"I mean it, Gorham. Your little joke has gone far enough. Get me out of here!"

Gorham stirred, his eyes brooding. "In the first place, none of this is a little joke, as you call it. Secondly, I didn't put you here. You did!"

"Oh sure!" Bryce snapped. "I was driving through the countryside of Connecticut, and thought to myself, 'Wouldn't it be wonderful to—' "

"Look!" Gorham thundered, startling Bryce enough that he fell back a step. "It was very difficult for me to get here. I can only stay for a short time. Are you going to sit there and whine, or do you want to hear what I've come to say?"

Bryce sat back down on the cot slowly. "All right, I'm listening."

"For a while, I thought we were making progress with you. Between me and Leslie and her father, I thought we were really going to convince you." Gorham sighed, and it was a deep, painful sound. "Then came the thing with Mannington and Leslie. Perhaps it was foolish of me to interfere—"

"Perhaps nothing!" Bryce blurted. "You blew the whole thing."

"Well, be that as it may, when it became apparent that you had become absolutely rigid in your determination to continue on in the same course, there was a meeting of the Council of Founding Fathers. It was their unanimous decision to take more drastic action."

"Wait a minute," Bryce cut in. "You didn't know for sure how I felt about the amendment until we were in the car. There were only a few seconds between when you disappeared and when I hit that wall of light. When did this meeting with the council take place?"

"Time, as you think of it, does not hold sway in that other sphere. Though it was only a few seconds for you, actually the deliberations of the council went on at great length."

Bryce was shaking his head. "And because I wouldn't kow-tow to you guys on this amendment thing, you zapped me into another world?"

"Your stand on the amendment was an important factor, but it was not the only one, and not even the most important one."

"Then what was?"

Gorham stood and began to pace the narrow confines of the root cellar. "Over the past few decades, the principles that we fought so hard to establish have been eroded again and again. In and of themselves, none of the losses were that critical. But the aggregate effect has become very serious. When added to all that has gone before, the proposed amendment is potentially devastating. It could be the straw that finally tips the camel over."

"Come on," Bryce scoffed. "I can see where it might reduce some of the checks and balances set up by the Constitution, but it's not that different from what we have now."

He stopped and looked at Bryce. "It is very much different than what you have now. But it's more than just that. There are evil people at work now. People who seek for power. People who clearly understand that the Constitution stands in their way. This new amendment is enough to give them the bridgehead they need to completely overthrow it."

"Then why not zap some of *those* people over here? Just leave me alone."

"I told you before," Gorham answered evenly, "don't under-estimate yourself. By some strange combination of circumstances, Bryce Sherwood has become a pivotal player in events—not only

133

the current events, but in the shape of things yet to come. He serves as a catalyst for much of what is to happen."

"Well," Bryce snapped, "so much for your policy of not directly interfering in the lives of others."

"Because of the gravity of the situation, the council received a special dispensation to remove you from the scene. Whether that will turn the tide remains to be seen, but with you in, there was little question of what would happen."

"I am truly flattered," Bryce said with soft bitterness. He sat back, letting it all sink in, one part of him on the verge of laughing wildly at the whole insane situation, another part of him chilled by the finality of Gorham's words. Finally he looked up. "So where am I?"

Gorham turned and sat back down on the orange crate. "It is very difficult to explain. Perhaps an analogy will help. What do you call it in your railroads, when two tracks split off from one another?"

Bryce gave him a baffled look.

"You know, where the two tracks come together and can be changed."

"You mean a switch?"

"Yes, that's it. A switch. It is a very small thing, yes? Just a fraction of an inch between the switch and the other track."

"Yes."

"People on the train go over a switch and don't even realize they have changed tracks."

Again Bryce nodded.

"And yet, they can end up hundreds of miles away because of that little switch."

"I understand all that. What has it got to do with where I am now?"

"The train is the same. Even the people on the train are the same, but because of that little switch, the train is now in a very different place."

He took a deep breath. "Think of the United States as the train, and the year 1787 as the switch. Suppose that after we

134

met at Philadelphia and drafted the Constitution in 1787 . . . ''
His voice trailed off, and his eyes took on a faraway look. Finally, he pulled back, looking at Bryce. "Suppose that the Constitution was never ratified."

Bryce leaped up. "But it *was* ratified!"

Gorham shook his head. "Not here it wasn't. In this world, the Constitution was never ratified."

Bryce just stared, his jaw slack. "It can't be!" he whispered.

"Well," Gorham said slowly, "it is! You are now in an America that has never had the Constitution."

For the next few minutes, Bryce sat with his head in his hands, listening as Gorham described the history of this new America.

When ratification failed, the colonies broke up into several factions. The three Southern colonies formed a monarchy. They tried to persuade George Washington to be their king, but he adamantly refused and died in 1799, broken-hearted to see all for which he had fought so hard unraveling at every seam.

The New England colonies formed their own confederation using a loose constitutional monarchy. Under Thomas Jefferson's direction, the remaining states formed a small nation they called the Atlantic States Alliance. Using the Constitution as the basis for government, for a time they did quite well. To the north, Canada formed its own confederation of small states.

But the three little nations in America were too small. Expansion became critical, and by the early 1800s all three countries were locked in battle over the western territories. Then in 1833, the generals in the Atlantic States Alliance overthrew the democratic government and set up a military dictatorship. They quickly overran the southern monarchy and consolidated their power base.

Bryce lifted his head to watch Gorham. He was far away now, staring off at nothing as he droned on in a dull monotone, as though even the very speaking of it caused him pain.

Battling Canada and the New England Confederation to a standstill, the generals finally signed the Treaty of 1836, which formed the Confederation of North American States—CONAS— a commonwealth of three socialistic, totalitarian states.

In the meantime, the peoples of the West used the paralyzing war in the East as an opportunity to form their own free nations. Western Canada broke off from the Confederation of Canadian States and created the Republic of Canada, or Free Canada, as it was more popularly known. The heavy Spanish population in the southern part of the country formed the Republic of Latin American States, which included what should have been California, Arizona, New Mexico, and Texas. Between these two nations were the twenty-seven states of the Rocky Mountains and Great Plains.

The pioneers had carried the now defunct Constitution with them and used it as the basis for governing themselves. They chose the name proposed by the Constitution, and the twenty-seven states became the United States of America.

"There was a map at the motel," Bryce interrupted for the first time. "Now I understand what I saw."

"Yes. So now you have two groups of nations—three totalitarian states in the East, three free republics in the West."

"And that explains the demilitarized zone I saw on the map."

Gorham nodded. "CONAS doesn't like having a free nation on their borders, beckoning to their citizens. So you have the Mississippi Demilitarized Zone—a twenty-mile-wide stretch of machine guns, electric fences, barbed wire, dogs, and land mines. Dozens are killed every year trying to cross it."

"What about my family?" Bryce asked softly. "Are they here?"

Gorham nodded. "I told you, it is the same train with the same people. It's just on a different track."

"Where are they?"

"Well, fortunately, they never left California. Who wanted to emigrate to the New England Confederation under the circumstances? Your family are all healthy and safe and doing fine."

136

Bryce looked at his hands, then finally back to Gorham. "Okay, I've learned my lesson."

The older man searched his face, but didn't answer.

"I said I've learned my lesson!" Bryce exploded. "You've made your point! I was wrong about the Constitution. I'm sorry I didn't listen to you sooner. I'm ready to go back to reality now."

"This *is* reality now."

Bryce rocked back. "You know what I mean."

"Didn't you listen to anything I've been saying?" Gorham shot back. "This is it! There is no other reality for you. It is not possible for me to take you back."

Bryce leaped to his feet and gave the cot a vicious kick, sending it crashing against the wall of the cellar. "You make it possible!" he yelled. "You're the one who got me into this."

Gorham just shook his head stubbornly in the face of Bryce's fury. "I tried to warn you, but you refused to listen. Now I can do nothing."

Bryce felt his fingernails digging into his palms. "You've got to, Gorham!" he pleaded. "You've got to get me out of this nightmare!"

Gorham's patience ran out. "And what if I could? Would I? Should I? Oh, sure, mentally you're deeply shaken, but has anything else really changed? If I could take you back this instant, are you ready to tell Mannington the deal is off?"

That caught Bryce totally off guard. "I . . . Well, yes, I guess I would—"

"Are you ready to go to work and fight as hard to see that the amendment isn't ratified as you did to get it passed?"

Again Bryce hesitated. He had been consumed with thoughts of getting back. What he would do if he made it there hadn't yet received much consideration.

"I rest my case," Gorham said soberly. "Little has changed. Not in the heart, where it really matters." He swung around abruptly. "And now I must go. I have stayed longer than I was supposed to already."

"So there is nothing you can do?" Bryce whispered.

He shook his head sadly.

Bryce leaned against the wall, shattered. Gorham's face softened. "Is there nothing you would know from me?" he asked softly.

Bryce looked up. "What?"

"You asked about your family. Is there no one else?"

Bryce's head came up slowly, the blue eyes suddenly wide. "Leslie! Is she here?"

"I told you. Same train, same people."

"She *is* here! Where?"

"I am only allowed to say this much. Her family still lives near Arlington, Virginia." He stopped, sighed. "Find her, Bryce. Before, you needed her. Now, she needs you." He shrugged and instantly began to fade. "You must be very careful, Bryce," his voice echoed ethereally. "As you learned in the motel, this is not just some dreamscape you are passing through. It is real. The people are real. The bullets are real. And you are a stranger in a difficult land."

Jessie and her son arrived shortly after dark. As they shut the door to the root cellar behind them, Bryce took more careful stock of the young man who had saved his life. He was in his early twenties, lean as a split-ash rail and dressed in simple overalls and a long-sleeved cotton shirt. He still carried the rifle in his hand. His eyes were those of his mother, the mouth too.

Bryce stuck out his hand. "I didn't get a chance to thank you yesterday. If you hadn't come when you did . . . "

He took Bryce's hand, pumped it once, then dropped it, obviously embarrassed.

"I'm sorry, Bryce," Jessie broke in. "I forgot you haven't been formally introduced. This is my son, Neal."

Bryce smiled. "I would never have guessed."

Suddenly Jessie was all business. "We've got the papers," she said, her voice low with excitement. She handed him a passport and some other papers.

Bryce examined them closely. His picture looked sick—unruly hair, thick stubble. But it would be hard to identify him later from the photograph alone. "Are you ready to go?" Neal asked.

Bryce had been thinking about nothing else for the last four hours. "I am."

"We've decided that the easiest way will be to cross into the Canadian Confederation, then head west until—"

He stopped. Bryce was shaking his head slowly.

"What?" Jessie demanded.

"I'm ready to take you to the United States," he said evenly, looking to each one of them. "But not north."

Neal shot his mother a quick look. She ignored it, watching Bryce steadily. "They know you came from the south," she said. "They'll be watching the southern border very closely."

"I've got to go to Virginia," Bryce said stubbornly. "Then I'll see that you get to the United States. I owe you that, for saving my life. But first, I'm going to Virginia."

CHAPTER 17

They drove south for two hours, keeping to the back roads, then slept fitfully in the truck until dawn. Leaving the old pickup hidden deep in a clump of underbrush, they walked into a small village on the main highway and joined a ragtag group of people waiting outside a small general store.

This had been Neal's idea, once he saw that Bryce was not going to back down from his determination to go south. Starting in July and August, the ASA imported itinerant farm workers from all over CONAS to help with the tobacco and cotton harvests in the South. There was always a shortage of laborers, and getting included was not that much of a challenge. At seven o'clock, an overweight, slovenly constable came to the store and began writing out travel permits. In their shabby clothes and unshaven condition, the three newcomers blended in and received their permits without a hitch.

Two hours later and a mile or two from the border, the rickety bus pulled to a stop in a long line of traffic. Bryce felt Neal tense alongside him. "This isn't normal?" Bryce asked, low and under his breath.

Neal shook his head as Jessie, sitting across the aisle from them, flashed a warning look. Bryce leaned back, feeling his heart suddenly pick up its tempo as he sensed the sudden fear and tension on the bus. If the others were nervous, where did that leave him and the Lamberts as they traveled on forged papers? In addition, Jessie had the Declaration of Independence sewn into the side of her suitcase. Bryce had balked at taking it, remembering the penalty for being caught in possession of it, but Jessie was absolutely adamant. It was not to be left behind.

There were nearly thirty people on the bus. Though Anglos dominated the group, there were half a dozen blacks, two or three Orientals, and a couple of Latin extraction. There were only three other women, and that worried Bryce a little. Jessie was not dressed conspicuously different than them, but he wasn't sure she could ever feign the air of forlorn, broken-spirited hopelessness that the others carried like a burden. There was a fierce streak of independence in her that radiated like the inner core of a nuclear reactor. Jessie was a fighter and a proud woman. And thank the Lord for that, he thought fervently.

It took nearly half an hour for the bus to creep forward until it approached the heavy, fortress-like building of the border checkpoint. When Bryce saw the high barbed-wire fence with its V-shaped barrier on the top stretching off in both directions, he shook his head in disbelief. Two days ago, he had driven across this border between New York and Connecticut at about sixty-five miles an hour with hardly a second thought.

The low murmurs that had filled the bus since they had entered the long line of traffic suddenly dropped off to silence. Bryce craned his neck and saw two uniformed soldiers approaching the bus, submachine guns hanging over their shoulders, pistol butts jutting from holsters around their waists.

Neal leaned slightly toward Bryce. "Don't look at them until they come to you. Just look submissive."

The bus driver swung open the door, and the two men came aboard. "Identity papers, passports, and travel permits!" barked the first. Suddenly Bryce's heart was pounding in his throat. This is not some dreamscape you're passing through, Gorham had reminded him. These are real people and real bullets.

He leaned back, pulling the dirty baseball cap lower over his eyes, then reached for his papers, forcing his mind into a numbing blankness.

Bryce jumped as there was a sharp rap on his shoulders. "Papers!"

He looked up into the hard coldness of the soldier's face and handed him the documents. He jumped again as his hat was ripped off his head and dumped in his lap. It took every ounce of willpower to hold his head up, eyes steady, as the man looked at him, then at the passport photo, then back at him. Then the eyes went to the identity card, then the travel permit. The man dropped them back into his lap. "Papers!" the man demanded, and Neal Lambert handed his across.

The burst of relief and wild exhilaration that hit Bryce was the most intoxicating thing he had ever experienced. He had jumped the abyss, he had come up from the blackness! He was alive!

Neal passed muster and so did Jessie. A look of triumph flashed between the three of them as the soldier moved on past them toward the back of the bus. Bryce put his hat back on, slouched low again and closed his eyes.

"Where did you get this permit?"

Bryce opened his eyes a crack. The first border guard was about six rows from the front, standing next to where two of the women sat. He had papers in his hand and was glaring down at the woman in the aisle seat. Even from where he was, Bryce could see the terror in her eyes. He sat up straighter, and Neal's hand shot across to grab his arm. He gave a quick shake of his head. Bryce dropped his eyes.

"I asked you where you got your travel permit?" the soldier shouted.

"At . . . at Norwalk." Her voice was high pitched, quavering.

In spite of himself, Bryce lifted his eyes. She was the youngest of the three other women, probably in her mid twenties. Bryce had watched them board at Norwalk, and had absently noted that in spite of the shabby dress and furtive air, this one was passably attractive.

The guard laughed, an ugly, rasping sound. "Of course. Norwalk," he said amiably. Then suddenly his voice hardened. "From the underground, right?"

"Oh, no! From the government offices." She clutched at his jacket. "Please. They told me everything was in order."

The woman next to her started to rise, but the guard straight-armed her back down. "You! Stay out of this!" Then to the first. "Stand up!"

The second guard laughed loudly behind Bryce and moved swiftly back up the aisle, weapon high, daring the crowd to interfere with his partner's little drama. Bryce turned his head quickly and stared out the window. Something outside had suddenly caught the interest of everyone else on the bus as well.

He heard a soft gasp and couldn't help himself. He turned his head enough to see. The girl's arms were up high, and the first guard was searching her for weapons, his hands moving slowly as they followed the lines of her body. She was rigid, eyes locked on a spot on the ceiling.

Again Bryce felt Neal stir in warning, but he couldn't pull his eyes away.

The first guard grabbed the woman's arm and yanked her roughly out into the aisle. "Off the bus!"

"Oh, no. Please!" She was near hysteria now, sobbing, pleading.

The other woman leaped to her feet and grabbed at his arm. "Please, let her go."

Now the second guard stepped forward and hit the older woman full across the face with the back of his hand. Her head snapped back and cracked sharply against the bus window. "Sit down!" he roared.

Bryce was on his feet, barely conscious that Neal was pulling hard at his coat. The lead soldier, who was dragging the weeping girl toward the door, stopped, shooting a warning glance in Bryce's direction. The second guard whirled, weapon snapping upward.

Bryce sat down slowly, averting his eyes. He heard the heavy footsteps approaching, felt Neal tense in the seat next to him. Bryce kept his head down, cursing his stupidity.

The black boots stopped directly in his line of sight.

"You got a problem, friend?"

"No, sir," Bryce murmured.

He sensed the movement, tried to duck, but the clubbed fist caught him directly alongside the head. Lights exploded and he reeled back.

"I'm talking to you, Mister! Look at me when I talk to you."

Bryce forced his head up slowly. The barrel of the submachine gun was two inches from his nose.

"You think she's pretty? Maybe you'd like to join her!"

"No, sir."

The hand flashed out, knocked his hat flying. Meathook fingers grabbed Bryce by the hair and yanked his head back hard. "What did you say?" he screamed.

"I said, no, sir."

He gave a vicious yank, nearly pulling Bryce's scalp off, then he let go and laughed raucously. "That's what I thought you said."

Then backing down the aisle slowly, weapon high, he let his eyes challenge everyone else on the bus. No one moved. No one looked at him. The first guard, who had watched the whole thing with faint amusement, waited until his partner pushed by him and stepped off the bus. Then he shoved the girl toward the door. "Get this bus outta here!" he snarled at the driver, and with one last glare at the passengers, he stepped off the bus with the sobbing woman.

Even as the bus carrying the itinerant workers rolled through the last of the barricades and headed south into the Atlantic States Alliance, a small white car pulled up in front of the Dew Drop Inn in Bollingbroke. Before the driver had shut off the engine, the man who had been nervously peeking out the front window of the motel office was outside and opening the door on the passenger's side.

He stepped back, snapping to attention as the short, distinguished-looking man got out of the car, stretched, and looked around curiously.

"Sir! Captain James Rodale, ISD commander for the Hartford district."

The other finished his survey, then finally turned back. His face was pleasant enough, the eyes dark and compelling. The dark hair, thick and wiry, was starting to gray around the temples; the suit was expensive and hand tailored. Rodale quivered slightly in excitement. Here, standing within a foot of him, was the minister of internal affairs for all of CONAS. That surely made him one of the five most powerful men in the entire Confederation of North American States.

"How was your flight up, sir?"

The minister nodded, looked up at the motel sign, then started for the office. "Any sign of the owner yet?"

"No, sir. She's disappeared along with her son. No one has seen them since Friday morning. The question is, did this Sherwood kill them, too?"

The minister stopped, looking at him. Rodale nodded grimly. "We're pretty sure Captain Talbot is dead, sir. Possibly Sergeant Walker too. Come inside and look at what we've got."

When the Hartford office had received the call Friday morning from a Sergeant Walker in Bollingbroke asking to speak directly to Rodale, a call which was cut off before Rodale got to the phone, the head of ISD in Hartford had done two things. First he had listened to the tape of the phone call again and again. Then he had brought a full investigative team and a completely equipped portable crime lab with him to Bollingbroke. Now it paid off. He rolled out the evidence one piece at a time for the minister—the bullet dug from beneath a newly plastered patch on the wall; the blood samples from the freshly scrubbed wall and carpet—samples that matched Captain Talbot's blood type; Sergeant Walker's fingerprints from the hall phone; fibers from the hall carpet where the bodies of both men had been dragged that matched the colors of the suits they had been wearing when they left.

By the time he finished, the minister was impressed. "You've done good work, Rodale. I commend you."

Rodale managed to keep his face sober, even though praise from such a source made his head reel.

"I'm sending up another dozen men. They'll be under your command."

"*Yes, sir!*"

"Scour the whole province if you have to, Rodale. I want our two men found. I want the woman and her son found." He swung around, and Rodale felt a sudden chill when he saw the fire smoldering in those dark eyes. "Are you sure about the name of this other one?"

"Yes, sir. When the sergeant called, he gave the name of Bryce Sherwood. That was also the name given to the telephone operator."

The minister reached inside his suit coat, brought out a long envelope, and handed it to Rodale. It wasn't sealed, and the captain opened it. There were three colored photographs inside, all head shots of the same person. Rodale looked at them carefully, one at a time. It was a man in his late twenties, quite good looking, light blond hair combed straight back and with a slight wave, blue eyes, strong jawline, pleasant smile. Finally he looked up.

"I don't want these circulated publicly yet," the minister said shortly. "Only your men are to have copies."

"Who is it?"

The minister looked up from staring at the pictures, his mouth a tight line. "This is Bryce Sherwood." He ignored Rodale's startled look. "The question is, is this the same man that was here?"

146

Bryce Sherwood and Jessie and Neal Lambert slipped away from the rest of the group as they shambled off the vehicle to line up at reeking public restrooms in a small park.

For the next three days they moved south through what had once been the states of New York and New Jersey, keeping to the countryside as much as possible, foraging as they went, sleeping in the wooded areas, hopping slow-moving freights under the cover of darkness. Twice they moved into small villages and made contact with the local resistance movement. Each time, Jessie and Neal would go in first, talk quietly, give appropriate code words and verification, and then Bryce would be invited in. There were never any names exchanged. They were never asked from where they had come or where they were going. Once identification was sure, food was supplied along with updates on local ISD activity or military patrols. There would be a quick handshake and fervent good wishes, and they were on their way again.

As they moved steadily southward, the characteristics of life in the Atlantic States Alliance began to embed themselves deeper and deeper into the mind of Bryce Sherwood. Everywhere he saw three primary qualities of life in this new America—spartan conditions, unremitting labor, and ever-present government control.

It was not abject poverty like he had seen on a tour he had taken with Senator Hawkes to India and Pakistan, but it was still life at subsistence level. There were few cars, and most of these were old. Houses were small and usually held several families. Food stores carried a few basics and whatever fresh fruit and vegetables might be grown locally, but little else. Bicycles were omnipresent. Walking, even ten or fifteen miles, was commonplace. He smiled grimly at that. The President's Council on Physical Fitness would be truly proud, for in the ASA, obesity was no longer a national problem.

It was the grim economic deprivation that drove the unremitting, relentless labor. There were some factories and light industry, but mostly it was muscle power—both animal and

147

human—that fueled the nation. The ASA was the bent back, the shouldered hoe, the sweat-streaked face.

The images began to burn into his consciousness like firebrands—a six-year-old with an angelic face digging in a trench alongside older brothers and sisters; a teenager, up to his knees in the muck of a dairy corral, loading manure into a cart with a wooden pitchfork; two sisters with long blond hair, barely twenty, heaving huge forkfuls of hay onto a horse-drawn wagon; a white-haired, gaunt old man staggering down a rutted road with a wheelbarrow full of potatoes.

But it was the oppressive, omnipresent government influence that was most depressing. Uniformed soldiers were everywhere, the bureaucracy stultifying. Identity cards were required to transact the simplest business. Getting permission to visit an adjoining village could take hours of standing in lines. Hospital stays required an endless nightmare of forms and permissions.

To Neal, who had never been out of the New England Confederation, it was an exciting time. He consumed the sights and new experiences with an insatiable hunger. He stood slack-jawed at the high-rise buildings of New York City and the traffic of Philadelphia. Jessie, on the other hand, seemed interested but unimpressed. She lived for one thing, and that was to get Bryce to whatever it was he had to do in the south, then turn west for the United States.

But to Bryce, it was like being fed a diet of one revolting food after another. He had seen worse things. He had even been in countries where the oppression was more severe. But this was America. This was the countryside he knew; these were the cities he had visited, the people he had mingled with. Before, he had never given any of it much thought. Now every new sight hammered at him like a constant stream of filth and garbage.

They entered Washington, D.C., on the evening of the fourth day. Correction, Bryce thought to himself. Not Washington, D.C. Just Washington. There was no District of Columbia. The states of New York, Maryland, and Virginia were now just provinces or districts within a province. Some of the familiar names had disappeared altogether.

As they moved slowly into the city itself, Bryce was sickened. The city laid out under George Washington's direction was still there, with its great mall cutting down the center, its wide, radial boulevards and spacious vistas. But that was the only recognizable thing. A squat, ugly government building stood at the west end of the reflecting pool, replacing the stately marble columns of the Lincoln Memorial. MINISTRY OF AGRICULTURE, read the sign as they passed. The Tidal Basin was almost completely hidden behind high-rise apartment buildings stuck into the grass like giant stakes around a muddy pond. There was no Jefferson Memorial, no Washington Monument. And across the Ellipse, where the White House should have been, was a sprawling gray palace bathed in spotlights.

Bryce slouched down deeper in the seat and closed his eyes, unable to look anymore.

CHAPTER 18

They were sitting in a small apartment in central Washington. In espionage parlance, this was what was known as a safe house, a place where people could hole up, find a place to stay overnight while on the run, or hold a meeting with people whom they weren't sure about and whom they did not want to know where they really did their business—which was the reason the four of them sat in the safe house now. It was sweltering and stuffy, even though it was past ten o'clock, which left them all in short temper.

"Look," Jessie finally said, with some asperity. "For the last five years, our group has been serving as a conduit to help you send people from the ASA north. We've taken great risks."

The man they knew only as Lewis shook his head stubbornly. "I know that, and that is the only reason you are here right now. But that doesn't change the fact that this man is an unknown."

No one turned to look at Bryce, who sat on a hard-backed chair in one corner.

"You yourself admit he has been with you only for less than a week."

"We have been through much together," Neal snapped.

"In less than a week?" Lewis sneered. "Do you think the ISD is so foolish they wouldn't have their agents appear authentic?"

Bryce laughed out loud at that. "Right. An ISD agent. That would about round out the picture."

Jessie stood up abruptly. She looked at Bryce, then to her son, then finally back to Lewis. "I want to show you something." She walked to where they had set their luggage in one corner.

Neal leaped to his feet. "Mom, are you sure?"

"I'm sure." She knelt, took a small pocketknife from her purse, and began to slit the stitching on her suitcase. When the opening was big enough, she reached inside and withdrew the thin sheaf of typewritten pages. Then she stood and tossed them on the table in front of Lewis.

Curious, he leaned over, then his eyes widened. He looked up at her, shocked.

"Go on," she said, "look at it."

For the next several minutes the room was completely silent. Twice more he looked up at the others in the room, his face registering disbelief. Finally, he pushed the papers aside, turned slowly, and looked up at Jessie, who had stood over him the whole time. "Where did you get this?" he said in a low voice.

Jessie turned and pointed at Bryce. "He brought it to us."

Bryce stopped across the street and half a block down from the headquarters building of the Virginia Provincial Educational District and took a deep breath. He took the envelope out, opened the letter, and read it again for the twentieth time. It introduced him as Mr. John H. Carrol from the Ministry of Education. As he read it, Lewis's words echoed in his head again. "These papers are of excellent quality, but you must remember, they are what we call shallow cover. There is no John H. Carrol in the Ministry of Education. If anybody decides to check on you, you're blown!"

That had sobered Bryce. If Bryce was blown, then Lewis and Jessie and Neal and who knew how many others were also at risk. Once Lewis had read the sacred document—for that was

151

how Bryce was starting to think of it—he had instantly and completely accepted the three refugees from New England. When they had told him of their plans to escape to the West, he agreed to provide critical support. When Bryce told him of his need to find a certain person around the area of Arlington, Virginia, who might be a teacher, he had gone to work immediately, and by late afternoon of the next day, Lewis had produced the letter Bryce now held in his hands.

There were two women at their desks in the Office of Teacher Placement. A man was partially visible in a smaller office. Bryce stepped up to the counter and cleared his throat. Both women looked up, then the older of the two stood and came to him.

"Yes, may we help you?"

Bryce nearly smiled, then remembered Lewis's reminder. Government officials hold power. Petty power, it may be true, but power nevertheless. Never ask. Demand. So he kept his face impassive as he took out the letter and slid it across to her. "I'm John Carrol, from the Ministry of Education."

The woman straightened, and Bryce noted that the other woman was staring at him. The first read the letter as Bryce held his breath. All she had to do was call and check and—

She looked up at him with new respect. "Let me get Mr. Buckner."

But the man in the office had already heard and was coming toward Bryce, smiling obsequiously.

"Yes, Mr. Carrol, how may we help you?"

"I want to see a current list of all the teachers in your district."

Buckner, a small, nervous man in wire-rimmed glasses, nodded quickly, at the same time reading the letter that was on the counter.

"Yes, sir." He turned and snapped his fingers. The first woman instantly went to a file and brought back a folder.

"Is there something specifically I could help you with?" Buckner said, as he slid it across to Bryce.

152

"The list will be fine." He looked the man squarely in the eye as he opened it.

Buckner backed away quickly. "If there's anything else, just call."

Bryce didn't like this role. He softened a little. "Thank you, you're very helpful."

The list was alphabetized, and with a leap of excitement he saw what he was looking for third name down. "Leslie Adams: Teacher, history and government studies, Hillsburg Secondary School. Home address: 667 Walquist Avenue, Hillsburg, Virginia, ASA." No phone was listed.

Remembering where he was and who he was supposed to be, he fought down the urge to shout in triumph. Buckner was watching him closely. So Bryce thumbed idly through several pages, as though searching, found a name in the L's that lived in Hillsburg, and took out a paper. He wrote that one down, then two more from the S's. Finally, he turned back to the first page as though he were finished and quickly memorized Leslie's address. He closed the folder, put the paper back in his pocket.

"Thank you, Mr. Buckner. You've been most helpful. Could you tell me which bus number goes to Hillsburg?"

"Bus seven."

Bryce suddenly realized the foolishness of what he had just done. He looked at his slip of paper. "Let's see, actually it's Marysvale I need."

"That would be bus thirteen."

"Thank you."

Only when he was two full blocks away from the school did he suddenly leap upward and punch his fist in the air. "All right!" he whispered exultantly.

Hillsburg was a small town—almost a village—adjacent to Arlington. Finding the Hillsburg Secondary School was easy. He went to the principal's office first—or headmaster, as they called him—and produced his credentials. The result was the

153

same. Instant respect and anxious compliance. No, there was no one in particular Bryce wanted to see. He would just walk around and talk with some of the teachers if that was all right, look at the school, see how things were going. He had to be firm with that, or the man would have trailed him like a puppy, wringing his hands nervously.

He actually talked to only one teacher before he saw her walking down the hall toward him. He stopped, unable to keep from staring. It was Leslie! The same graceful walk, the same dark hair, though it was cut a bit more severely than he remembered. And her clothes, though all right, were clearly not the same as before.

She smiled faintly at him as she passed, obviously a little embarrassed by the frankness of his stare. There was no flicker of recognition.

"Uh . . . say," Bryce blurted. "Excuse me."

She stopped and turned back slowly.

Flustered now, all he could think of was to fall back on his cover. "My name is . . . uh . . . John H. Carrol. I'm from the Ministry of Education."

He saw the quick wariness in her eyes that was the standard response whenever he pulled rank. "Yes?"

"I'm visiting the school, talking to teachers, just seeing how things are going now that school has started."

"Oh?"

"Would you have a minute or two we could talk?"

She hesitated, then nodded, her face impassive. "Of course."

They were sitting in the faculty lounge. Her hands were folded in her lap, her legs were crossed. She met his eyes only occasionally, responded only to his direct questions, volunteered no more, no less than he asked. He decided to push a little.

"We've had some recurring reports about the classes in government."

"Oh?"

"Yes. Parents are reporting that some students are coming home with revisionist notions."

"Like what?"

Good question! He shrugged. "Like saying that the government may be too repressive."

She looked at him steadily.

"Well?" he asked.

"Well, what?"

"Do you think the government is too repressive?"

"Have *my* students been reported as saying that?"

"I didn't say that."

"Oh."

This was maddening. This wasn't the Leslie he knew. This woman was dull and listless. Evasive. If there was one thing Leslie had not been before, it was evasive. "You didn't answer my question," he finally said.

"What question?"

"Do you think the government is too repressive?"

"And you didn't answer my question."

Bryce laughed right out loud, startling her. Maybe she was evasive. But this stubborn streak—that was more like the girl he knew.

She watched him for a moment, then stirred. "Is that all?"

"No."

"Oh." She sat back, her eyes dropping to watch her hands.

"I would like to have dinner with you tonight."

For the first time, he penetrated the wall she had erected. And what was worse, for the first time he saw fear in her eyes.

By seven o'clock, the temperature had dropped down into the eighties. The humidity was also down, and the summer evening was beautiful. As Bryce turned up Walquist Avenue and started watching for Leslie's house number, he was actually whistling softly to himself. Not that he had unrealistic expectations about the night. He shook his head. The coldness with which

155

she had accepted his invitation after he had made his veiled threat was like a hard slap across the face. But he had found her, he had made contact, she had agreed to go to dinner with him. That was more than he had ever hoped he could do in one day.

It was an old house, probably thirty years or more, and run-down and dreary. A screened porch ran across most of the front. The paint was faded. One corner of the screen mesh on the door had torn loose. The grass was not dead but was badly parched, and a few scraggly looking petunias and azaleas grew along the walk. It was a sharp contrast to the neat and well-cared-for rambler in Arlington where Leslie lived before. With a sudden sense of gloom, he turned up the walk.

As he lifted his hand to knock, he stopped. A movement at the far end of the porch caught his eye. He turned, stepping back a little, so as to see more clearly through the screen. An older man sat in a rocking chair, hands folded in his lap, chin down on his chest. Bryce would have thought he was sleeping if it weren't for the fact that the rocker was going back and forth very slowly.

He knocked sharply, watching the man. His head came up slowly and turned toward Bryce, and Bryce's jaw dropped. The hair was white and thinning, the cheekbones high and protruding, adding to the sense of gauntness about the face, but there was no mistake. It was Leslie's father! His hands moved, and Bryce saw that they were twisted and deformed.

The effect was palpable, a jolt that shook him deeply. There was no question that Paul Adams had seen him, but he made no move to get up. He just watched Bryce steadily, the rhythm of the rocker never stopping.

Footsteps sounded in the house, and Bryce turned as the door opened and Leslie stepped out. She looked at him with the barest of acknowledgment, turned back, said something to someone inside, then shut the door firmly behind her. Finally he got a nod. "Good evening," she said. It was cool. Not curt, but cool.

"Hello."

She was dressed in a navy-blue skirt and pink blouse. It was hardly Neimann-Marcus, but it showed off the slimness of her figure and nicely accented her dark hair. It was a definite improvement over the severity of the dress she had been wearing at the school.

Instead of coming directly toward him, she turned and walked to the old man in the chair, bent over and kissed him on the cheek. Bryce barely heard the soft murmur of her voice. "Goodbye, Dad."

He said something to her, too soft to catch, and one of the twisted hands came up and brushed her cheek. She took the hand in both of hers and kissed it quickly. It was a tender gesture, full of love and affection, and Bryce blinked, surprised at a sudden burning in his eyes.

In a moment she was back to him, ignoring his questioning look toward her father. She started down the walk briskly, not waiting for him. Bryce looked once more at Paul Adams, then moved quickly to catch up with her.

"I'm sorry I don't have a car," he said as he fell into step beside her. "Is there a good place to eat in Hillsburg?"

She shot him a withering look. "Only a government worker would apologize for not having a car."

Bryce winced at his blunder, then just as suddenly laughed softly to himself. Maybe it would be all right after all. This was more like the Leslie he knew.

"What?" Her lips were pressed into a tight line.

"Nothing."

"Do you enjoy laughing at me?"

He shook his head quickly. "I wasn't laughing at you. I—I just remembered something, that's all."

From the look on her face, she took that about as well as a cat takes to having its tail pulled, but she said nothing, just increased her pace. "Look, Leslie—"

Her head jerked up.

157

"Sorry. Look, Miss Adams, I know you're not wild about this whole thing. How about if we just go get a root canal instead?"

She looked at him blankly.

"Sorry, just a little joke. My attempt at some humor."

She somehow managed to contain the gales of laughter.

"Look, I really am sorry. I didn't mean to badger you into this."

She stopped. "How sorry?"

Wow! This wasn't conversational hand grenades. This was a full-blown artillery duel. He grinned. "Not that sorry."

Off she went again, her heels popping sharply on the sidewalk. They walked on for several moments in silence before he tried again. "I . . . Look, hinting that I would write a negative report on you if you didn't accept my invitation was really a cheap shot. I wouldn't really have done it, you know."

The look she shot him out of the corner of her eye was like getting jammed with a needle. That and seeing the broken hulk of her father on the porch was enough to change his mind about the wisdom of this whole idea. He stepped forward quickly, turned to face her, and stopped. She stopped too, head up, lips tight with defiance.

"I really am sorry. I didn't know what else to do." He took a quick breath. "Actually, I didn't come to the school today to check up on teachers. I came only to see you."

That caught her off guard, and he pressed his advantage.

"If I give you my word that there will be no report of any kind, no coercion, no pressure, then will you consent to have dinner with me?"

Her eyes were still like flint. "You have my consent, remember?"

He shook his head. "No, I have your compliance, not your consent."

"You take what you get, Mr. Carrol!" she snapped.

He shrugged, suddenly tired of what he was doing to her. "Then I don't want it." He stepped back. "I'm sorry for the whole mess. Good night, Leslie."

He turned, thrust his hands into his pockets, and started away.

"Wait!"

He turned back slowly.

"Why *did* you come today?"

He let out his breath in a long weary sigh. "I met you once before." He shook his head at her sudden surprise. "No, you would never remember. But I did and . . . I wanted to meet you again."

Suspicion, surprise, and curiosity were all tumbling around in the depths of her eyes as she gave him a long, appraising look.

"But it was stupid of me to do it this way. Maybe sometime we can meet under better circumstances." He risked a quick smile. "Like maybe when you're really desperate to go out to dinner or something."

Still she looked at him. "You really *do* mean it!" she said, still disbelieving.

"Yes, I do."

"Why?"

This time he laughed out loud. "What? I can't even back out without you interrogating me?"

She didn't smile. "Why are you telling me this?"

Suddenly he was very serious. "Because as much as I'd like to have dinner with you, I'm getting a little tired of people throwing their weight around. I suddenly looked at myself and didn't like what I saw."

"Neither did I," she said bluntly.

"Oh, come on," he said soberly, "don't hold back on me. Give it to me straight."

That won him the closest thing that he had yet seen to a smile.

"Really," he went on, "I don't blame you in the least for being really burned with me. So . . . " He shrugged. "Maybe some other time."

159

"Maybe," she said slowly. He met her steady gaze, seeing what he hoped was some hint of softening.

"Of course, if you *were* to change your mind . . . " He let it hang hopefully in the air.

"Then what?"

He kept his face very serious. "I'd promise to use my napkin and not steal any silverware."

There was no answering smile, not even the glimmer of one. "You give your word there is nothing more to this than just dinner?" she asked gravely.

Bryce nodded, as sober as she. "Yes."

She took a deep breath, still hesitant; then, while it did not reach her mouth, a smile did touch her eyes. "All right, then. You have my consent, Mr. Carrol."

"Just call me Bryce, please."

She was staring at him, and for a second he was caught completely off guard. Now what had he done? Then the realization hit him with a cold shock. "I mean . . . Mr. Carrol is all right. John would be better. But my name is John B. Carrol. B as in Bryce. My family and friends call me Bryce."

Their date would hardly go down as a smashing success, but by the time they brought dessert—a raisin pudding with some kind of sauce—Bryce had to admit it had gone better than expected. She had finally picked the restaurant, as much, he suspected, because it was within easy walking distance as for the food. It was a small, corner cafe with red-and-white-checked tablecloths and a waiter/cook who looked like he'd just mustered out of a thirty-year stint with the merchant marines. The food was plain but passable. The prices, like those at Jessie's motel, were ridiculously cheap.

As they were walking in, Bryce suddenly remembered that Lewis had only given him a little over ten dollars in ASA currency. But he had no need to worry. He ordered a spaghetti dinner for a dollar fifteen, she had a chicken and broccoli casserole for one twenty-five. Lukewarm, watery soft drinks were a dime.

Short of standing on his head in the corner and singing an aria from *The Marriage of Figaro*, Bryce did everything he could think of to keep the conversation light and moving. He decided his charm was considerable because he managed to get her to smile three separate times, and once she laughed right out loud. But it was a painful task for him. Those brief moments of sunshine came hard. Most of the time she was withdrawn and quiet. It was hard to pin down an exact word for it—aloof, wooden, subdued. None of them completely fit. But whatever it was, it was a long way from the vibrant aliveness of the Leslie Adams he had known prior to last Thursday.

Through what little she did say, he also learned that the Adams family of this world was completely different from the one he had known before. He learned nothing about her father, and in fact she quickly steered the conversation away from him both times Bryce brought him up, but she revealed that her mother worked at a clothing factory. He also found out that Leslie was an only child. There was no sister named Kellie and no bright and mischievous brother named Keith. This was typical of many city families in CONAS. The economic realities of life were too harsh to encourage larger families, but it left him with a deep and profound sense of loss.

But none of that affected him as much as watching Leslie herself. He found only the briefest glimmers of the old Leslie he had come to love, and something began to happen somewhere deep inside him. As he had moved south across the countryside, he had been sickened by what he saw. But this was more than that. One could talk about the poverty, one could rail against the ever-present government oppression, one could shake one's head at the never-ending, backbreaking labor forced upon the people, but this! This was the bottom line. The ultimate impact of the system was on the individual human spirit, and when he

161

saw what it had done to Leslie, the sickness began to give way to a deep and smoldering anger.

As they finished, there were several moments of awkward silence, then Bryce pushed his chair back. "Well, shall we go?"

She stood up. "Thank you for dinner."

He nodded, smiling. "Thank you for accepting. You had every right to refuse."

"I know."

He winced, then she softened it with a smile. "But I'm glad I didn't."

With that he even winked at the merchant marine as they walked out of the restaurant.

On the street, she stopped. "There is no need to walk me back," she said abruptly. "I can find my own way."

He opened his mouth to protest, then clamped it shut again. "Whatever you say."

Her lips parted in surprise.

"I told you," he smiled ruefully, "no pressure. If you say head for the bus stop, I head for the bus stop."

For the first time he saw something really soften in her. "Thank you."

"You're welcome." Again there was an awkward moment of silence, but neither of them turned to go. "Look, Leslie," he finally went on, "I would really like to see you again. Maybe we could just go for a walk or something sometime?"

Again there was the long, searching look.

"You have my promise," he added quickly. "Anytime you say the word, I'm gone."

She put her hands in the pockets of her skirt, looking at the ground.

He felt a sharp pang of disappointment. "I understand. Bus stop, here I come."

Her head came up. "I didn't say that."

"What did you say?"

Again there was the hesitation, then she smiled a little. "When?"

162

His heart leaped. "Well, I'm in no hurry. How about tomorrow?"

She laughed. "Okay, tomorrow."

"After school?" He was really pleased. "I could even meet you there, walk you home—"

"No!" She saw his surprise at the way she had blurted it, and went on quickly. "It . . . It would be better at the house."

"Fine. How about five o'clock?"

"Yes. Five o'clock would be fine."

Charles Buckner had deliberately stayed late at the office. He reached for his phone for the seventh or eighth time, only this time the director of the Office of Teacher Placement for the Virginia Provincial Educational District had made up his mind. He picked it up and dialed the number out of his desk-top directory. He drummed his fingers as the phone started to ring. He and Quenton Norris had been roommates at the Washington Teachers College, but Norris was still a big shot in the Ministry of Education, and Buckner was still a minor official in a provincial office.

The phone clicked. "Hello."

"Quenton! Charlie Buckner."

"Well, Charlie, hello. This is a surprise. How are you?"

Buckner was encouraged by the warm cordiality in the other's voice. "Good, thank you. And you?"

"Fine. How's everything out in Arlington?"

"Well, pretty good. I just had a question for you."

"What?"

He lowered his voice. "Quenton, I thought you promised me you'd warn me any time someone from your office was going to drop in on us for a check."

The voice on the other end lowered just as swiftly. "That's right, why?"

"Well . . . " He took a breath. "Yesterday we kind of got caught off guard. We had this guy named John Carrol drop in on us and—"

"Hold it," Norris said, reaching for a pencil. "We don't have anyone by the name of Carrol in our office."

CHAPTER 19

"We're really happy you've found her," Jessie said the next morning when she and Lewis heard Bryce's report. She hesitated a moment. "Did you talk to her about going to the United States?"

That startled Bryce. Thoughts of the United States hadn't even crossed his mind. "No. She knows nothing about that."

"Good," Lewis said. "We think you ought to go slow with that." He too hesitated now, and Bryce could see they both had something on their mind. "We've been doing some checking," Lewis went on. "Her father is Paul Adams."

"So?" From his face it was obvious he expected Bryce to be impressed.

Jessie leaned forward in surprise. "You've never heard of Paul Adams?"

Bryce shook his head.

"Even in the New England Confederation we know about Paul Adams."

"What?"

"He happens to be the most famous dissident in all of CONAS."

"Dissident?" Bryce gave a quick, derisive laugh. "Hardly. Not the Paul Adams I saw."

"He used to teach at a university," Jessie explained. "He and three others spoke out against the government. They sent them to prison, then to work camps."

"Have you seen his hands?" Lewis asked.

Bryce's head snapped up. "Yes."

"He used to be an excellent pianist, almost concert level. No one knows exactly what happened in the camps, but . . . " He shrugged. "Well, you saw his hands."

"You must be careful," Jessie urged. "He has been home for several years now, but the government may still be watching him."

Bryce was only half listening. He was remembering Leslie's face when she reached down and kissed the grotesque hand that had caressed her cheek.

Leslie had said to come at five. Bryce deliberately timed it so he was there at four-thirty. The suit and tie of the day before had been replaced by jeans, a short-sleeved sports shirt, and tennis shoes. He looked down at the ragged shoes. Compared to the hundred-and-fifty-dollar shoes his mother had given him last Christmas, these weren't much, but then somehow in CONAS, jogging and tanning salons had not fared so well.

As he started up the walk, he noted with satisfaction that Paul Adams was sitting in the rocking chair where he had been the day before. Bryce knocked softly on the screen, then stepped inside. A book sat unopened on Paul's lap, but the head turned and the eyes watched him steadily as he walked up to him.

"Mr. Adams? Hello. I'm Bryce Sher . . . uh . . . Carrol. I'm a friend of Leslie's."

It was no mystery from whom Leslie had gotten her eyes. His were the same deep green flecked with brown and were filled with the same bright alertness. The previous impressions of a broken shell of a man were certainly not confirmed by the piercing look he was getting now.

"May I sit down?"

There was a quick nod, half a smile, and he started to rock again.

"I've come to take Leslie on a walk. Guess I'm a little early."

"It's warm today."

The richness of the voice caught him by surprise. It was deeper than the other Paul's. Bryce shook his head. The other Paul. This Paul. It was crazy. They were the same man. Then he shook his head again. He was staring at the hands. If a man was the product of what happened to him, this was not the same man.

"Doing some reading, I see," he said, looking at the book.

Paul nodded, looking down, and the hands gathered in the book. It was old and scarred, but there was no title on the leather, either on the front cover or the spine. One twisted thumb began to rub along the cover, back and forth, back and forth. Again Bryce found himself staring. They—whoever "they" happened to be—must have broken every bone. The palms were twisted and deformed, the fingers bent and twisted, the knuckles bulbous knobs. Could these misshapen lumps ever have played the piano?

Bryce's head came up as he realized the rocking had stopped. He looked away quickly, embarrassed to have been caught staring. Suddenly the revulsion welled up in him like bile, and he lifted his eyes to meet the other's gaze.

"They say you were a marvelous pianist," he said softly. "I wish I could have heard you."

There was a quick impression of surprise followed by a long pause, then the deep richness of the voice spoke again. "It was a long time ago."

"Which would only make the memory sweeter now," Bryce replied.

There was another slow nod, then the rocking began again.

"Why?" Bryce burst out. "I can understand prison. I understand work camps. But why your hands?"

For a long time there was no response, and, embarrassed again, Bryce nearly stood up and left to wait for Leslie out front. Then Paul Adams spoke, very softly. "Evil men," was all he said.

Bryce sat back. "Evil men did this to you?"

There was a quick shake of the head.

167

"What?"

"Evil men hate beautiful things."

And in a sudden flash of insight Bryce understood. "They hated you because you played the piano?"

The gnarled old hands opened the book, pushing it slightly toward Bryce. He leaned over to see better. It was filled with short lines of poetry handwritten in a beautiful script.

"Music and words," said the voice. "Beautiful things in a sea of ugliness. They could not bear it."

"I understand." And he did. More powerfully than he ever had before. And the anger that had started the previous evening with Leslie suddenly was a hard, tangible ball in the pit of his stomach.

Bryce jumped as one of Paul's hands swung over and rested on his knee. Bryce looked up in surprise and was even more startled. The eyes, sunk deep in hollow cheeks, were peering at him, and they were filled with triumph. There was no other word for it. His eyes were filled with a blazing triumph!

Paul Adams leaned back. "But they cannot break the fingers of your mind."

A sudden sound brought Bryce's head around. Leslie was standing in the doorway to the house, staring at them, her eyes round and wide and glistening with tears.

They were sitting in a small park a few blocks from her home. They had talked little as they had come, she answering his questions about her day briefly and noncommittally. Bryce sat on the grass. Leslie was in one of the swings of the playground, not moving, just smoothing the sand with the bottom of her foot.

Finally she looked up at him. "How long had you been there?"

"About five or ten minutes." He stopped. "How long were *you* there?"

She lowered her eyes, the dark lashes almost hiding them. "I heard voices. I . . . I shouldn't have listened." Suddenly tears

168

welled up again, and she shook her head, angry with herself. "I've never heard him talk about it before," she whispered. "He will with Mama, but never with me."

He wasn't sure how to answer that, so he just watched her. "What did you say that got him started?"

"I asked him about his hands." He looked away. "They're horrible."

She closed her eyes. "I know. I have nightmares about them."

They sat that way for almost a minute, both lost in their own thoughts. He finally looked up when he realized she was looking at him steadily.

"Who *are* you?"

That visibly startled him.

"And I'm sorry," she cried, "but John B. Carrol, or John *H.* Carrol won't do anymore. Who are you?"

Bryce felt his stomach drop.

"Are you from the government?"

He shook his head quickly. "No. I'm not John Carrol, and I am not from the Ministry of Education or any other government agency for that matter."

"Why should I believe you?" she said bitterly.

"My name is Bryce Sherwood. I'm . . . I'm from a long ways from here. Boston, to be exact."

"What are you doing here? What do you want?"

He sighed, knowing that he could no longer lie to her, but knowing also that he could hardly reveal but very little. "Like I told you yesterday—I met you a long time ago. I've never forgotten. I wanted to meet you again, so I used the letter to find you. I'm sorry. It was stupid."

"How can I believe you? How do I know you're not lying now?"

He stood to face her, took a deep breath, and let it out slowly. "Because you were there when I talked with your father."

That stopped her. She blinked quickly, remembering. "That's the only reason I'm here talking to you now," she said, then

169

instantly she was fierce again. "But I'll do anything to stop him from being hurt."

"I am not here to hurt him. Or you."

She looked away, torn with indecision.

"Leslie, I'll tell you what. You're worried that I will hurt you or your father. Well, all you have to do is call the Ministry of Education and tell them I was using false papers. You can have me taken out at any time. I'm now as vulnerable as you."

She didn't turn back, just kept smoothing the dirt with her foot over and over. "Do you want to know the crazy thing?" she finally said softly.

"What?"

"As we were leaving today, when he called me back . . . "

"Yes?"

"He asked me if you could stay for dinner."

Now Bryce was staring. "You're kidding!"

Suddenly her eyes were brimming with tears. "Four years. It's been four years since we had someone for dinner. Mama won't believe it."

"So what did you tell him?"

She smiled through the tears, and suddenly she was so lovely Bryce had to force himself not to reach out and touch her cheek.

"I told him you steal silverware and that we don't have that much to lose."

CHAPTER 20

Captain James Rodale, district commander for the Hartford District of the Internal Security Division, was awed. Here he sat, in the heart of Washington, in the office of the Minister of Internal Affairs. Out one window was an impressive view of the presidential palace that housed the prime minister. Out another stood the National Assembly Building.

Nearly as intimidating as the presence of the minister himself was the personage of the third man in the room. Colonel Anthony Burkhart, Chief Director of ISD for all of CONAS—it was a name that every ISD agent throughout the world knew and respected. His picture hung in Rodale's Hartford office next to that of the prime minister. Now Rodale was in his presence.

The three men watched the minister's secretary pour coffee and waited until she exited. Then the minister turned to Rodale. "Okay, Captain, let's hear what you've got."

Rodale stood, cleared his throat, and looked first to Burkhart and then to the minister. He gave the report of his findings in quick, terse sentences. He also summarized his conclusions, ticking them off quickly. When he finished, the other two men sat quietly for a moment, sipping their coffee. Finally, the minister took a silver cigarette box on his desk, offered it to Rodale and Burkhart, then took one himself.

When all three had lit up, the minister sat back, inhaled deeply, then blew the smoke out in a cloud over his head. "You really think Sherwood didn't kill the captain?" he asked finally.

Rodale shook his head emphatically. "Everything points to the Lamberts as the killers. First, we know that the body was carried in their truck. Second, the son was seen at the place of burial. Third, the Lambert boy had a rifle of the same caliber that killed the captain. And fourth, the Lamberts are on the list of suspected resistance people in the Bollingbroke area. There were some things we found in the motel that would be enough to send them to prison. Maybe the captain stumbled onto something when he came looking for Sherwood."

He paused, but neither man spoke, so he went on. "Sherwood is a puzzle. He drops into the picture from nowhere. No one in the village knew him, we're pretty certain of that. We have those odd attempts to make a phone call the night before. And yet we're certain he is traveling with the Lamberts now. The driver of that itinerant worker bus identified them as the three who got on his bus in a little village south of Bollingbroke."

He shook his head. "Like I say, Sherwood is a puzzle."

The minister nodded, then straightened and looked directly at him. "How would you like to come to work for Colonel Burkhart, Captain?"

Rodale started, staring at the minister, then at the head of ISD.

Burkhart smiled. "We're bringing your investigative team down too. We'd like you to stay in command of them."

"Yes, sir!"

The minister looked to his head of ISD. "Anthony, tell him what's happening."

Rodale leaned forward, watching the colonel closely, thrilled to be part of something that had "big" written all over it.

"We know who Sherwood is," the colonel said abruptly, then smiled faintly at Rodale's surprise. "More importantly, we know where he is."

"Really? That's great, sir!"

Burkhart accepted that without expression. "He showed up here about a week after the New England thing using false papers from the minister of education. We got positive ID on him day before yesterday. He's taken up with a teacher out in Hillsburg, a little town in Virginia province."

The minister took another deep drag on his cigarette, then blew the smoke gently upward. "The teacher is the daughter of Paul Adams."

Rodale had just started to pick up his coffee cup. He set it down slowly. "*The* Paul Adams?"

Both men nodded, and Rodale gave a low whistle.

"That's why you're here," the minister said. "We're going to put a blanket of surveillance over Sherwood so tight he can't even untie his shoelaces without us knowing what color they are . . . " His eyes narrowed and bored in on Rodale. "And so loose that he won't have the slightest—and I emphasize, *the slightest*—suspicion that we are on to him."

"I understand, sir," Rodale said slowly, realizing that he was about to either make or break his career.

"Good." The minister stood abruptly. "I've got another meeting, so I'll leave you two to work out the details."

Burkhart nodded.

The minister smiled down at the director of ISD. It was a pleasant smile, but when he spoke his voice was like a sudden blast of air rolling off the Arctic tundra. "Let's find out what our friend is up to, shall we?"

It was Thursday, September 22, three weeks to the day since Bryce had skidded his car into a wall of light and his life into another dimension. He was thinking about that as he chewed on a blade of grass outside the Hillsburg Secondary School, watching the last of the uniformed students filter away from the campus. There had been no more sign of Gorham since the root cellar, and though something inside Bryce fiercely resisted giving up hope, nevertheless that hope was dimming every day, and the possibility of being locked in this time and place for the rest of his life was becoming more and more a reality.

He looked up, then stood quickly. Leslie was just coming out with another teacher. Both had an armload of books and papers.

"Hi." He waved to the other teacher, then took the books from Leslie.

"Hello." She smiled up at him warmly and slipped her hand through his arm.

It was the only thing that made the thoughts of staying bearable. In the last ten days, his relationship with Leslie had blossomed. In fact, he had kissed her last night for the first time. At first she had pulled back, startled and surprised, then suddenly she had put her arms around his neck and kissed him back, softly and without reservation.

It had not come easy, for somewhere deep inside her was the suspicion, the lingering fear, that somehow he brought danger to her family. And at that thought, Bryce frowned. He was intimately involved with the resistance movement and there was a dead ISD captain buried somewhere in the Connecticut woods. If they found Bryce and connected him with Paul Adams in any way . . .

Maybe it was best to pack it up and head west with Jessie and Neal. They were pressuring him with increasing insistence now. So far he had stubbornly put them off, unable to face the thought of leaving Leslie, even if it was the best for her. Neal had finally suggested he bring the Adams family with them, but Bryce thrust that aside immediately. The risks of being caught were high. Paul Adams would go directly back to the men who had shattered his hands. And thus with each day, Bryce's dilemma and frustrations deepened.

Suddenly he realized Leslie was looking up at him with a quizzical expression. He forced a quick smile. "What?"

"What in the world were you thinking that had you so far away?"

He gave her a long, searching look. "I was thinking about how different things would be now if you hadn't agreed to have dinner with me that first night."

She laid her head against his shoulder and just nodded, squeezing his arm. They walked on for several moments in silence, then she said, "Mom wants to know if you can stay for dinner tonight."

He shook his head, causing her to look up in surprise. "Only if your mother will let me buy some of the food."

"You know better than that."

Bryce nodded glumly. He had already tried it before and lost. The Vera Adams of this dimension was just as sweet and kind and hardheaded as the Vera Adams of the other. She had adamantly refused to let him help out with the food budget and also refused to let him help with the dishes afterwards.

"She will be eternally grateful to you for what you have done for Daddy," Leslie said softly. She squeezed his arm. "And so will I. You've done enough to earn dinner at our house for the rest of your life."

Bryce pushed back from the kitchen table, groaned, then patted his stomach and rolled his eyes. "Just lay me on a stretcher and carry me straight to the mortuary."

Leslie pulled a face at him. "Well, that's a wonderful compliment for the cooking."

He ignored her and just kept looking at her mother. "And let it be written on my tombstone: Here lies Bryce Sherwood. He ate the pie, gave a sigh, and died with pleasure in his eye."

Vera laughed, but Leslie just groaned. "Oh, brother! Now you can carry us *all* out on a stretcher. That was awful."

"That kind of poetry certainly would never have gotten you in trouble in the work camps," Paul Adams agreed dryly.

"Well, I liked it," Leslie's mother said firmly. "Thank you, Bryce."

He smiled at her warmly, amazed at how quickly he had come to feel completely at home with her. He still found Paul Adams a little overpowering. Even during light conversation, Bryce's eyes would stray to the twisted, misshapen hands, and all that

175

this man represented would well up again. But with Vera he felt perfectly at ease.

Leslie's mother pushed back her chair, then stood. "Paul, why don't you and Bryce go in the living room? Leslie and I will get the dishes done."

Bryce stood and picked up his plate. "I think it's about my turn to do some dishes around here."

"No," Vera said firmly, taking it from him.

Leslie nodded as she stood and began clearing the table. "You and Daddy go out and talk. We'll just be a minute."

Paul Adams got up slowly, his eyes twinkling. "You are not a good influence in this kitchen, young man. Next thing you know, these two are going to start expecting me to do the same."

"Both of you, get!" Vera said, shooing at them with a dish towel.

As they settled in the living room, Paul leaned back in his chair and closed his eyes, and the silence stretched out between them for almost a full minute.

"Any idea why Leslie doesn't fully trust you yet?"

Bryce looked up in surprise. The man could still be very deceiving. He could sit for ten or fifteen minutes, his eyes staring off at something, a hollow vacancy filling his face, then pow! he would come off the wall with a comment that caught Bryce completely off guard.

Bryce almost tried a quip, changed his mind and merely shrugged.

Paul said, "It's more than the fact that you used false pretenses to find her."

Again Bryce tried not to show his surprise. Had Leslie told him about the John Carrol thing?

"She's afraid for me."

Bryce sighed again, this time with great weariness. "Yes, I know."

"Are you going to make trouble for me?" he said slowly, and suddenly the green eyes bore in with fierce intensity.

176

"No, sir," he said quietly. "Nor Leslie. I wouldn't do anything that would harm your family."

There was silence for several seconds as the eyes continued their steady probe, then finally they closed again. "I know." He laid his head back. "Don't give up on her."

Bryce was staring at him but the eyes stayed shut.

"Just give it time."

"I plan to." And at that moment, he made up his mind what he was going to tell Lewis and Jessie and Neal. "I really plan to," he said again, with more firmness.

Paul Adams's mouth pulled into a tiny smile. "I know that too," he said softly.

CHAPTER 21

"Look," Bryce said, deciding there was no use in prolonging the issue, "I've got to be honest with you." He spread out his hands. "I can't go with you."

They were in another safe house, this time in Arlington. Bryce had gone to see Jessie Lambert the previous night as soon as he had got home from Leslie's and told her they needed to meet with Lewis. This evening, he had waited until dark, then caught the bus to Arlington, met Jessie and Neal, then spent nearly an hour moving through the city, carefully checking to be sure they were not under surveillance. Once they were in the safe house, Bryce plunged in the moment Lewis sat them down around the kitchen table.

"You don't need me. Sure, I'm from the United States, but that doesn't help you much. I don't know the country between here and there. I've never crossed the demilitarized zone. I'm just not going to be that helpful."

Jessie shot a quick look in the direction of Lewis and her son. There was a definite impression of surprise, but it was certainly not dismay, which of itself caught Bryce off guard.

"Have you talked to Leslie or her parents about this?" Lewis asked.

Bryce shook his head firmly. "No, they know nothing about it. Nothing."

Again there was the quick exchange of glances, and Bryce had the sudden suspicion that he was missing out on something.

He looked at Jessie, realizing how much he owed this quiet woman and her son. "I feel lousy, after all you've done." He turned. "And you, Lewis. You've given me clothes, money, papers, found me a place to live—and now this." He sighed. "But I just can't walk away from Leslie."

Jessie shot Lewis one more searching look, at which he smiled slightly and gave a quick nod. She turned back to Bryce. "Suppose we told you we don't want you to go."

Bryce's head came up slowly, causing Neal to laugh softly at his expression.

"Suppose we told you we're not going either," Jessie continued.

"What?" Bryce was staring. That's all they had talked about since they had fled the New England Confederation. "Why not?"

Both mother and son looked to Lewis. He took a deep breath, then plunged in. "If we could make it to the United States it would be wonderful—" There was a long pause. "For us."

"What does that mean?"

"It would be great for whoever ends up going, but who else does it help?"

"I still don't understand."

"How widespread do you think the resistance movement is here in CONAS?"

Bryce shrugged, a little surprised by the question. "I don't know."

"If you count the New England Confederation, the Confederation of Canadian States as well as the Atlantic States Alliance, we estimate that we have somewhere between five and seven thousand actively involved."

Bryce gave a low whistle. Seven thousand!

Neal leaned forward eagerly. "And for every person actively involved we have five to ten more who support us."

"And," Jessie broke in, "the vast majority of the population hate the government. They are sick to death of the oppression, the stagnant economy, the constant fear."

179

Bryce looked back and forth between the three of them. "What are you suggesting?" he asked warily.

Again the three of them looked back and forth. Again there was the imperceptible nod, then suddenly Lewis stood and walked to the door leading off to the bedroom.

Half a block away, in a small van crammed with electronic gear, Captain James Rodale leaned forward over the radio, listening intently to the sudden silence. He could clearly hear the footsteps of the man they called Lewis, but nothing else. He grabbed his walkie-talkie. "All units stand by," he whispered. "If they start to move, close in fast."

He had done his work well, putting a rolling surveillance on Sherwood and the Lamberts all the way in from Hillsburg. It took an incredible amount of manpower, one person following for a block or two, then passing them on by radio to the next shadow. But Burkhart had given him the teams, and he used them well. He was sure his people had not been spotted.

At that moment the door to the van opened and Colonel Anthony Burkhart stepped inside.

"Glad you're here, sir." Rodale turned and took the notes from a stenographer. In addition to taping the conversation taking place in the safe house, Rodale was keeping summary notes of the dialogue. He handed the sheets to his commander.

Burkhart nodded crisply. "The minister should be here in a few moments." He dropped his eyes and started skimming quickly. His eyes narrowed and his lips pressed into a tight line as he read.

Suddenly over the speaker came the sound of a door opening and shutting and more footsteps. Rodale held up his hand for silence.

Lewis opened the door and stepped back. From the hallway came a medium-built man in his mid-thirties. He was dressed in jeans, T-shirt, and sneakers. His hair was sandy and tousled, the eyes a light blue and filled with soberness, his body that of an athlete in superb shape.

"Bryce," Lewis said, "let me introduce Wesley Quinn . . . "

The man stepped forward, extending his hand. Bryce stood and accepted the grip, which was firm but not crushing.

" . . . a representative from the Agency for Internal Security."

"Good to meet you," Bryce said, liking the man's face almost immediately.

"The AIS, or Agency for Internal Security," Lewis went on, noting Bryce's lack of reaction to the title, "is the primary espionage agency for the government of the United States of America."

That got the reaction Lewis had hoped for. Bryce's jaw dropped. "The United States?" he echoed.

Lewis chuckled and moved back to the table, gesturing for them all to sit down. "We thought that might get your attention." Then instantly he sobered. "Wes is taking a tremendous risk to be here, so let's jump right into it, shall we?"

Wesley Quinn took the chair directly across from Bryce, leaned forward on his elbows, and started to talk, quietly, with little dramatic expression—but the words staggered Bryce.

"I'll be brief and to the point. The United States of America, along with the Republic of Latin American States and the Canadian Republic, or Free Canada, as you call it, are tired of sharing the continent with states that threaten our way of life. We're tired of states that seek the overthrow of our governments. We're tired of states that try to subvert our peoples through propaganda and infiltration. And we're tired of states that publicly declare that their goal is to bring all of North America under their dominion."

He stopped, but Bryce was still just staring at him, so he took a quick breath and continued. "We are not willing to declare open hostilities—unless of course, they do first—but earlier this year a secret agreement was signed creating a Western Alliance of Free States. One of the articles of the agreement states that the Western Alliance will actively support any viable movements within CONAS that seek to change the existing order of things.''

He leaned back, letting that sink in.

''So you're saying . . . '' Bryce stopped, the enormity of the thought suddenly hitting him. He turned to Jessie, then Lewis.

Lewis nodded soberly. ''If we leave CONAS, we help no one but ourselves. If we stay, our influence could become immeasurable.''

Quinn picked that up. ''For the past few months we've been exploring options, looking for some way to crystalize the various resistance movements within CONAS.''

Neal, excitement crackling in his eyes, swung around to Bryce. ''Wes thinks they can smuggle Mom out of CONAS to the U.S. She'll travel through the three nations of the West on a massive fund-raising drive. There are tens of thousands of people who have escaped to there over the years. Our goal is to raise ten million dollars or more to help finance the movement.''

''Like Golda Meier did for Israel,'' Bryce said.

''Who?''

He shook his head. ''It doesn't matter.''

''In the meantime,'' Lewis broke in, ''the rest of us stay here. We'll unify the various freedom movements, try to marshal the support of the people, set up the necessary support structure for a full-scale revolution.''

''Do you know what you're saying?'' Bryce blurted. ''You don't just wave your hand and overthrow a government, especially a government with as much entrenched power as CONAS has.''

The AIS agent from America nodded soberly. ''We know that, but for the first time we think the conditions are right. No one is kidding themselves; it isn't going to be easy. Even the different freedom movements within CONAS tend to distrust one another.''

Jessie reached across and laid her hand on Bryce's arm. ''But it will never happen unless we start somewhere.'' Her eyes were moist and full of quiet determination. "We've got to begin sometime!"

Bryce sat back, his mind racing. This was treason talk. What had already been said in the room was worth an automatic death sentence for every one of them. Suddenly, he thought of Nathaniel Gorham's accusation in the root cellar. Had Bryce really changed that much, or was he just reeling from the intellectual shock of his new environment? There in the cellar, he hadn't been sure. Now? In the last three weeks he had traveled the land. He had tasted the fear. He had seen the twisted hands and battered lives. The image of a terror-stricken girl cowering before two border guards flashed into his mind. And then he thought of Leslie. He thought of the anger that seethed in him every time he saw what the system had done to her. Always before, when he thought of freedom and the Founding Fathers, it had been in the abstract. Now he understood the fires that drove those early patriots, and suddenly Bryce wished Gorham were here, in this room, at that very moment, asking him those questions again.

He cleared his throat. "What do you want me to do?"

Wesley Quinn gave him a long steady look. Finally, he spoke. "The conditions have been right for a rebellion for many years, but up until now we've lacked the spark that will ignite the tinder. We've needed something that will seize the imagination of the people and fire their will. The document you brought will help. It's electrifying! Even in the United States we do not have a copy of the Declaration of Independence. When the time is right, we'll publish it for the people. It can become the rallying cry for the revolution."

He sat back, and every eye in the room was fastened upon him. "But something more is needed, something more than a document, something more than just a cause." He stopped, the blue of his eyes darkening with sudden intensity. "What we need is the right person."

Bryce laughed right out loud. "Surely you don't think I'm that person? Look, if you need someone to pass out pamphlets

183

on the street corner, or even throw a Molotov cocktail at a tank or two, maybe I'm your man. But . . . "

He stopped. Quinn was shaking his head slowly. "You're not the person we had in mind."

"Oh." Embarrassed for jumping to such a conclusion, Bryce dropped his head. "Then who?"

"Paul Adams," came the quiet reply.

In the van filled with electronics gear, the minister of internal affairs clenched his fist and slammed it against the wall, causing the man monitoring the transmission and the stenographer to jump sharply. "I've heard enough!" he thundered. He swung around to Colonel Anthony Burkhart. "Bring them in!"

Rodale, standing next to Burkhart, leaped into action, grabbing his walkie-talkie. "All units! All units! This is a go. Close in on the targets. I repeat, close in on the targets."

"You'd better not lose one of them," the minister said, his voice suddenly deathly quiet. "And I don't want Sherwood so much as bruised."

"Paul Adams is known all over the continent. He is admired and loved." The AIS agent from America jabbed a finger at Bryce. "We'd like to call a meeting of all the leaders of the various resistance movements in the next few weeks. They won't come—they're too independent, too worried about being caught . . . unless we can tell them Paul Adams is with us. If Jessie can tell the people in the West that Paul Adams is leading the movement, we'll double the contributions. The governments of the Western Alliance will know we have a viable movement with Paul Adams leading it." He suddenly sat back, wearily. "I could go on and on. Paul Adams is the key to everything, Bryce, and you are the key to Paul Adams."

Bryce shook his head stubbornly. "You don't understand. I can't ask him to risk his life again."

Quinn shook his head slowly. "You asked me what you can do. I'm telling you now. Get us Paul Adams!"

There was a soft tinkling sound from somewhere behind them, and suddenly Lewis was on his feet, waving his hands urgently. "Someone's coming!" he hissed. In one leap he was to the light switch and plunged the room in darkness.

But Captain James Rodale had done his work too well. As the five of them scrambled frantically down a back staircase and through the small patch of fenced yard, floodlights suddenly bathed them in brilliant whiteness. Blue uniformed policemen appeared everywhere, rifles steady, and in less than thirty seconds it was over. Five stunned conspirators were handcuffed to the chain-link fence, and Rodale had won his triumph.

Bryce leaned against the fence, feeling the metal of the cuffs cutting into his wrists, not much caring in his dazed shock. The words of the ISD captain had hit him like a fist to the stomach. "You are hereby charged with conspiracy, consorting with agents of an enemy power, treason, and murder." In that moment Bryce understood perfectly that their conversation in the safe house had been monitored and what that meant to all of them.

But that was nothing compared to the jolt that hit him when the captain turned and spoke to two shadowy figures in business suits standing just beyond the circle of lights. "What about the Adams family?" he called. "Shall we move in on them now?"

Bryce didn't hear the reply. Suddenly his stomach was twisting violently and he felt that he was going to be sick. All of his promises. All of his assurances. For nothing! He had betrayed Leslie and her father.

"All right," the captain said to his men. "Move them out. Separate cars. Separate cells. None of the prisoners are to talk to each other or communicate in any way."

They led the others away one at a time. A uniformed policeman stepped up to Bryce, released the handcuff from the fence, and put it on his own wrist. As they started for the van, the two men in suits finally stepped out into the light and moved toward where the biggest of the cars was parked. The taller man Bryce didn't know. But as the shorter one came fully into the brightness of the floodlights, Bryce stiffened and gasped.

He was short and wiry, built like a marathon runner. The hair was dark and thick and just starting to gray at the temples. The dark eyes were brooding and grim as death. He stopped for a moment and looked directly into the shocked face of Bryce Sherwood. "Well, well," Elliot Mannington said softly. "Look who we have here."

Then he swung around to the second man. "Colonel, I am late for a meeting with the prime minister right now. But as soon as I'm back, I want to see Bryce in my office."

"Yes, sir."

Mannington turned back to Bryce, his voice hard. "We'll have our little talk then, and let me tell you, mister, it had better be good."

CHAPTER 22

The events that followed were a blur in Bryce's mind—the ride in the police van, the arrival at the prison, the hasty booking process, then being shoved roughly into a foul-smelling cell. Now as he sat on his cot, head in hands, two things kept going through his mind over and over—the first was Elliot Mannington, the second was Leslie Adams and her father.

He had been so stunned by the sight of Mannington that he had done nothing more than gape at him. The thought that Mannington might also be present in this sphere had never entered his mind. And yet he knew that was simply his own shortsightedness. Leslie and her father were here. Gorham had said his parents were also here. Then why not Mannington?

But who was he? Now, other details began to come back to him—the unmistakable aura of power and authority that surrounded him, the obvious deference the others had shown him, even the one they called the colonel. And why should he be present at the arrest of a small group of underground resistance fighters?

There were no answers, and finally Bryce would push the questions aside. But that only opened up the way for the waves of guilt as he thought of Leslie and her family. Even at this moment they might be here in the prison. Did Leslie know? Did she know it was Bryce who had led the hounds to their door? From the beginning she had been afraid he meant danger for them. But no, he was so confident, so sure he had escaped from

New England without detection. He had looked her father straight in the eye. "I wouldn't do anything that would bring you or your family danger. I only care for Leslie. Trust me!"

The bitterness welled up in his throat like a lump of bile.

"Things may not be as bleak as they seem, Laddie."

Bryce whirled. Just inside the bars of his cell, slowly materializing in the semidarkness, was the figure of Nathaniel Gorham.

"Gorham!"

The old man's fingers flew to his lips. "Shhh! You keep bellering like a calf for its mother and you'll have the whole prison awake."

Bryce instantly dropped his voice to a whisper. "Where have you been?"

Gorham ignored that. "We must talk very quickly. Mannington will be returning very soon now and sending for you."

"Mannington!" Bryce hissed. "Who is he anyway?"

"Mannington is what is known as the minister of internal affairs. The ISD comes totally under his jurisdiction. He is one of the three or four most powerful men in the Confederation of North American States."

"Great!" Bryce said in despair. "What other little surprises have you got in store for me? What about Senator Hawkes? Is he here too?"

"Benjamin Hawkes is a minor official in the New England Confederation up in Boston."

"And Sterling Jennings? I mean, who else is going to jump out at me?"

"Who's Jennings?"

"Former secretary of defense. He was with Mannington the night they offered me the ratification chairmanship."

"Oh, yes." Gorham shrugged again. "I don't know. He's one of the officials in the Ministry of Foreign Affairs. Doesn't really matter."

Bryce sat back, digesting that.

"You've not asked about the most important one."

"Who?"

Gorham looked at him steadily.

"*Who?*"

"Did nothing strike you as strange tonight when Mannington confronted you?"

Bryce was suddenly nodding, the memory coming back like a flash. "Yes. He called me by name, spoke as if . . . " He was staring at Gorham. "He *did* know me!"

"That's right. Leslie and Paul Adams are here in this dimension. Elliot Mannington is here." He paused, then finished softly. "And so is Bryce Sherwood."

"That's impossible!"

Gorham put up his hands. "Look, let's not start that again. I'm afraid my little analogy with the railroad track and the switch has misled you. There are not parallel tracks, not two separate, coexisting dimensions. There's not another Bryce Sherwood somewhere out there right now sailing off the coast of Cape Cod. It doesn't work that way."

"Then how?" Bryce started, his head swimming. "How can all of this be?"

Gorham sighed. "When you hit that wall of light, it was as if you had instantly been hurtled backwards in time to 1787, the point where the railroad switch was located. Then in another instant you hurtled forward again. You were on the same train, with the same people, only now it's in an America that never had the Constitution."

"So I've had a whole life here?" He rubbed his hand across his eyes. "Then why can't I remember it?"

"Look," Gorham said, with growing exasperation. "You were put here by direct decree of the Council of Founding Fathers. I'm sorry if every detail doesn't happen to fit into some neat, logical compartment for you. But that's the way things are. Get that through your head, because time is running out fast now."

Bryce finally straightened. "Who was I—or am I, then?"

"You are Bryce Sherwood. As a boy you were brought to Boston by an uncle. That's where you were raised. From there it's much the same as what you know. You graduated from

189

Harvard Law School. Benjamin Hawkes spotted you and hired you as an assistant. That's how Mannington met you."

He stopped, and Bryce felt his heart sink.

"For the past four years, you have been the special assistant to Elliot Mannington III, minister of internal affairs."

"Special assistant? What does that mean?"

"You're Mannington's fair-haired boy. It's a low-profile but high-responsibility position. He uses you for things he doesn't fully trust anyone else to take."

The implications of what Gorham was saying were exploding in his mind, and none of those implications were very cheering. "So here I am, special assistant to the minister of internal affairs, caught conspiring with a group of resistance fighters? No wonder he said what he did tonight."

"Are you?" Gorham asked sharply.

"Am I what?"

"Conspiring with the resistance movement?"

"No," Bryce retorted bitterly. "Actually, I'm in here for loitering."

The sarcasm had no effect on the old man. "There in the meeting tonight, you asked the American agent what you could do to help them. Did you really mean it?"

Bryce was suddenly angry. "If you knew I was there, why didn't you appear then, warn us about the police? What does it matter now what I said?"

"It matters very much. Did you mean it?"

Bryce took a deep breath, meeting the probing gaze. "Yes."

"I didn't appear earlier because I was not allowed to. That meeting was a test to see if you had really changed." He stopped, and a smile stole across his face. "Now you've passed the second one as well."

"What second one?"

His eyes were gleaming. "Do you realize that you haven't demanded that I take you back to the other dimension tonight. Not once. Do you realize that?"

That rocked Bryce back. "I . . . I guess I assumed it isn't possible."

"No. It's because you've forgotten yourself. For the first time, you're wrapped up in something bigger than your own needs." He straightened suddenly. "Because of this, the council has authorized me to help you."

Bryce just stared at him. "How?" A sudden hope leaped up in him. "Can you get to Leslie and her father, help them get away?"

Gorham shook his head.

Bryce suddenly felt sick again. "Is it too late?"

"No. No action will be taken against Leslie's family until after your meeting with Mannington tonight. They're still safe."

The relief that hit him was like a blast of fresh air in the cell. "Then what? What do we do?" he asked.

Gorham pulled at his lower lip. "Once, in a speech you wrote for Senator Hawkes, you quoted something from Winston Churchill. Do you remember?"

Bryce started to shake his head; then, in an instant, it flashed back into his mind. He nodded and began to quote softly: " 'We fight not for glory, not for riches, not for honor; we fight only and alone for freedom, which no good man surrenders, save with his life.' "

"It's one thing to say that in a speech," Gorham said slowly. "It's something else again to say it when you're facing a death sentence in a prison cell, right?"

Bryce nodded slowly, the chilling reality of the possibilities hitting him hard.

"I won't fool with you, son. What I am about to suggest carries great risk. It could put you in the gravest danger."

"Will it help Leslie and her family?"

"They too are in grave danger. You are now their only hope."

"*Is* there hope?" Bryce burst out, almost pleading.

"There is always hope for those who dare."

Bryce sighed.

"Well?" Gorham asked quietly.

"There are no guarantees, I assume."

There was an almost imperceptible shake of the head. "I'm not a guardian angel. I can help, but only to a limited degree."

"I guess your generation didn't have any guarantees either, did they?"

Gorham considered that, then smiled faintly. "Only the guarantees that spring from faith in God and the knowledge that we gave ourselves to a righteous cause."

Bryce suddenly straightened. "That's good enough."

Gorham was suddenly all business. "Good. Then listen carefully, for everything now depends on what happens between you and Mannington."

CHAPTER 23

The minister of internal affairs was sitting behind his massive desk, face impassive. He waited until the guard took the handcuffs off Bryce, then dismissed the man with a wave of his hand. Colonel Anthony Burkhart stood slightly behind Mannington, eyes alert. Bryce suspected that he was armed and that that was why they allowed him to be freed from his restraints.

"You know Burkhart," Gorham had told him in the cell, "but not well. Don't underestimate him. You don't get to be head of ISD through being inept or stupid."

Bryce waited until the door closed behind the guard, then swung around to face Burkhart. "You idiot!" he burst out.

His intent had been to startle, and he fully achieved his objective. Both men's mouths dropped open in surprise. Bryce bore in, pressing the advantage. "Weren't you monitoring the conversation? Didn't you hear what they said?"

"Of course," Burkhart said, still caught off guard, "but—"

"But nothing!" Bryce roared. "We were on the verge of setting up Paul Adams, setting him up once and for all. But more than that. You heard the American agent. He was ready to bring in the leader of every major resistance movement. Every one!" He threw up his hands and turned to Mannington in disgust. "And then in comes Colonel Burkhart with blazing sixguns."

Burkhart's eyes had narrowed dangerously now, and Bryce could see he had skated out onto thin ice. But he was committed now. Into the breach and damn the torpedos. He sighed wearily and dropped into a chair. "Did you really authorize this, Elliot?"

"Don't call him Mr. Mannington," Gorham had warned. "You are one of the inner circle. You must be natural. You must be confident."

Confident? Bryce nearly hooted aloud at that. His heart was pounding so hard his ribs hurt.

Mannington was watching him steadily, the dark eyes hard to fathom. For a moment, Bryce was tempted to press, but he decided there was a fine line between playing his role properly and suicidal overconfidence.

"Well," Mannington finally said, his voice low and almost conversational, "let's suppose before I answer that question that you explain to Anthony and me how it is that you can leave for a short vacation, turn up at a motel where two ISD men are murdered, and—"

"Two?" Bryce cut in. He looked puzzled. "Wait a minute. You didn't find the sergeant?"

"No we didn't," Burkhart sneered. "Do you know something we don't?"

"But I told you where they were holding him. You didn't get him?"

"Come on, Sherwood," Burkhart snarled. "Stop playing coy with us. We haven't heard one word from you for a month."

"But . . . " He looked to Mannington for support. "Didn't you get my report?"

"What report?" he said flatly.

Bryce sat back, stunned, or so he hoped it looked. "But—I don't understand. I finally got clear and called in a full report on the fourth day. I told you exactly where they were holding the sergeant." He shook his head. "But he'll be gone by now. They were taking him to Boston, smuggling him aboard a freighter—"

"You're lying!" Burkhart snapped. "We had no report from you."

Bryce shot to his feet. "Look!" he cried hotly. "Don't call me a liar! You've already blown this operation. Find out who took my report!"

Both men glared at each other until Mannington broke in. "Day and time?" he said to Bryce. "We can easily check."

Bryce paused, wrinkling his brow. "Let's see, I left here on Thursday, August thirtieth. So it would have been the second of September. Yes, the second. Somewhere around 2:30 A.M. I had to slip away while the others were asleep."

Burkhart picked up the phone. "Get me Major Powers." There was a pause, then, "Major. Check the logs for the second of September—"

"I could be a day off," Bryce spoke up, "but I'm almost positive it was the second."

"Start at midnight on the second and check twenty-four hours in either direction. We're looking for a telephone contact from Mr. Sherwood." Pause. "Yes. I'm in the minister's office. Bring it immediately."

Bryce held his breath. Now came the test of Gorham's ingenuity. When he had outlined their strategy, Bryce had instantly protested. There had to be some kind of irrefutable evidence if the story was going to stand. Gorham had merely smiled. "I think I can handle that," he had said. Now they would see, because if the Elliot Mannington of this dimension was as shrewd as the Elliot Mannington Bryce had previously known, there could not be even the tiniest flaw.

Mannington turned to Bryce as Burkhart hung up the phone. "While we're waiting for the major to check, why don't you start at the beginning and tell us exactly what is going on?"

Bryce took a deep breath. They had had only a few minutes to rehearse this, and this was where it would all be decided. He sat back down again, face thoughtful. "Well, as you know, you gave me a week off to go to Boston for a vacation with my uncle and his family. I had no plans other than lying in the sun and doing some sailing."

He looked up into Mannington's dark eyes. "I did know, of course, that recently you have been very concerned about the increasing penetration of CONAS by foreign agents from the United States."

Mannington nodded. "Go on."

And so Bryce launched. For the most part, it was built on the framework of what had actually happened. He changed only one or two details, embellished only enough to build his case.

His car had broken down. It was night, so he hiked back into town. Realizing he would have to wait until morning to get it fixed, he took a room at the Dew Drop Inn. At first, Jessie Lambert and her son seemed exactly what they appeared to be, operators of a small motel and cafe in a very small town. But later, unable to sleep, Bryce had gone to see if the proprietors might have some aspirin for a splitting headache. As he reached the office, he heard the soft murmur of voices. Curious, he stopped to listen and had been stunned to realize he was eavesdropping on a clandestine meeting of the local resistance group.

Realizing the seriousness of what he had stumbled upon, Bryce had tried to call ISD, but just as he got the operator on the line, the son came out into the hallway of the motel. Thus Bryce had gone into his stupidity act, giving a false number, acting as though the operator wasn't making sense. When the boy didn't leave, Bryce gave up. He would find another phone first thing in the morning and report to ISD what he had learned.

Mannington seemed content to listen, but Burkhart interrupted frequently, and often with deliberate rudeness. He challenged the story, demanded details, called for exact times and other corroborating information. The first attempt at cross-examination by Burkhart nearly unnerved Bryce, but the fact that 98 percent of his story really happened made it easier. And the further he went with the colonel unable to shake his story, the more confident he became.

"Evidently the telephone operator got suspicious and called ISD." He turned to Burkhart and frowned. "I know part of ISD's strategy is to terrorize and cow people into submission, but that captain . . . I'm sorry about what happened to him, but if he hadn't been such a conceited, arrogant idiot, he'd still be alive today."

"I'll mention that to his family," Burkhart said coldly.

"The next morning I had just gotten out of the shower," Bryce continued, ignoring that. "The boy, this Neal Lambert, was still curious about me and was hanging around, so I was trying to act as natural as possible. Suddenly the captain and the sergeant burst onto the scene. Next thing I knew, I was pinned up against the wall with Captain Talbot's pistol jammed into my ribs. At first I stalled, because we were in the room with the boy and his mother. That didn't help the captain's mood. Finally, he and the sergeant took me in my room. That's when I tried to tell them who I was. I showed my ID."

There was no need to try to enhance his emotions to make it more believable; the horror of that morning was on him again. "The captain didn't believe me, accused me of having false papers. When I demanded that they call you, the sergeant slugged me in the stomach. I guess I wasn't completely without blame, because I really got angry then. I told them what I thought of their high-handed tactics."

He took a deep breath. "That's when something snapped in the captain." Bryce proceeded quietly now, giving the precise details of what happened next—his coming within an ace of being shot by the captain, Neal Lambert bursting into the room, the blast from the rifle, the hurried flight to the mountains in the back of the pickup. As he talked, he watched both men closely. Burkhart was still skeptical but finding it harder and harder to cross him. Mannington seemed more and more impressed, or so Bryce desperately hoped.

"As I sat in the root cellar all that next day, waiting for the woman and her son to return, it finally hit me what kind of opportunity I had been handed. Suddenly, by an ironic twist of events, I had been thrust right into the heart of the resistance movement. I didn't have to establish any validity with them. I had won that with the blast of that rifle in the motel room."

197

He looked to Mannington. "We've been trying to penetrate the inner core of the resistance movement for years, with little success. That's when I decided this offered us an opportunity that would not come again."

Mannington just nodded, his expression inscrutable.

"We fled south. I looked for an opportunity to call in, but I didn't dare risk exposure. Finally on the fourth night I got away long enough to call. In my report, I told you exactly what had happened and asked for your permission to continue the mission. There was to be a code word given in the 8:00 P.M. radio news broadcast every day for the next week if you wanted me to pull out. I listened. There was nothing, so I continued. I also told you in my report that the risk of making further calls was too great and that I wouldn't report in again until I had something definite."

He lifted his hands. "But if you never got that first report . . . "

"We'll talk about the report when the major gets here," Mannington said, almost half musing. "Continue. Tell me what happened next."

And so he continued, describing the events in the days and weeks that followed. He told of how the resistance movement was trying to find a way to get to Paul Adams and how they had hit on the idea of the approach through his daughter. Thus the false letter from the Ministry of Education.

He talked steadily for the next ten minutes and was just coming to the events of that evening when there was a knock at the door.

The major entered, followed by a lieutenant who looked scared to death. Both were stiff as ramrods as the major handed Burkhart a folder. Bryce tensed and had to forcibly struggle to keep his face calm and outwardly confident. Burkhart opened the folder. The major leaned over and pointed something out to him. Burkhart's eyes scanned quickly, and he gave a soft grunt.

Bryce felt a sudden, blinding surge of relief. Burkhart was not pleased.

"Well?" Mannington demanded impatiently.

The colonel stepped to the desk and laid it before his boss. Then he whirled back to the lieutenant. "You were the duty officer on the night of the second of September?"

The lieutenant stiffened even more rigidly. "Yes, sir!"

"You took the phone call and made the entry in question?"

"Yes, sir!"

"Were you aware of the standing orders of the minister that any contact from Mr. Sherwood was to be reported directly to him immediately?"

There was a sheen of sweat on the lieutenant's upper lip. "Sir, as is indicated in the log, I typed the report myself and sent it to the minister's office, marked for his eyes only."

"And to whom did you give this report, lieutenant?"

"To one of the couriers, sir. An older man."

Mannington was reading the log. "A Sergeant Nathaniel Gorham."

Bryce started slightly, then fought hard to bite back a smile. So that was how Gorham had pulled it off. How he had known enough back then to call in the report baffled Bryce. But then he had once said that time, as Bryce knew it, didn't hold in the world of spirits.

The lieutenant started to tremble. "Yes, sir. Sergeant Gorham."

The major was sweating now too. "He had the proper ID and security clearance. That's noted there too."

"All right, then get this Sergeant Gorham in here," Burkhart snapped. "I want to talk with him."

The major swallowed hard. "There is no such man on the roster, sir."

Burkhart leaned forward, his mouth open; then his jaw snapped shut.

The major rushed on desperately now. "Lieutenant Royas, as is customary, filed a backup copy of the report." He handed another folder to Burkhart.

Burkhart opened it, stared for a moment, then swung around to Mannington. "The backup file is properly marked, but there's nothing in it."

The major was now about the shade of a casaba melon. "We can only assume the Signals Division has been penetrated, sir. I assure you that whoever is responsible will be found and dealt with."

Bryce was on his feet, eyes blazing. "You mean someone else knows about this? My cover has been blown?"

Even Colonel Burkhart was deeply shaken now. "I don't know what this means," he said in a low, tight voice. "But I will find out."

The minister of internal affairs stood slowly and leaned over his desk until his face was a few inches from that of his ISD head. "I think that is a very good idea, Anthony," he said softly. "I want a full report by 7:00 A.M. tomorrow morning."

As the other three exited, Mannington sat back down, his face flushed and his hands pressed tight against the desk top. Finally he turned to Bryce. "Well, it looks as though I owe you an apology."

Bryce waved it aside. "My only concern now is, who knows about who I really am?"

"Hopefully, we can find that out." He sighed. "So what now?"

Bryce took a quick breath. Here came the plunge. "Elliot, I have a suggestion."

"What?"

"Maybe we can still salvage this. Why don't you send me back to my cell while Colonel Burkhart tries to track this leak down? And maybe it would be wise to bring in the other prisoners for interrogation as well. That way my being called out won't look suspicious. Then, come morning, we can decide where to go from there."

Mannington gave him a long searching look, then finally nodded.

For some time after Bryce left, Mannington sat in his chair, smoking one cigarette after another. Finally he lifted the phone.

A few moments later there was a soft knock at the door, and the guard was there with another of the prisoners.

"Leave him manacled," Mannington said gruffly. "Return for him in five minutes."

The guard saluted and exited. As the door shut, Mannington was instantly out of his chair and around the desk, smiling. They shook hands firmly.

Mannington stepped back and looked at the man before him. Agent in place, a mole, a sleeper—those were the terms in espionage parlance. Though this man was listed in the files of ISD's Special Operations Branch by the code name "Red Fox," not even Colonel Burkhart knew his real identity. Mannington was his control, his field operations officer, and his one and only contact. It had been thus for nearly six years since Mannington had hand-picked him and sent him out to make his way in a dangerous and clandestine world.

Mannington took the silver cigarette case from the desk and offered it to the other. The man lit up, then took a deep draw, watching Mannington closely, his eyes filled with questions.

The irony of it all made Mannington laugh, for he had been nearly as startled to see this man come out of the safe house as Bryce Sherwood had been to see Mannington step into the light.

He went back around the desk and sat down, lit a cigarette of his own, then laughed again. "Who would have dreamed that you would be caught in a net meant for other fishes?"

The other shook his head in disgust. "Well, you just blew six years of work."

For a moment Mannington considered telling Red Fox about Bryce Sherwood, then suddenly thought better of it. Mannington was a firm believer in covering every bet. One way to do that was to keep most of the cards to yourself.

He smiled again. "I'll be sending you for interrogation along with the others. But don't be dismayed. I think there may be a way to salvage this whole thing without too much damage."

CHAPTER 24

By 8:25 the next morning, Bryce had again been hauled out of his cell past the silent, grim faces of the others down the cell block and taken back to Mannington's office.

The guard shoved him through the door, and then immediately things changed. Mannington was waiting with a smile and a full breakfast spread out on the desk. Bryce tore into it with relish, feeling guilty as he thought of the others, but knowing that refusal to eat would look peculiar. Burkhart came in a few minutes later and stood nearby, watching Bryce as he finished, his eyes brooding.

Burkhart, with occasional glances at Bryce, reported the findings of the night. The lieutenant who had logged in the entry had passed an exhausting and grueling interrogation, including the use of a polygraph. There was no question but what he was telling the truth. His recall of the contents of the report perfectly corroborated Bryce's story. The investigation Burkhart had thrown over his entire operation was thorough and exhausting, but it turned up nothing. There was no indication of how the reports had disappeared.

Mannington grunted as Burkhart finished, then turned to Bryce. "So, where does that leave us now?"

Bryce sat back and pushed the rest of the breakfast aside. "I've been thinking about that all night." Which was certainly true. He had slept little, elated beyond belief that they had pulled it off, but deeply sobered by the challenges with which it now put him face to face.

"Go on."

"My biggest fear is, who took the report? Who knows I am really working for you?"

Burkhart nodded grudgingly. "I also have been asking that question. It doesn't make sense. If it was the resistance movement, Bryce would not be here now talking to us. He would be dead."

Bryce gave a quick shudder. "Exactly."

"So?" Mannington said.

"So," Bryce plunged in eagerly, "I don't think I'm blown. That means we may still have an opportunity to let this thing unfold. I have a suggestion. If I can persuade Paul Adams to join us, we could very likely snare every major leader of the resistance movement from all over CONAS, to say nothing of the possibility of exposing the entire network of AIS agents."

Mannington shook his head slowly. "It would be extremely dangerous for you."

Just how dangerous you hardly know, he agreed silently.

Burkhart was thoughtful. "But on the other hand, we've known about this so-called secret agreement of the Western Alliance. We know they're anxious to support any movement that will create problems for us."

Mannington was nodding. "It would be a perfect way to lure those countries into a trap. It would be terribly embarrassing for them. And it could even give us an excuse to retaliate against them in new ways."

"So," Bryce said quietly, "isn't that worth the risks?"

"Yes," Mannington said, suddenly decisive. "Yes, it is."

"You said you had a suggestion," Burkhart spoke up. "Why don't you lay it out for us?"

And so Bryce proceeded to tell them what he thought they should do.

An hour later, as the first steps of Bryce's plan were being put into motion, Colonel Anthony Burkhart came back into the office of Elliot Mannington, Minister of Internal Affairs.

Mannington gestured to a chair, then took out the cigarette case and extended it to the other. Finally, Mannington spoke. "So, Anthony, tell me how you peg this whole affair."

The other was silent for a time, brooding again. He took a deep breath, shook his head. "I don't know. Too many things don't make sense. I have the nagging feeling that something isn't right, but I just can't put my finger on it."

Mannington nodded. "Exactly." He paused, thoughtful. "I have three theories."

Burkhart straightened a little to watch his boss more closely.

"One, there is a conspiracy within ISD, of which you are aware and with which you, Colonel Burkhart, are in collusion." He laughed softly at the sudden paleness on Burkhart's face. "That's the least likely, of course." But his voice suddenly hardened. "But if it proves to be true, it would show you to be a very foolish man, Anthony."

Burkhart did not respond. Denials would be seen only as weakness.

"Second possibility. There is outside penetration into ISD or possibly an internal conspiracy of which you know nothing." He puffed deeply and blew the smoke into the air above his head, watching it idly. "But that doesn't add up either. Why would Bryce Sherwood be in on such a conspiracy? The ISD is not his bag. Nor is he theirs. In fact, few people except you and the prime minister even know of him. I like it that way. Keeps him low key. Allows him to do some critical things for me. But he knows very few ISD people, rarely even goes over there."

"Besides," the colonel finished for him, "what has he to gain? Only the top three or four people in my organization are as high as he is now. The risks would be tremendous for very little gain."

"Right again, so theory two seems weak. Unless, of course, the conspiracy has nothing to do with Sherwood, and the disappearance of his report just happens to be one tip of an iceberg we accidently discovered."

Mannington puffed on his cigarette, then stubbed it into an ashtray. "Theory three is that somehow Bryce is up to something and has managed to pull off a very, very clever deception."

"But how? I've gone over and over that possibility. There's no question but what the duty officer is telling the truth. He did get that report. And what is most puzzling, who was this Gorham? And even if he was working with Bryce, how could Bryce ensure that he would be the one to get the report? There are always three or four couriers on duty, and they rotate as the messages come in. There's no way Bryce could control that."

Mannington was pulling at his lip, equally troubled, but pleased that his ISD commander had been thinking about this as much as he had.

"And here again," Burkhart was saying, "there seems to be no motive. Unless it's to somehow to pull a coup against you, but that doesn't make much sense either. That would take the subversion of the entire ISD, plus he would have to have the support of others on the Central Committee, and there is not the slightest hint he has been working with them."

"So," Mannington concluded, "what is the answer?"

The colonel shook his head, and both men fell silent for a long moment before Burkhart responded. "Isn't there a fourth possibility?"

"What?"

"That Sherwood is telling the truth exactly as it happened and that he has given us the opportunity of a lifetime."

Mannington smiled—a brief, humorless smile that did not touch his eyes. "Of course. That is the most likely. And we must proceed on that assumption."

"Of course," Burkhart said evenly.

"It answers the most questions."

"Yes, it does."

Mannington formed a steeple with his fingers and peered into it moodily. "But as you know," he said slowly, "I never like to sit with my back to an open window."

"Only the foolish do," Burkhart agreed. "What would you like me to do?"

"Let it run as Bryce has outlined it. But I want a detailed contingency plan on my desk by tomorrow morning. How do we guarantee that Bryce is not going to hand us any little surprises?"

Burkhart rose. "You'll have that today."

"Good."

As the colonel exited, Elliot Mannington sat back, making the steeple again, staring into nothingness. He had not come to this position by being careless nor by ignoring his instincts. And every instinct was whispering that something wasn't quite right.

As the heavy army truck leaned slightly into a curve, Bryce let the motion carry him enough to bump Jessie Lambert's shoulder. They were headed up a sizable grade, and the engine was in a high-pitched roar. For the first two and a half hours out of Washington, the two guards riding in the back with their prisoners had stayed completely alert, watching for the slightest provocation, jabbing hard with a gun barrel to emphasize their grunted commands for silence. But for the last fifteen minutes, the monotony of the ride had started to tell. Bryce saw that the larger man was fighting a valiant battle against heavy eyelids.

"I'm going to try to take the guard's weapon," he whispered loudly, though he almost could have shouted it and not been heard over the roar of the truck's engine. Jessie's head barely came up, but he saw the alarm in her eyes. There was an almost imperceptible shake of her head, which he answered with an emphatic nod.

The five of them were chained together with leg irons, and also individually handcuffed. Bryce, Jessie, and Wesley Quinn were down one side of the canvas-covered back, and Neal and

Lewis were on the other. In addition to the guards back with them, there was another in the cab of the truck, and the driver was armed as well.

"Tell Wes to take the other one once it starts."

Though she obviously did not approve, Jessie waited until the truck lurched again, then passed the message on to Quinn. Out of the corner of his eye, Bryce caught the AIS agent's quick nod. Within moments, Neal and Lewis had read the unspoken warning in Bryce's eyes. They were ready, though for exactly what they weren't sure.

Somehow sensing that the mood in the truck had changed, the one guard's head came up, and he eyed them warily. Bryce leaned forward to look directly into the eyes of the man. "Where are you taking us?" he shouted.

The second guard came back to full alertness as the first waved the muzzle of his rifle in Bryce's direction. "No talking!"

"We have a right to know where we are being taken."

This time the muzzle came up level, and steady as a rock. "Shut up! Do not talk!"

"Is it to the Blue Creek Work Camp like they say? We have a right to know."

Bryce took a quick breath. He had finally persuaded Mannington that the guards should not be informed about what was going to happen lest things look too pat. When the time was right, Bryce would tell the others about his involvement with Mannington, but in the meantime he didn't want to be shot by a suddenly suspicious group of resistance fighters.

For the same reason, he had insisted that the guards carry live ammunition. It greatly increased the risks, but again, blanks would be a dead giveaway. He pulled a face at the lousy pun. He had finally agreed to one concession. The guards had been given the strictest orders that none of the prisoners were to be harmed. He hoped that would be enough of an edge to carry the day. That was assuming, of course, that Colonel Burkhart had passed on those instructions.

Bryce felt a sudden lurch in his stomach, for Colonel Burkhart was not the highest man on his list of those he could trust.

The nearest guard had lumbered to his feet and was coming toward Bryce, his eyes murderous. The second man was standing now too, weapon raised. The guard stopped in front of Bryce, coming down into a half crouch. He jammed the muzzle hard against Bryce's ribs. "I said no talking!" he screamed into Bryce's face.

Bryce raised both hands into the air, the fear suddenly as much real as pretended. "We have a right to know where we are going," he said stubbornly.

The man, face flushed with anger, reached out with his free hand and grabbed Bryce by the throat, his fingers digging viciously into his windpipe. "Shut your mouth! Do you hear me!"

Bryce brought his hands down with all the power he could muster, letting the chain of the handcuffs catch the man squarely on the bridge of his nose. At the same time, he thrust his body to the side and away from the man's rifle. There was a scream of pain, a deafening blast, and Bryce felt the bench at his side splinter. At that moment, the second man made his mistake. He leaped forward to help his partner. Lewis and Wes Quinn were up and clubbed him from behind simultaneously. He went down hard, the rifle clattering away.

"Get their weapons! Get their weapons!"

Bryce wasn't sure who had screamed it. His ears were ringing, and the man's weight had pinned him against the bench. Dimly he was aware of the truck lurching hard as the driver slammed on the brakes. He grabbed frantically for the weapon, trying to keep the man's writhing body pinned against him. But suddenly he felt the weapon pull free. He looked up in time to see Neal wrench the rifle away and jam it up against the man's ribs. Quinn already had the other rifle pointed at the head of the second guard.

"Shhh!" Quinn commanded as he moved toward the back of the truck as far as the leg chains would let him. There was the sound of a door opening in front of them, then quick footsteps. The guard Bryce had hit groaned, but Bryce clamped a hand over the man's mouth. The footsteps stopped.

"Dave! Manny! Are you okay?"

Lewis threw both hands to his mouth, cupped them, and made a muffled, strangled sound. The flap lifted a crack, then was thrown back. But all the guard saw was the muzzle of Quinn's weapon pointing directly at his head. "Drop it!" Quinn yelled.

There was a moment's hesitation, then instant realization that the odds were definitely not in favor of heroism. The weapon clattered to the pavement.

Neal swung around, parted the canvas that hung over the window to the cab, and slammed the butt of the rifle against the glass. As it shattered, he shoved the muzzle of the weapon through the opening and into the face of the startled driver. "Okay, friend," he said quietly. "Get the keys to these chains and come around slowly or your three friends are going to get blown away."

And as rapidly as it had started, it was over.

They drove the truck five or six miles up a small dirt road, stripped the four men of their clothing and shoes, and sent them down the mountain in the opposite direction. It was then the argument began. Lewis and Quinn were for heading south, into the province of West Virginia, where Lewis knew of a stronghold of freedom fighters who would provide them safety, food, and rest. Jessie and Neal argued that they should follow the mountains north, into the New England Confederation, where they knew the people and could set up a new base of operations.

Bryce listened quietly for a moment, then walked around to the back of the truck and got one of the uniforms. He began donning it. Quinn and Lewis stopped in mid-sentence to stare at him.

Finally Jessie and Neal turned, then started in surprise.

"What are you doing?" Jessie demanded.

"North or south, it doesn't matter to me. Just tell me where to find you."

"Where are you going?"

"And you'll have to commandeer a vehicle. I'm taking the truck back to Washington."

"*What!*" All four shouted it as one.

"If we were going to the Blue Creek Camp, we should have been arriving around nightfall, right?"

Quinn nodded.

"So that gives me about four hours to get back and get the Adams family."

This time it was Lewis who found his voice first. "That's insane!"

"Probably," Bryce agreed, finishing the buttons on his shirt. "But once the ISD learns we've escaped, they'll pick up Leslie and her family first off."

"Look," Quinn started, "I understand why you're doing this, but—"

But now it was Jessie who sided with Bryce. "No!" she said flatly. "He's right. They won't stand a chance."

"You yourself said Paul Adams was the key to everything," Bryce said evenly to Quinn.

Lewis nodded dubiously. "But that was if you could persuade him to come with us."

"Well, things have changed. I've got to get them out. We'll try to convince him later."

Neal was shaking his head too, but he didn't say anything, and Bryce had the quick impression he was responding negatively to the challenge involved more than the idea.

Quinn blew out his breath. "You'll have to dump the truck once you hit the city."

"I know. Where do I meet you?"

Quinn looked to the two Lamberts. "They know you're from New England. That's the first place they'll look for us. I say we head south."

210

Jessie hesitated.

"Come on, Jess," Bryce said softly, "time's running."

"Okay, south it is."

Lewis stepped forward and laid his hand on Bryce's arm. "If you're in the clear, find the village of Quaid's Crossing. It's about a hundred miles east of Charleston. Stop at the general store. Ask if there are any jobs in Richwood. They'll direct you from there."

"Thanks."

"You'll also need transportation. I have a car in a garage not far from your apartment." He gave him quick directions as to its location and where the keys were hidden.

Bryce blew out his breath, then shook their hands one by one, except for Jessie, and he gave her a quick, hard hug.

"Good luck," Quinn said for all of them.

"Thanks."

And with that, he climbed into the truck and headed down the mountain toward his rendezvous with Elliot Mannington and then his dinner appointment with the Paul Adams family.

CHAPTER 25

"So you did it!" Mannington spoke even as Bryce climbed down from the army truck in the old warehouse somewhere on the north outskirts of Washington.

He nodded.

"Any problems?" Burkhart asked.

Bryce turned slightly, pulled on one corner of his shirt, and showed them the burn marks where the muzzle of the rifle had been lying when it went off. "It was a little closer than I care to think about, but no one got hurt." He turned to Burkhart. "Your men are barefoot in the mountains, but they should be back to the highway about dark."

The third man with Mannington and Burkhart grunted softly, and Burkhart turned. "Bryce, this is Captain James Rodale. He's directing the field operations."

Bryce nodded. This was the man who had arrested them the night before, but he made no move to shake hands. Nor did Rodale.

"So there was no question about it being a setup?" Mannington asked.

"None. It could just as easily have gone the other way. And for the moment, they're elated to be free. They're on their way to a place somewhere in West Virginia."

"Where?" Rodale said eagerly.

Bryce ignored him. "Is there still surveillance on the Adams family?" he asked Burkhart.

The head of ISD gave a slight nod.

"Well, pull them off! If Paul spots one of your men now, it could blow the whole deal."

Burkhart shook his head slowly. "We can't just pull back all surveillance on your say-so. We—"

"I didn't say pull them back," Bryce shot back. "I said pull them *off*." He swung around to Mannington. "Everything now hinges on Paul Adams. If he comes with us, we can pull in the others. But at this point, I can't guarantee he will."

"Oh, he'll come," Burkhart said. "He's a fanatic. He'll see this as the perfect opportunity to get back into the spotlight."

"And if he does," Captain Rodale broke in grimly, "we can't take any chance of losing track of him."

Burkhart was now appealing directly to Mannington too. "If Adams or the others ever suspect Bryce—and we still have to remember that someone knows who he is and what he's up to— they can dump him in a minute. Then where are we?"

Mannington seemed content for the moment to listen and referee. He turned back to Bryce, one eyebrow lifting questioningly.

"Look," Bryce said, not trying hard to hide his disgust. "It was that kind of paranoid mentality that nearly blew the whole game yesterday. We've managed to patch it up again, but all it will take is one more stupid slip and I *will* be blown."

"Is there some reason you are so eager to have all surveillance removed?" Burkhart asked softly.

Bryce threw up his hands. "I give up! Just because Paul Adams is a scarred and broken shell physically doesn't mean he's not still as shrewd as a wolverine. So you get your little binoculars and your earphones, and you hover around us like a cloud of flies over a piece of rotten meat, and then when he tells me to take a flying leap, we'll all sit down and have a good cry together. That's assuming I'm still alive."

"*Will* Adams agree to all this?" Mannington finally said.

Bryce shrugged. "I don't know. There's no question about the bitterness he feels for the government. But the work camps are still pretty vivid in his memory too." He shrugged again, this time also shaking his head. "I don't know how to predict it. As you know, I haven't made any kind of approach to him yet, so thus far he's clean as a new plate. We have nothing on him."

He turned on Burkhart. "Did you get me a radio?"

The colonel nodded.

"Good. Lewis has a car I'll be taking. Could you ever hide the radio in there somehow?"

Rodale nodded for the both of them. "We could put it behind the back seat. That would be easy."

"All right. Then I can call in every night, whenever possible. You can track my location from that. Or put a homing device in the car, if you're so worried about losing us. Just pull off the live dogs so Adams doesn't smell a trap!"

Mannington laughed quietly. He and Burkhart had already discussed at some length how to make sure they didn't lose track of one Bryce Sherwood. They had already gone into Bryce's apartment and imbedded a small but powerful transmitter in the battered suitcase they hoped he would take, and another one in the heel of one of his shoes. Now to have Bryce hand them such a simple solution, Mannington had to chuckle at Burkhart's disappointment.

He turned to Burkhart. "Bryce is right. We can track him with the car. Pull off the men."

Bryce blew out his breath gratefully. "Well, thank heavens someone listens to reason."

Rodale started to say something, then clamped his mouth shut and turned and walked to the car and picked up his radio.

"How long do you think it will take before you'll know on Adams?" Mannington said, ignoring the sullen look his ISD chief was giving him.

Pursing his lips, Bryce considered that. "I'm not sure. If the opportunity presents itself, I'll start feeling him out tonight. But I've got to go slow, see how it develops."

"I agree." Mannington gave him a shrewd and appraising look. "How much is this interest you're showing in his daughter genuine and how much is just doing your duty as an obedient espionage agent?"

Bryce laughed, trying not to show his surprise. Anyone who underestimated Elliot Mannington was a fool. He grinned, a bit sheepishly. "Let's just say I haven't found the duty to be unpleasant."

Now it was Mannington who chuckled. "I thought as much."

Bryce sobered. "But frankly, she's going to prove to be as difficult as Paul himself." He gave a little self-deprecatory laugh. "I think the interest is mutual, and that may help. But she is extremely protective of her father. She'll do anything to stop him from going back to the work camps."

"That's understandable. But I'm like Anthony," Mannington mused. "I think if you appeal to Paul Adams's ego and his sense of destiny, he will swallow the bait whole."

"So where are your friends headed in West Virginia?" Burkhart asked, still not ready to totally surrender.

"You think they'd tell me that already?" Bryce asked incredulously.

"I thought they trusted you."

"They do trust me, but at this stage of the game it's information on a need-to-know basis only. If one of us gets caught . . ." He shrugged. "I make contact in a little village called Quaid's Crossing. I'll get further directions from there."

That seemed to satisfy Burkhart, and Bryce felt himself relax a little. He straightened. "Now, one other thing." He looked at Rodale, who was still at the car, and lowered his voice. "Any progress on finding what happened to my first report?"

Burkhart shook his head and so Bryce turned to Mannington. "So what are you doing to make sure my next reports don't disappear?"

"We're taking care of it," Burkhart said coldly.

"Look, colonel," Bryce flared, "it's not your neck out there on the block. Your people already dropped the ball once, so I want to know what—"

Mannington held up his hands. "All right, that's enough. We've taken every precaution. You'll be on a secure communications link reserved strictly for your calls. Believe me, we are as anxious to keep you safe as you are."

Bryce looked dubious but finally let it pass. "Anything else? If not, I'd better get going. I don't want Adams and the others comparing notes later and finding out that I spent an inordinate amount of time getting back into the city."

"Where's this car you're talking about?"

"Oh, yeah." Bryce gave him directions, knowing full well that in addition to a homing device, the car would likely be rigged up with a microphone somehow. But there was nothing he could do about that.

As he finished, Mannington stepped forward. "I don't need to tell you, Bryce. This is perhaps the single most important mission we have ever undertaken. The fate of the nation depends on its success."

"Yes, I know," Bryce said quietly. "I know."

By four o'clock, Bryce had gone to his apartment and showered, changed clothes, and walked quickly to the garage where the car was. It was an older model and beat-up. But the engine turned over immediately and ran smoothly. He nodded in satisfaction. He looked quickly behind the back seat and found that Rodale's men had already done their work. The radio was small and compact but looked efficient and powerful. He tried it, got a brief response from the operations center, then locked the garage again and left.

He stepped off the bus several blocks from Leslie's house and started a leisurely stroll through the area, but his eyes were constantly searching for any sign that Rodale had not fully complied with his wishes. He spent nearly an hour circling through the neighborhood, one part of his mind occupied with the search for any ISD presence, the rest of it filled with the tumbling melee of his thoughts.

As Bryce had left Leslie's house the previous night . . . He stopped and shook his head. Was it really only last night? It seemed like a week ago. But as he had left her house, he had had only one thought on his mind—get out of the commitment to head west with the others. He would stay with Leslie, perhaps even settle into some kind of normal life.

How vastly things could change in twenty-four hours! From the moment the alarm had sounded in the safe house, Bryce had been plunged into a maelstrom of peril, conspiracy, and battle for survival. His mind was numbed by the constant, high-voltage tension, his body ached for sleep. And yet . . .

What he was feeling was something akin to "runner's high," only so much more intense, so much more consuming that it left him a little breathless. He was numbed, yes, and unquestionably exhausted and strung out to a fever pitch, but there was something more. There was not the slightest question in his mind that one slip in the next days and weeks could, and would, bring him face to face with death. It was deeply sobering and yet positively exhilarating to discover that it didn't matter. Not enough to make him turn back.

As Bryce started up Walquist Street, finally satisfied that there was no surveillance, his brow furrowed deeply. And what now did this neophyte convert to freedom say to the family that meant so much to him? He had thought of little else on the way down from the mountains.

There was one sure way to remove them from danger, and that was to not say anything to Paul Adams and then to tell Mannington he had refused to join the movement. The man had been through hell. He had already paid his dues to freedom. Who could blame him if he declined, considering the risks?

Bryce gave a quick, frustrated little shake of his head. On the other hand, in these past twenty-four hours he had come afire with the realization that they just might do it. With Gorham's help he had snatched victory right out from under the nose of Elliot Mannington. Now, Bryce was convinced they just might pull it off.

217

The thought of that sent a shiver of excitement through him. And if they did make it, if they did pull off their own Concord and Lexington, would Paul Adams thank him for being kept safe? Would Leslie?

Bryce sighed deeply as he turned up the walk toward her house. Though mentally he was still agonizing, deep inside he already knew what he had to do. And it filled him with dread, for he very much feared he could lose Leslie in the process.

CHAPTER 26

Bryce managed to keep his mood light and the conversation safe during dinner. But this time, as they finished, he adamantly refused to take a no answer on his offer to do the dishes. He shooed Vera and Paul out onto the front porch, donned an apron, and picked up a dish towel. During the meal, Leslie had shot him several questioning looks, somehow sensing that something was troubling him.

Now as she put some powdered dish soap into the sink and started the water running, she looked up at him. "Is everything okay?"

He laughed softly, simultaneously cursing and loving her perceptiveness. "Couldn't be better," he answered lightly.

"I don't believe you."

"Well, thanks a lot."

She turned off the water, swirled the soap suds idly with her hand, then finally looked up again, the wide, green eyes much troubled. "Bryce?" She was pleading with him now. "What's wrong?"

He set his dish towel down, gathered her into his arms, and kissed her gently. "Only that I'm finding myself falling deeply in love with a certain teacher from the Hillsburg Secondary School."

For several moments she looked up at him, probing his face. Then she sighed and went back to toying with the suds.

"There is an appropriate response to that last line," he said softly.

"I know."

This time he found it more difficult to force the lightness into his voice. "I don't think that was it."

She spoke so softly he almost missed it. "I know," she said again.

And with a deepening sense of gloom, he stepped back and picked up the towel again. They didn't speak again until they were finished.

As they came out into the living room, Vera was just turning on the television.

"The ballet is on tonight," Leslie murmured, still subdued. "Do you mind if we just stay here and watch it?"

So we don't have to be alone and try to talk things out? he thought. But he just nodded. "That's fine." What had to happen tonight was going to be tough enough without her probing further to see what was bothering him.

They sat on the couch, across from her parents who were in the two easy chairs. On the television, the camera focused on the orchestra as it began that unique cacophony of sounds peculiar to a group of instrumentalists warming up. Suddenly Bryce rubbed the back of his hand. "Hmmm," he said, looking at it. "I've got something sticky on me, from the dishes I guess. I'll be right back."

He went in the kitchen, turned on the water briefly, then moved quickly to the small desk where there was a pad of paper and a holder with several pens and pencils. "I need to talk with you alone," he wrote swiftly. "Can we go outside?" In the other room, the orchestra's tuning sounds died out.

He folded the paper into a small square, waited a moment until he heard the sound of applause, and then, as the orchestra began to play, he walked back into the living room. All three glanced up at him idly, then turned back to the television. He slipped the note under Paul's arm as he passed, then gave him a quick, warning shake of his head as he looked up in surprise.

Paul waited almost a full minute before he quietly retrieved the note, and, holding it low, unfolded and read it. He looked at

Bryce, then away. Three minutes later, he suddenly stood. "Sorry, dear," he murmured, as he bent down and kissed his wife on the cheek. "I'm too fidgety for television tonight. I think I'll go dig around in the flowers for a while."

Vera looked up at him surprised, but then, as though she was used to such unexpected turns, smiled. "Need some help?"

"No. You've been waiting to see this. I'm just going to putter."

Bryce waited for almost five more minutes, then withdrew his hand from Leslie's. "I guess I've got the same case of the fidgets as your father. I'll go out and keep him company."

There was a long, appraising look, filled with sadness. "All right," Leslie finally said softly. "We'll have some ice cream after this is over."

"Good." He walked out of the house into the backyard. Paul was bent over in the roses, using a small hand rake to stir up the ground around the plants. Bryce picked up a hoe and took a few desultory whacks at some small weeds. It was nearly sunset, and the late September air was still and pleasantly comfortable. But most important, unless Rodale and Burkhart were much more thorough than he thought, they were also free from any possible electronic listening devices.

Bryce stopped, leaned on his hoe, and gave Paul a long searching look. "Sir, may I ask you a question?"

Paul smiled, sitting back on his heels. "If you'll answer one for me."

"Okay."

"Why is it you insist on calling me sir? Paul is just fine."

Bryce laughed softly. "I'm sorry. I know you've asked me twice now, but . . . " He laughed again, a little embarrassed. "But when I think of who you are and what you've done, somehow it seems disrespectful for me to call you Paul."

"I did no more than others."

"Maybe so, but I don't call them Paul either."

He chuckled. "I give up. Okay, what's the question?"

Bryce took a deep breath. "Have you ever heard of the Declaration of Independence?"

Paul set the rake down slowly, his eyes narrowing. "Why do you ask?" It was said slowly, almost as though it were forced from him a word at a time.

"Because I've seen it."

"There is no such document." It was flat and harsh, almost angry.

"I've seen it," Bryce repeated slowly.

He shook his head stubbornly.

"*I have it!*"

For several seconds the penetrating eyes glared at him from the deep sockets that heightened the sense of gauntness in the face, then he picked up the hand tool and began digging at the earth again. "There is no such document," the deep voice said again in a soft whisper.

Bryce dropped the hoe and moved over to him, sitting on the grass to face him. "I know what you think. But I'm not trying to trap you. There's something I must tell you."

"I don't want to hear it." The look in his eyes was suddenly frightened, cornered.

"I give you my word that all you have to do is listen. Then if you tell me to go away, I will."

"I don't want to listen to you."

"If you don't hear what I have to say," Bryce started, "what I *must* say, then—" His eyes dropped to the twisted, shockingly deformed hands, and he drew in his breath quickly, suddenly unsure of himself.

Paul Adams was watching Bryce's face, and then his own eyes dropped to look at his hands. "Then what?" he said in a hoarse whisper.

Bryce shook his head.

"Then what!" he said sharply.

"Then the evil and ugly men of the world will have won again."

For almost a full minute there was silence except for the quiet scratching of the metal against the soil and the sound of a bus engine far off in the distance. Paul did not look up, just kept

222

digging, but finally he said, with sudden firmness, "If you must, you must."

Bryce leaned back, letting his breath out in a long sigh. And suddenly at that moment he knew he had to tell it all. From the beginning. He looked up. "This is going to sound insane."

There was the tiniest crinkle of a smile around the corner of Paul's eyes. "Perhaps that's best, for I think it is insane of me to listen."

And so he began. He had never told anyone all of it. Jessie Lambert had heard part. She knew about the wall of light and the second dimension, and miraculously she had believed him. They had never talked of it again, nor had she even hinted of it around Neal or the others. But now Bryce started long before that. He spoke of a fantasy world, of a great nation on the North American continent, forged from the fires of revolution and built on a remarkable document called the Constitution. He described the nation of 235 million people and what they had accomplished.

Then with a sigh, shifting uncomfortably on the grass, he began to speak of a young man—bright, aspiring, an aide to a U.S. senator—and of his attempts to change what he thought were faults in the system.

As Bryce talked slowly and without emotion, Paul Adams stopped his digging in the soil. The rake was laid aside. He sat down next to the tree. At first he watched Bryce intently, then he leaned back and the deep-set eyes stared off into space, as they had that first day Bryce had met him on the porch. He never interrupted, never asked a question, just listened with an intensity that was frightening.

Paul gave Bryce a flash of incredulous disbelief as he began to speak of a young woman challenging the bright young lawyer in front of national television. The look only deepened as Bryce went stubbornly on and told of the night a hitchhiker had appeared, and of what had followed. But as Bryce continued, describing the final bitter argument between him and Leslie, his journey north alone, and the events that followed, Paul seemed

223

to retreat deeper and deeper within himself. The face became as stone, completely impassive and unreadable. And even as Bryce outlined the plans Lewis and Wesley Quinn had proposed for Paul Adams and of the ensuing arrest and confrontation with Mannington, he showed no reaction. None. He might have been carved from the trunk of the tree against which his back rested.

Finished at last, Bryce sat back, a tremendous sense of burden lifted from him. Believed or not, insane or not, it was a catharsis to tell it all, to put it into words, to completely uncork the bottle.

Idly, almost as if his hand belonged to another person, Paul's fingers began plucking up individual blades of grass and letting them drop into his lap. Like Leslie, Bryce thought, remembering how she had done the same thing that day in the park.

Suddenly Bryce stood, feeling foolish, awkward, embarrassed, discouraged.

"I'm sorry. I know it's . . . " He lifted his shoulders, let them drop again. "Like I said, it's insane. Maybe I'm insane."

For the first time in almost fifteen minutes, the figure stirred. "Several times," Paul said in a low voice that was almost a hollow echo, "in the camps, I thought I was insane. Now," he finished sadly, "I no longer know what is sanity and what is insanity."

A tiny ray of hope lit Bryce's face. "Then . . . ?"

Finally Paul was looking at him again. He shook his head slowly. "It is an incredible tale."

Bryce laughed shortly, mirthlessly. "You're telling me? At least you didn't laugh in my face. That's what I would do, if I had heard it from someone else."

"I believe *you* believe it."

"Thanks," Bryce said, suddenly profoundly discouraged, knowing he had lost. "I suppose I ought to be grateful for that." He stood again. "I think it's best if I go now. Tell Leslie I'm sorry." He forced a smile. "But somehow ice cream seems a little anticlimactic right now."

224

The frail figure got slowly to its feet. "We'll talk more tomorrow," he said wearily.

Bryce just nodded forlornly. "I'll be leaving tomorrow," he answered. "I'll come around to say good-bye to Leslie."

It was nearly midnight when Paul Adams stole quietly out of bed, put on his robe, and tiptoed to the door. He stopped as Vera stirred and made a soft sound in her sleep, but she quieted and lay still again, and he went out and shut the door carefully behind him. As he moved down the hall, he paused momentarily at the next door. A slight frown wrinkled his brow as he thought of his daughter and the young man who loved her. Then he slipped out of the house and into the soft patterns of moonlight and shadow that dappled the backyard.

He moved to the deeper shadows beneath the tree, where he had sat earlier that evening and listened to the fantastic tale of Bryce Sherwood. With a tired sigh, he lowered himself against the rough bark of the trunk and closed his eyes, trying to sort it all out. Subconsciously, he began to massage the twisted knots of one hand with the bumpy fingers of the other. For half an hour or more he sat like that, motionless except for the slow and gentle movement of his fingers.

He started, hearing a soft sound nearby, feeling a quick surge of fear, but almost instantly he smiled at himself. There was nothing but the familiar shapes of flowers and shrubbery around him. There were no sounds but the softness of the breeze rustling the trees.

Then suddenly, he cried out. In the darkness, directly in front of him! Something was there! He tried to scramble backward, away from it, but he was already against the trunk of the tree and only succeeded in scraping his skin against the rough bark, even through his robe.

With eyes gaping and heart pounding hard, Paul Adams stared, frozen into immobility. It was almost as though the moonlight itself was taking form. Gradually the figure of a man became fully visible, glowing softly in the shadows. The face was narrow and angular, though the eyes were kindly and held open amusement. The white hair was pulled back and tied at the back of his neck. The man wore a long coat, and there were ruffles at his throat and wrists.

As the figure became fully visible, he bowed slightly at the waist. "Good evening, Dr. Adams."

Paul swallowed hard, pulling his legs up underneath him in preparation for flight.

"There is no need to fear. I assure you, I mean you no harm."

"What . . . Who are you?" he stammered.

The man smiled kindly. "Don't you know?" The voice was as soft as the night breeze.

Paul gave a quick, frightened shake of his head.

"Think about it."

And then understanding came. "Nathaniel Gorham," Paul breathed.

Gorham nodded, quite pleased. "It is a pleasure to have the privilege of meeting you, sir."

CHAPTER 27

Paul Adams stopped on the sidewalk, just short of the screen door that led onto his front porch. "Are you sure the house has been bugged?"

"No." Bryce took a deep breath. "I'm only going on the probabilities. Neither Mannington nor Burkhart make many mistakes. You've probably been monitored for some time, possibly since your return from the work camps, but almost certainly in the past week since they got onto me."

"And it's got to happen in there?"

Bryce nodded. "If it is bugged and Leslie and Vera react in a way that seems forced or unnatural, we're dead before we start."

The older man sighed. "I've never lied to Vera."

"We're not going to lie," Bryce said patiently. They had gone over this at his apartment, after he had finally gotten over the shock and then the elation of having Paul Adams show up at his door at 6:30 A.M. to tell him what had transpired during the night. "But we can't tell them everything. Not here. Not even in the car because it may be bugged too. We'll tell them about Mannington later, but not until we're sure, absolutely sure, that there is no chance Mannington is listening."

Again there was the sigh of resignation. "All right." He opened the screen door. "This isn't going to be easy, you know."

"You're telling me," Bryce answered glumly.

"Leslie . . . " Her father stopped, then shook his head slowly. "I don't know what she'll do."

The line along Bryce's jaw tightened. "Well, waiting isn't going to make it any easier. Let's go."

The women were waiting in the living room, faces tense, eyes full of anxiety. Paul had left a note that Leslie was not to go to school, nor was Vera to go to work, until he returned. Little wonder they were on edge.

Paul walked over and sat down next to Vera and took her hand. Bryce stood awkwardly near the bookshelves, not meeting Leslie's worried, questioning gaze.

Paul took a deep breath and plunged right in. "For several weeks we have suspected that Bryce Sherwood, alias John H. Carrol, alias John B. Carrol, was not all that he was representing himself to be."

Leslie's eyes dropped, and Bryce saw that her fingers were twisting at her belt.

"We were right," Paul said quietly. "He is not from the ministry of education, which he has already confessed. Nor is he from the government, sent here to spy on an aging old dissident—" he shot a look at Leslie, "as some of us thought." He took a deep breath. "Actually, he is a member of the resistance movement."

There was a quick intake of breath from Vera, a sudden wide-eyed shock from Leslie.

"He has come to us—to me, with an offer, an opportunity."

Vera paled and was staring at Bryce, suddenly frightened.

"It's something that will have a profound effect not only on me, but on both of you as well. You need to hear what he has to say."

Leslie's eyes were suddenly blazing. "No!" she cried.

"Yes, Leslie," Paul said softly, "we must at least listen to him."

She whirled on her father. "Stop it! Stop it this instant!"

The vehemence caught all of them by surprise, even her mother.

"We do not have to listen to him! We must not listen!"

Bryce stepped closer to her. "Some things cannot be stopped, Leslie."

"Go away! Leave us alone!" she cried.

"As a matter of fact," he said quietly, "I am leaving this morning."

She blinked, and her lower lip trembled slightly. "Then go," she said in a bitter whisper. "I knew all along that you meant nothing but danger to us."

"Nothing?" he asked in a low voice.

She looked away. "Please! Can't you just leave us alone?"

"I invited him to come this morning," Paul broke in with sudden determination. "We *will* hear what he has to say." He looked up. "Go ahead, Bryce."

Bryce did so, quietly and fighting to control the pain he felt as he saw the anger and alienation on Leslie's face. He told them of Lewis and Jessie and Neal. He spoke of Wesley Quinn, an agent for the United States government, and of his proposal and the pivotal part that Paul Adams could play in it all. He said nothing of Elliot Mannington and Colonel Anthony Burkhart.

"They're waiting for me somewhere in West Virginia," he finished quietly. "If I bring Paul Adams with me, we'll begin immediately. If I don't . . . we'll go ahead on our own, do the best we can."

Leslie was crying softly now. "You have no right to ask him to go with you," she said. "No right!"

Bryce shook his head. "And you have no right to ask him to stay."

"He's my father!" she shouted.

Bryce stepped up to her, looking down into the angry face. She looked away but he gently took her chin in his hand and turned her back. "No, you listen!" he pleaded with infinite gentleness. "Leslie, I know how you feel. I understand your fear for him, the horror of all he's gone through. But daughter or not, you have no right to make this decision for him."

Bryce's voice softened even more. "If *he* says no, I'll turn and walk out that door without another word. I know what he's done. There's not a man alive who will think the less of him if he stays

229

here. He's paid the price. Far more than you or I. That's right!" he said fiercely, as she started to shake her head. "Far more than you or I. And so, I cannot speak for him." He straightened, sorrowed by what he had to say. "And neither can you."

There was a deep sigh of pain from Vera as she turned to her husband. "You have already made up your mind, haven't you?"

He shook his head. "No. If we tell Bryce to go without us, he will do so and life will go on for us . . . " He stopped, then finished more slowly. "Life will go on for us as it was before."

"Oh, Paul," she said, her voice suddenly catching. "Do I know you better than you know yourself? How can you say you haven't decided?"

He turned and took her face in those gnarled, twisted hands and lifted it to him. When he spoke, his voice was deep with emotion. "Vera, if you know me as well as you say you do, then you know that if you ask me to stay, we will stay. I've put you through enough. I have no right to ask any more of you."

Tears welled up and overflowed, and Bryce had to swallow hard as he saw the love that passed between these two aging and battle-scarred partners. "And you, Paul," she answered in a whisper, "you know my heart is your heart, and if your heart says go, then I will go." She wiped quickly at a tear-stained cheek and forced a smile. "Will there be something I can do this time? I so much hated the waiting last time."

Leslie leaped to her feet. "No!" It was a stifled sob, a strangled sound of pain and agony. "You can't!" And suddenly Leslie was standing in the middle of the room, as alone as she had ever been in her life.

With surprising alacrity, her father was up and had her in his arms, soothing her, stroking her hair gently. As she buried her head against his shoulder and began to shake with convulsive sobs, he spoke gently. "It looks like your mother and I have decided, Leslie." She shook her head fiercely against him, but he smiled gently. "Yes, I think we have. And now the question is, what about you?"

She straightened slowly, looking up at her father, then over his shoulder at Bryce. Their eyes locked, hers red and swollen, his filled with anguish. But it was Vera Adams who spoke. She stood and turned to Bryce. "How much time do we have to pack?"

Bryce shrugged. "The sooner we leave, the better chance we have of getting away clear."

Paul took his wife by the hand. "I don't have much worth taking," he said, "but I'll help." And smiling briefly at the two young people standing in the living room, they left and went down the hall.

For a long moment, Bryce and Leslie did not look at each other; then finally, Bryce held out his hand toward her. "Will you walk with me?" he asked softly.

He held his breath. He had some things he wanted to say. If he had to, he would say them here, beneath the microphones and into the tape recorders of Colonel Anthony Burkhart, but he much preferred to say them only to Leslie.

She searched his face for a long moment, brushed angrily at the wetness on her cheeks, then shrugged and turned, ignoring his outstretched hand. She walked slowly out the front door.

He caught up with her on the sidewalk and fell into step, and they walked for several moments in silence. Finally, Bryce stopped. She walked several steps more, then stopped, not turning around.

"Leslie . . . "

She waited.

He sighed, not sure where to start. Finally she turned, her face tear stained, her eyes filled with pain—and pleading.

"You know," he said, in a low voice. "It's more than love."

Her chin came up, and he saw the questioning in her eyes.

"With your mother. It's more than just standing by the man she loves. She believes it too."

She finally spoke. "Believes what?"

"In what your father is doing. That the cause is worth the cost. That's what she meant when she said, 'Your heart is my heart.' "

Leslie turned then and began walking again slowly. As Bryce moved up beside her, she said, very softly, "I know."

He reached over and took her hand and pulled her around to face him, and this time she didn't pull away. But neither would she meet his gaze. "If somehow you could ever come to love me—"

Her head came up.

He had to stop, the sharp intensity of what he was feeling for this woman taking his breath away. He sighed and started again. "If somehow you could ever come to love me as deeply as I love you, there might be a day when we could have what your parents have."

He saw the tears starting again.

"But even that wouldn't change how we feel about this other thing." Suddenly he shook his head, half muttering to himself. "I can't believe this. Here I am, trying to convince *you*? If I ever go back, I'd like to have a video of this moment."

"If you ever go back where?"

He brushed that aside and plunged in with renewed determination. "Leslie, I know what drives your father. For the first time in my life, I know what it's like to be driven by that kind of commitment. Here at last is something to fight for, something to throw myself at with all the fury I can muster. If only you could feel that too, then . . . " He let it trail off. Then what? Then we can walk hand in hand into the jaws of hell singing love songs? Then you can join me in front of the firing squad? What, it suddenly hit him, was he offering this woman?

"Then what?" she asked.

He shook his head.

"Then what!" she cried, grabbing his other hand and holding them both with a sudden fierceness.

"Then we can stand together in this." He laughed bitterly at how empty that sounded. "I've heard better offers than that from used-car salesmen."

Her eyes dropped. "I've always stood in awe of my father," she said, barely whispering. "His commitment, the courage to go through what he has and never back down—it frightens me."

"It frightens me too. He is a remarkable man."

"I don't think I have that kind of courage."

"And I think you are one of the most courageous women I have ever met." He laughed softly. "After all, you went to dinner with me that first night."

She didn't smile. "I'm terribly frightened, Bryce. For me. For my father and mother." She suddenly threw her arms around him and gripped him tightly. "For you."

He reached down and put a finger under her chin and lifted her head. "You don't have to be frightened for me," he said gravely. "I've already got that base covered very well."

She swallowed and managed a tremulous smile. "And you'd take me under those conditions?"

He stared at her, then nearly threw back his head and shouted with joy, but again he forced a solemn look. "Will there be any kind of dowry?"

She slugged him hard against his chest, then instantly sobered again. "Can you really forgive me if I'm not all that my father is?"

It took a moment for what she was saying to sink in, then he swung her up and around once, laughing aloud. He put her down and took her face in his hands. "As long as you let me do this—" he kissed her eyes, "and this—" he kissed her nose, "and this—" and he kissed her full on the mouth, and she kissed him back hard, fiercely, with all the pent-up emotions that were welling up inside her.

He pulled back and looked at her in wonder. "As long as you let me do that," he said, a little breathlessly, "I'll forgive you if you're not exactly all that your father is."

233

CHAPTER 28

The next five or six days were some of the most glorious Bryce had ever spent. They had left the Washington area before noon on that first morning, driving leisurely, two couples in love, knowing that this idyllic time would be short-lived and ever too brief. That night, they made the contact in the general store of Quaid's Crossing, a tiny village on the western slopes of the Allegheny Mountains. From there they were taken by a solemn-faced teenager deep into the hill country where an old logging camp had been converted into a temporary headquarters for the freedom movement.

Only Jessie Lambert and Neal were there to welcome them and introduce them around. Lewis had gotten the others settled, then headed immediately back for Washington. In the swiftness of the arrest at the safe house and the escape the next day, he had had no chance to warn his people. All of his networks were now vulnerable. Equally important, documents had to be retrieved or destroyed, hidden arms secured and moved to the mountains of West Virginia. Only a few of the most strategically placed people would remain. The rest would be told to make their way to the camp to join the rest.

Wes Quinn had also left immediately to meet with other AIS operatives somewhere out West near the demilitarized zone for a full briefing and to receive further instructions from their superiors.

Though Bryce was mentally ready to plunge immediately into the massive task at hand, he was not disappointed at the temporary lull. September closed out, and the first days of October dawned crisp and clear. The mountains were turning now, and as far as the eye could see it was a sea of brilliant color—oranges, yellows, reds, crimsons. He and Leslie would hike the hills for hours at a time, talking quietly, laughing, sometimes just holding hands, caught up in the total wonder of each other.

The only thing that marred life at all was when Bryce each night would go to the car, uncover the radio, and call in his report to Elliot Mannington. But he could say truthfully that little was happening at the moment, and so the reports were terse and the unpleasant reminders of the game he was playing were quickly put aside.

Coming to know the others in the camp was pleasant and revealing as well. There were nearly fifty people now, and each day a few more trickled in. Tents and makeshift shelters were scattered through the trees. The few old buildings left from before were given to the families with children. Although the camp had tried to persuade Paul Adams to take one of the nicer cabins, as a mark of their respect and honor for him, he had quietly but adamantly refused. He and Vera and Leslie slept in sleeping bags in a tent beneath some quaking aspen.

The majority of the people in the camp were younger and unmarried, with more men than women. But there were two widows, besides Jessie Lambert, and three people past sixty. There were also ten children under fifteen, and by the third day, Leslie and Vera had a school going for half a day, much to the parents' delight and the children's dismay. Often Bryce would sit in the back of the rough classroom just to watch Leslie as she worked with them. He got an equal amount of joy out of watching her with the other single girls in the camp. They would go down to the stream together to get water, or stand around the cook stoves, chattering like high-school girls about the various camp romances and other such things. It thrilled Bryce to see how alive and vibrant Leslie was becoming in this mountain setting.

Though the camp was in a state of waiting, the arrival of Paul Adams had infused everyone with a sense of excitement. Every night after dinner, bundled up in jackets and sweaters against the chill of the night air, they gathered around a huge fire pit to laugh and sing, or sometimes just to sit and talk quietly, sobered by what the future held for them.

The change from a mere state of mental shock to a deep, inner commitment to the cause of freedom had come for Bryce as he saw life in CONAS, life in an America without the Constitution. For Leslie, that change came during these sessions around the fire. For the most part, the people had come because they were fed up with the system—the constant oppression, the stultifying poverty, the incredible waste and inefficiency. But there were also the more dramatic stories of life in the Confederation of North American States. A young couple with three small children had had their food permit revoked for attending church. They had survived for six months by foraging at night and buying what meager supplies they could on the black market. A widower, a grizzled old farmer, had struck a police constable for trying to force sexual advances on his granddaughter, then had fled to the hills with her and her parents, one step ahead of a prison sentence. Three were university students, disillusioned with poor facilities and endless propagandizing. A sensitive young girl with sad brown eyes had watched her parents lose the farm that had been in the family for six generations to a collectivized factory and die within the year in abject poverty.

One night, after the others had gone to bed, Bryce and Leslie sat quietly in front of the glowing coals. He could tell she was pensive and lost in thought. He put his arm around her and pulled her close. With a murmur of contentment, she snuggled into his shoulder.

"Tell me what you are thinking," he said, putting his face against her hair.

She stared into the coals for a long time before she spoke. "I was thinking," she said softly, "that there are none so blind as those who will not see."

"Meaning what?"

"Meaning that I have been teaching history and government for over four years now. I taught those young people the official state dogma. I outlined the glories of our socialist system. I knew it wasn't true, but I taught it so that I could keep my job, help our family survive since my father could no longer work. Occasionally some of the students, usually those with inquiring minds, those in whom the hunger for truth had not been totally crushed, would ask difficult questions. The contradictions between what they were taught and what they saw at every hand were too obvious. Life in their world—the real world—somehow didn't quite match up to what the textbooks said. And I would answer their questions as I was supposed to. I would try to gloss problems over, brush them aside, look the other way."

"You had little choice."

"My father had a choice!" she retorted.

There was nothing to say to that, and so he just pulled her in more tightly.

"But now . . . " She paused, then sighed.

"What?"

She sat up, looking into his face. One hand came up and touched his cheek. "This has been a wonderful time, these past few days." Her eyes softened. "I love you so much."

He kissed her gently. "And I can't believe how much I love you."

She kissed him back, but then turned to gaze deeply into the coals again. "But now, now it's more than loving you, and wanting to be with you. Now I'm coming to understand my father."

"Yes," Bryce agreed. "I know exactly what you mean."

"I'm beginning to feel that same absolute determination that we cannot—must not!—simply sit back and accept cruelty and injustice. If we do, we become part of it."

Bryce ran his hand gently across her hair, loving to touch her, loving this woman of grace and beauty and growing determination. "In the early history of this country," he said quietly, "the history that has been suppressed by the government, there

237

was a man who felt that same fire your father feels. His name was Patrick Henry. People were frightened, afraid that if they took a stand it might mean war. As a matter of fact, he lived in Virginia, at Richmond."

"What did he do?"

He stopped, remembering. He had first memorized this speech for a high-school debate class. It had gone over so well he had used it again and again in his college debate meets. He had even quoted it once to a jury for dramatic effect. He looked at Leslie and took a quick breath. "One day a crowd had gathered at a church. They were vacillating, fearful to do anything."

He looked into Leslie's eyes. And then with emotions he had never before felt, he began to quote the words that he had not thought about for several years. "Henry got up on the steps of the church, and this is what he said: 'We have done everything that could be done to avert the storm which is now coming. An appeal to arms and to the God of Hosts is all that is left us! They tell us that we are weak, unable to cope with so formidable an adversary. But when shall we be stronger? Shall we gather strength by irresolution and inaction? Shall we acquire the means of effectual resistance by lying supinely on our backs and hugging the delusive phantom of hope, until our enemies shall have bound us hand and foot?' "

Suddenly Bryce was no longer thinking of the British and of colonialists standing in front of St. John's Church in 1775. He was thinking of CONAS and Elliot Mannington and the deformed hands of Paul Adams.

His voice rose in intensity. " 'We are not weak, if we make proper use of those means which the God of nature hath placed in our power. We shall not fight our battles alone. There is a just God who presides over the destinies of nations, and who will raise up friends to fight our battles for us. Gentleman may cry, peace, peace!—but there is no peace. The war is actually begun. Why stand we here idle? Is life so dear, or peace so sweet, as to be purchased at the price of chains and slavery? Forbid it, Almighty God!' "

Bryce Sherwood sat back, a little shaken by his own emotions. Finally he looked down again into the eyes of the woman he so loved. " 'I know not what course others may take,' " he finished softly, " 'but as for me, give me liberty or give me death!' "

The silence of the night closed in around them. Leslie's eyes were glistening as she reached out and took his hand.

Suddenly a little embarrassed at his own passion, he shook his head. "I'm ashamed to say that for a while I used to think that speech was too corny, too passionate, a little too fanatic. Now . . . "

"When the time is right," she said in a husky whisper, "you must share that with the others. Write it out so that it can be taught in the schools, preached in the churches, trumpeted from every pulpit and lecture hall in the land."

He nodded soberly, then with the greatest of gentleness he put his hand over hers. "And you, Leslie Adams. What of you?"

She smiled up at him. "What would you have of me?"

"I would have you to be my wife."

She leaned her head against him, suddenly crying. "And I would have Bryce Sherwood to be my husband," she murmured happily.

But within the hour, the idyllic respite came to an end. After he had walked Leslie to her tent, Bryce reluctantly moved down the small dirt road and into the trees where the car was hidden. As he turned on the radio, gave the codes, and started his brief transmission, the gravel-voiced man who always took the call suddenly broke in. "Stand by for a message." Surprised, Bryce grabbed the small notebook and then for the next two minutes copied the unintelligible set of numbers and letters that spewed forth. Puzzled and with a gnawing sense of dismay, he dug under the back seat of the car and retrieved the code book.

It took him nearly five minutes more to translate it. When he was finished, he sat back, his face grim. Finally he shook his head, stowed the radio, and walked swiftly back to the tent where Paul Adams lay sleeping.

"You must go," Paul said firmly. "He leaves you no option."

"No!" Leslie cried. "What if something has gone wrong? What if this is a trap?"

Bryce read the message again by the faint light of the lantern. "Urgent that we meet tonight. Six miles west of Quaid's Crossing on road to Richwood. Small bridge over Charlie Creek. Two A.M. Create whatever cover required but absolutely imperative that you come. Blue Goose."

He sighed. Blue Goose was Elliot Mannington's personal code name. He reached over and took Leslie's hand. "It will be all right. If it was a trap, he wouldn't pull me out at night like this. He knows where we are. He can get me anytime."

"I agree," Paul said. "And we can't have him getting suspicious now. You've got to go."

Vera reached over into the corner of the tent to a pile of clothing and retrieved a black sweater that belonged to Paul. "Here," she said with quiet practicality. "Your jacket is too light colored. This will be better."

He smiled at her gratefully, took off his jacket quickly, and donned the sweater. He got up into a crouch, reached out and squeezed Leslie's hand.

She forced a smile, then kissed him hard. "Be careful," she whispered.

"I will." He straightened and slipped out the tent flap. Paul followed.

"I think you'll be okay, but watch him."

Bryce nodded. They gripped each other's hands firmly.

"Good luck."

Bryce swallowed, feeling the queasiness in the pit of his stomach. "Thanks."

240

He parked over a mile away from the bridge, cut left through the fields and meadows until he struck Charlie Creek. Then, keeping low, he moved back toward the highway, searching the night for any sign of others besides himself. By 1:30 he was hidden in a patch of wild raspberry bushes underneath the bridge.

Twenty minutes later he heard the sound of an engine and slipped up the bank to look. There was little moonlight but Bryce could still see the gleam of the car about a hundred yards down the road. Three shadowy figures got out, but only one started toward him. By the time the figure reached the bridge, Bryce was satisfied that it was Elliot Mannington. He swung up and over the guardrail and onto the road.

Mannington stopped, peering forward into the darkness, then Bryce heard an audible sigh of relief. "Bryce?"

"Yes."

"Thank heavens." He stepped forward and gripped Bryce's hand, pumping it vigorously. There was a short pause, and Bryce could feel the urgency in Mannington. "Look, I'm sorry to pull you out like this. I know it heightens your risk, but something has come up. I didn't dare communicate it over the radio."

"I think I'm okay. The camp was asleep. The car is far enough down the road, and I let it coast out for some distance before I started the engine."

"Good." And then he plunged right in."Bryce, it's imperative that you get things moving," he said bluntly.

"Why? What's up?"

"The prime minister." Mannington swore. "That stupid idiot!"

Bryce tried not to show his surprise. Coming from one of his loyal cabinet members, that was pretty strong talk.

"He's been under increasing pressure in the last few months," Mannington went on. "There are some on the Central Committee who are quietly starting to talk about the need for new leadership. Not in front of him, of course. But he knows."

Bryce waited. This was hardly what he had come down expecting to hear.

241

"He's decided that this operation holds the key for consolidating his position, solidifying his power."

"*We* do?"

Mannington gave a scoffing sound, completely disgusted. "Yes. And if we don't help him save his tail, we—and I mean you and me, Burkhart, all of ISD—could face serious consequences."

"But what? How?"

"October twenty-first is National People's Day."

"Yes." Whatever the heck that was, Bryce thought. Founders' Day, perhaps. Or something like May Day in European countries. He'd have to ask Paul.

"The prime minister is scheduled to give a speech on national television."

Again Bryce just nodded, still totally baffled.

"He wants to use that speech to announce the arrest and capture of the major leaders of the resistance movement. In fact, his plan is to parade them on national television, put them on trial right there for all to see."

"What!" Bryce's jaw had dropped open.

"That's right." He sighed wearily. "And in one fell swoop he will have silenced the criticism, put down his opposition."

Bryce leaned over the bridge railing, not hearing the soft murmur of the water below him. His mind was racing.

"There is no option, Bryce. By October nineteenth we have to move in and take whomever we can get."

"But that's not even three weeks from now. Lewis and Wes Quinn aren't even back yet."

"They should be back today."

Bryce started. They had received word of that in the camp, but how did Mannington know? To cover his dismay, he said quickly, "But even then, three weeks!"

"I know. That's what makes me so angry." He slammed one fist against the railing. "We've worked too hard to let it unravel now. But come the twentieth, I've got to hand him someone.

242

His power may be weakening, but he can still be a very powerful enemy. He'll take us down with him."

He took Bryce's arm and swung him around. "Push them, Bryce. You've got to get those resistance leaders here before the twentieth, or everything you've worked for will be lost."

"I . . ." Bryce thrust his hands into his pockets. "I don't know if I can. Three weeks! That's not much time."

Mannington grabbed him by both shoulders and shook him gently. "You've got to, Bryce. You've got to!"

CHAPTER 29

Bryce was back before dawn. Not too surprisingly, Paul Adams was waiting for him on the dirt road below the camp. They walked slowly, talking softly, their breath leaving frosty clouds in the air as they moved through the trees and out onto a ridge overlooking the valley below. The sun was fully up and comfortably warm by the time they came back down, and Bryce greeted a much-relieved mother and daughter with an enthusiastic hug.

But after breakfast, the two men left again, heading up for the same ridge, talking as quietly and as earnestly as before, as the outline of a daring plan began to take shape in their minds. That was where Leslie found them two hours later.

"What?" Paul said in alarm, standing quickly at the sight of his daughter coming swiftly up the trail toward them.

"They're back," Leslie said, a little out of breath. "Lewis and Mr. Quinn are back."

It turned out to be more than Lewis and Quinn who had arrived. They had brought with them Quinn's control officer. A control officer not only served as an espionage agent's immediate superior officer, but he also directed the agent in the field. He was the communications link between the AIS and the field agent, procurer of needed supplies, provider of a safe escape route should the cover be blown. In short, the control officer was supervisor, nursemaid, emergency fallback, and, when necessary, psychiatrist and counselor. Hal Hoffman certainly didn't look the part of a senior officer of the United States intelligence service. He was thin, balding, and soft spoken, and he wore steel-rimmed bifocals that gave him a bit of an owlish look. And yet, almost instantly, he conveyed a feeling of tremendous competence and confidence, and it quickly became obvious that the position of leadership in the group had shifted to him and to Paul Adams.

Seven people were present—Hoffman, Wes Quinn, Lewis, Paul, Bryce, and Jessie and Neal Lambert. As the introductions were finished and they settled back, Paul spoke up. "I think there is one thing we need to hear from Bryce before we go any further," he said.

Hoffman nodded. "Okay, shoot."

And so Bryce proceeded to reveal to them who he was and of his relationship with Elliot Mannington. At first there was stunned surprise, then sharp questions about why he had not revealed this sooner. He talked earnestly and quietly, showing them the advantages of having a double agent who was directly connected to the minister of the interior.

Surprisingly, it was Lewis who reacted most bitterly. Jessie very quickly believed him. Neal followed her lead as well. The others were taken aback, but it was obvious that Hoffman instantly saw the possibilities. But Lewis was furious that Bryce had not told them sooner.

Hoffman listened to it all, let the feelings all come out, then finally spoke. Bryce's revelation was accepted. They would now use that strategic position to their advantage. Lewis grumbled a little more, but when Hoffman moved right on, he gradually calmed down and seemed to accept it.

"We are here," Hoffman began, "not to plan a single battle or even a campaign. What we are facing is long, drawn-out, protracted warfare. For the most part, it will be waged here in the Confederation of North American States. But it could erupt and draw the Western Alliance into open conflict with CONAS.

We are prepared for that eventuality—in fact, some would welcome it. But because of that, we must do more than outline tactics. We are here to plan strategy—long-range, well-thought-out strategy."

He turned to Paul. "We have already taken one of the most important first steps in that strategy. Mr. Adams—Paul—I cannot tell you how pleased we are that you have agreed to join us. Word of your coming is already sweeping this country like wildfire. America too."

Now everyone was nodding. Quinn expressed the feelings of all. "Your name stands high in the minds of the people. Your example is known to us all. To stand with you in this effort is a great honor for me and for us all."

"The honor is mine," Paul said softly, his voice tinged with emotion. "I had almost given up the fight. It seemed so pointless, as though all I had done was for nothing." He turned to Bryce and smiled. "Until this stubborn young firebrand came into my life and reminded me of my duty. And now to be here with you. To hear you speak of strategy and long-range plans. To talk as though we may actually win someday. I don't know if this old heart can stand the joy I feel at this moment."

For a moment no one spoke, each touched by the humble commitment of this battered old man. Then Hal Hoffman broke the silence. "We are pleased that your wife and daughter are here too." He laughed and looked at Bryce. "Though we understand that half the fire in this young firebrand happens to be kindled by your daughter."

Bryce flushed as the others laughed.

"Your wife has already cornered me and asked if she can be of help," Hoffman said, turning back to Paul.

"My wife is a woman of great courage."

"We think she can," Quinn said quickly.

Jessie was nodding vigorously now.

Paul was a little surprised. "What? What could she do?"

Hoffman leaned forward. "Bryce has told you of our plan to send Jessie to America to start a fund-raising drive?"

"Yes."

"Let Vera come with me," Jessie broke in eagerly. "Think what it will mean if the wife of Paul Adams is actually there to speak to them."

Bryce was nodding now too, the kernel of an idea growing.

"Will she go?" Lewis asked.

Paul slowly looked from one face to the other. "I will ask her. It would be difficult to see her leave, but she is so eager. Last time, when I was arrested, she could do nothing but sit at home and worry." His face was suddenly determined. "I will ask her."

"If she agrees," Hoffman said, "we'll send them tomorrow. The sooner they begin, the better for us."

"How will you get them out?" Lewis said.

"We've already got the route set," Quinn answered. "We've used it before. It's safe. There would be little danger." He stopped, obviously not wanting to give any more than that.

The need to know, Bryce thought with a sudden chill. Information was given only as needed, for one never knew when he or she would be caught and put under interrogation.

"What about sending Leslie too?" Bryce suddenly asked.

Paul turned slowly to stare at him, then understanding came into his eyes. "You would do that?" he asked softly.

Bryce took a quick breath. "What we talked about today, you and I? It will add greatly to the risk here."

The deep-set eyes were grave as Paul considered that and then sighed. "Yes. Yes, it would. We will ask her too." He sighed again. "But you know Leslie."

"Yes, I know Leslie."

"What do you mean?" Hoffman broke in. "What increased risks are you talking about?"

Bryce and Paul looked at each other, and Bryce nodded his encouragement. "Tell them."

Paul sighed, then looked around the circle. "We know that Elliot Mannington wants us to lure all of the resistance leaders into a trap."

They nodded solemnly.

"Suppose," he said slowly, "suppose we use his trap to set a trap of our own." He leaned forward now, almost eagerly. "Earlier, Mr. Hoffman, you spoke of war and strategy."

"Yes."

"Would you agree that the more dramatic and successful the beginning blow of any war, the more likely it is that you marshal the will of the people behind you?"

Hoffman barely moved his head up and down, but Bryce could see that his mind was racing.

"Well, suppose we let Mannington do just exactly what he plans?"

Wes Quinn and Lewis snapped forward at the same instant. "You mean let him capture the resistance leaders?" Quinn blurted.

Paul and Bryce were both nodding. Bryce picked it up now. "We'll not bring the actual leaders in, but others from their movements. People who will volunteer to be captured and put on trial."

"But why?" Neal asked, shaking his head. "What do we gain by that?"

"Well," Paul continued, "still supposing, suppose that when the prime minister goes on national television on the twenty-first of October, to have his little show, just suppose that we had a team that took over the station at that point."

The others were staring at him wide-eyed.

"And," Bryce finished, "just suppose that at that point Paul Adams were to go before the cameras and give his own speech to the nation?"

The moment Bryce saw Leslie coming, he knew he was in trouble. She came up to the group of men in which he was standing and slipped her arm through Bryce's. "I'd like to talk with you, if I may," she said, as she smiled prettily at the others. But he wasn't fooled. He could hear the sound of battle in her voice, and as they walked away, he tensed.

"Don't I at least get a hearty meal before the execution?" he finally said soberly, as they moved out of earshot.

She gave him a dirty look but just shook her head and led him into the trees where they could no longer be seen. Then she stopped and turned around to face him.

"All right," he said glumly, "let me have it."

She suddenly went up on tiptoes, throwing her arms around his neck. Her kiss caught him completely off guard, and for a moment he didn't respond to the soft warmth of her lips. But he recovered quickly.

"I love you, Bryce Sherwood," she whispered.

Thoroughly surprised, he searched her face. "And I love you too," he said tentatively. He had come expecting an explosion. He liked this much better.

She stepped back, looking at him gravely. "Is life so dear, or peace so sweet, as to be purchased at the price of sending me off to a safe place to trail after my mother and Jessie Lambert so that you don't have to worry about me?"

He winced, knowing he had relaxed a moment too soon. "Leslie, I . . . Did your father tell you about our proposal to the council?"

"Yes, he did."

"The risks are going to be—"

She put her hand over his mouth. "I understand, and I love you for trying to do what you did. But we'll hear no more of my leaving. Not if you really know that my heart is now your heart. Agreed?"

She took her hand away, but he grabbed it again, and kissed it gently, searching her face over the top of it.

She cocked her head, giving him a warning look. "Agreed?"

"I can't stand the thought of something happening to you," he said softly, pressing her fingers to his lips.

"Then why don't you come with us too? Jessie and Mom can give the speeches while you and I go up and down the aisles

249

with handkerchiefs and collection plates. That way, we'll both be safe."

He pulled a face. "Ouch!"

"Okay, then, we'll hear no more of my leaving. Agreed?"

He sighed. "Agreed."

"Good," she said matter-of-factly. "Now, is it true you're going to be leaving the camp?"

"Yes."

Her eyes dropped, then came up again. "When?"

"Tonight. We've got to meet the resistance leaders face to face. It's going to take some hard selling."

"I understand."

"I sent another message to Mannington. I'll meet him again tonight and give him the news. Then Neal and I will leave directly from there. Your father and Hal Hoffman are the second team. Lewis and Quinn are the third. But we'll all be back by the fifteenth." He brightened. "And come the twenty-second of October, you and I are going to go into the nearest village, kidnap us a pastor, and give this camp the best darn wedding they've ever seen."

She managed a smile, but there was no heart in it. She looked up at him, her eyes wide and anxious. "Where have they asked you to go?" she asked, faltering for the first time.

"To the New England Confederation. Neal knows the people there."

"Where they are looking for the murderers of an ISD captain."

"Yes."

"Oh, Bryce," she cried softly, "help me to be brave."

He looked at her incredulously. "Help *you* to be brave?" he echoed. "My dear lady, you are clearly and unmistakably the direct stock of your father and mother. And it simultaneously thrills me and scares me to death to think you might pass on some of that same fire-tempered steel into the hearts of our children."

She stepped back. "Our children," she whispered, in sudden awe.

"Yes." He laughed. "I only hope they obey me better than their mother does."

"Will they ever see freedom?" she asked softly.

He sobered immediately. "If they don't," he responded with sudden determination, "then I pity the country that tries to hold them."

As they came out of the trees a few moments later, holding hands, Lewis saw them from across the main clearing and walked swiftly toward them.

"Oh-oh," Bryce murmured.

But he worried for nothing. Lewis stammered for a moment, then finally raised his head and met Bryce's gaze. "Look, I just wanted to say I was sorry for what I said in there. It caught me so off guard, I—"

"I understand," Bryce said quickly. "I wish now I had told you sooner, after all you've done for me, but—"

"No, you were quite right. You would be crazy to run around telling just anybody about that. But I didn't want to leave without telling you that I'm sorry and that there are no more questions in my mind." He stuck out his hand. "I'm grateful to be working with you."

"Thank you," Bryce said. And as he moved away, Bryce looked at Leslie. "Well, that was nice."

"Yes it was." She put her arm around him. "You'd better go say good-bye to Mother. She'll almost certainly be gone before you get back."

"And tell her to see if she can buy a wedding dress in America. Would you like that?"

Leslie did not look up at him. "We'll talk about the wedding after the twenty-first," was all she would say.

251

By one-thirty the next morning, the sky was overcast, and Bryce had to move more slowly through the thick darkness toward Charlie Creek. Neal stayed back at the car to wait. Bryce had received no acknowledgment of his message and wasn't sure whether this would be for nothing.

But this time Mannington was waiting for him. "Well?" he demanded, even as Bryce walked onto the bridge.

"They bought it!" Bryce blurted. "They actually bought it."

"Really?" There was obvious relief.

"Yes. I told them the longer we wait, the greater the chance there is for detection. They agreed. We're leaving now, all of us, to contact the various factions throughout CONAS. We'll set the meeting for the nineteenth of October."

"Wonderful!"

Bryce sighed. "There is one possible hitch, though."

"What that?"

"There's a new player on the scene. A man named Hal Hoffman—he's AIS and Quinn's control—"

"So," Mannington cut him off, "that's where he was going! We knew he had entered CONAS, but we lost him shortly after he came in."

Bryce kept his face impassive but once again mentally vowed to walk very carefully around this man. If they assumed all of Mannington's eggs were in the Bryce Sherwood basket, they were grossly mistaken.

"So?"

Bryce gave him a blank look, having lost the train of thought.

"What's the possible hitch?"

"Oh. Hoffman is really nervous about bringing all the leaders to one place at the same time. He suggested two separate meetings."

Mannington swore softly. "We can't allow that. You've got to convince them."

"I tried. And surprisingly, Paul Adams agreed. He admitted that there was a vulnerability factor, but he argued strongly that if we are ever to unify the entire movement, we must have everyone at once."

"That's right! Good for Adams."

"Hoffman finally agreed, but there's a chance some of the leaders may not see it that way. I don't know if we'll get every one."

"Do you know what I'd give," Mannington said, speaking half to himself, "just to get Paul Adams, Hal Hoffman, and Wesley Quinn?" He suddenly straightened. "But we'll do better than that. Much better. This is wonderful news, Bryce. The prime minister will be pleased."

"I'm headed north into New England to start making the contacts tonight. The others are spreading out in other directions. Tell Burkhart to lay off. If the borders are too tight or any of them suspect they've been spotted, we'll never pull this off on time."

"Those orders have already been given."

"Good. I won't call in again until we get back. I obviously can't take the radio along with Neal Lambert."

"That's fine. The prime minister is moving ahead as though the broadcast on the twenty-first will be just another speech, but he'll have everything ready for a national trial."

Bryce just nodded, not answering that.

He straightened. "Watch yourself, Bryce. This will be the most dangerous stage. But if we do it . . . " He clenched his fist and punched the air. "If we do it, there'll be no stopping us, no stopping us at all!"

"We're going to do it," Bryce said evenly. "I can feel it. We *are* going to pull this off."

As Elliot Mannington got back into the car, his driver turned. "Back to Washington, sir?"

Mannington took out the two slips of paper that held the messages that had come the previous night. The first was Bryce's call. It had surprised him to hear from Bryce so quickly. But the second message had come as a total shock.

He looked at it again. "Extremely urgent we meet tomorrow 05:30 in Charlottesville safe house. Red Fox."

Mannington leaned forward across the seat. "How long to Charlottesville from here?"

"Maybe three hours," the driver answered.

"I need to be there before five-thirty."

"Yes, sir."

As the car leaped forward, Mannington read the message one more time, then tucked it into his pocket and sat back, deep in thought.

CHAPTER 30

It was an hour before dawn on the morning of October nineteenth when Bryce slipped out of his tent. The air was crisp,
and there was already a white sheen of frost covering the ground.
Above him the stars were like crushed diamonds dusting the
black velvet of the sky. He looked around quickly, then moved
carefully out of the trees and across the main clearing toward
the dirt road that led down to where he had hidden the radio.

He stopped suddenly as a figure stepped out from a clump of
underbrush, then shook his head. "What are you doing up
already?" he whispered as he stepped forward and slipped his
arm around Leslie's waist.

"Did *you* sleep?" Leslie whispered back.

He shook his head.

"Well, then."

He gave her a quick kiss.

"If I promise not to make a sound, do you mind if I walk
down with you?" she asked.

"Yes."

She looked up sharply, then dug at him when she saw him
grinning.

"Well, how I am supposed to keep my wits about me with
you sitting close by?" he asked.

"Give it your best shot."

He laughed softly and pulled her close as they continued
down the hill. She sat down on a rock and watched soberly as

he moved into a heavy tangle of fallen trees and undergrowth, then backed out with the radio. He turned it on and sat back, waiting for it to warm up.

"He's not going to love you very much when all of this becomes clear," she said softly as he blew on his hands and started adjusting the knobs.

"I know."

Not too surprisingly, as he put on the earphones and gave the call-up codes, it was Mannington's voice that answered almost instantly. "Have you got the scrambler on?" he asked.

"Yes."

"Good. What's your report?"

"Everything's set. The last man got in last night."

"So how many?"

"Twelve out of the fifteen possibles. That doesn't count Lewis or Hoffman—" he looked up at Leslie, "or Paul Adams or Neal Lambert and myself. One bit of bad news. We lost Quinn."

"What?" Mannington blurted.

"He went into the Washington area to work with Lewis's people. He called in today, said something urgent has come up. We'll have to go ahead without him."

"Too bad," Mannington said. "But if we get Hoffman we can pull in Quinn later."

"I wish they were all coming, but this will wipe out seventy-five percent of the leadership in one crack."

"It's good enough. Better than I had hoped, actually."

"Are your people in place?" Bryce asked, watching Leslie's face.

"Yes."

"Any signs of alarm?"

"None," Mannington said flatly. "We've been moving our forces in at night for the past three days. We've stayed completely clear of any contact with locals. We're set."

Bryce took a quick breath. "All right, then. Tell them to be careful where they're shooting. I'm not excited about coming out of this dead."

256

"These are the best men we've got," Mannington responded. "They don't make mistakes. The prime minister wants his little show on television, not dead bodies to display." There was a pause. "Are all the others out of the camp now?"

"Yes. Everyone not directly involved in the meetings was sent down to the valley for security reasons. Leslie Adams is still here with her father. Lewis's wife is also here, and the wife of one other man who does our cooking. There are twenty people in camp, counting myself and the three women. Come in fast and quiet and I think we can keep the casualties to a minimum."

"Are you sure there are only the six guards posted?" That was a new voice, and for a moment through the distortion of the scrambler Bryce didn't place it. Then he pulled a face. It was Colonel Burkhart.

"Affirmative, Colonel. There are others down in the valley watching for any newcomers or unusual activity, but the six up here are all we've got."

"Good," Burkhart said, "We've got those six located and will take them with knockout gas capsules. They won't make a sound."

Bryce felt the nervousness start to hit his stomach again. "Anything else?"

Colonel Burkhart's voice responded again. "Yes, let's synchronize our watches. I show four-oh-seven exactly, on my signal. Ready." There was a slight pause and Bryce lifted his watch and peered at the dial. "Mark!" Burkhart said. "We'll hit the camp at exactly five-thirty."

"Good. The first meeting starts at six-thirty. Five-thirty should catch them just waking up."

"Great!" Mannington said jubilantly. "Keep your head down and we'll see you in just about an hour."

As he put away the earphones and stowed the radio, he looked up at Leslie.

"Well?" she asked in a low voice.

"It's done. They are in place and waiting."

257

Neither of them spoke as they walked back up to the camp to start waking the others.

By 4:45 every one of the seventeen men and three women in the camp were gathered in the darkness of the mess hall. Hal Hoffman cleared his throat, and the soft murmur of voices instantly came to a halt. "Okay," he said. "You've heard Bryce's report. Everyone knows exactly what to do."

There were several who nodded, but no one spoke.

"Let's look as natural as we can. Let them catch you completely by surprise. Those of us who are to run, run like you're scared." He paused. "That shouldn't be too difficult."

There was a quiet ripple of laughter.

"Those who have been assigned to go for your weapons, make it look good, but for crying out loud don't actually get them. We don't need any martyrs at this point."

"These are crack troops," Bryce added, "and they've been instructed to keep the shooting to an absolute minimum. But you get too excited and start blasting away at them, and they'll blast right back."

"Lewis and I," Hoffman said, picking it up again, "are to be the only ones who fire back at them, and that will be only enough to keep it looking authentic." He looked around at the dim faces in the darkness. "If we all do our part, like we've rehearsed, this will go off like clockwork. Any questions?"

There weren't.

"All right then." Hoffman turned to where Bryce and Leslie stood next to her father. "Bryce, you'd better get moving. You need to be completely clear before this begins."

"Yes, sir." He straightened. "I still feel like my place is here, with the rest of you."

Hoffman shook his head. "Wes said the same thing when we sent him into Washington. But don't worry; you'll get your turn day after tomorrow."

"All right, ladies," Paul said briskly. "Get your things and leave with Bryce."

Lewis's wife stepped forward and kissed him quickly. The other wife was crying quietly as her husband held her. Leslie threw her arms around her father and hugged him tightly. "This is for Mom, too. You know what she'd say if she were here, so be careful, Daddy. Elliot Mannington will be very happy to get his hands on you."

"Yes," he admitted frankly. "But don't worry. I'm to be the star at that circus they're calling a trial day after tomorrow. You can bet the prime minister won't let me miss that."

She kissed his cheek. "I love you."

"And I love you, Leslie. Go with care."

Two days before, Hal Hoffman had carefully gone through Bryce's car and located the homing device and the microphone that had been planted beneath the dashboard. He had disconnected the microphone and showed Bryce how to remove the little transmitter that would allow radio tracking on the location of the car. Then they had driven around to the next canyon and hidden the car deep in the underbrush.

Now, Bryce and the three women with him climbed steadily up the path that led away from the camp toward that canyon. As they crossed a ridge and started the descent, he suddenly held up his hand. In the quiet of the morning air they all heard the sound clearly—the crackle of rifle fire.

Bryce peered at his watch. It was 5:31. "That's it," was all he said.

They stood motionless for the next minute, listening intently. Bryce counted softly to himself as the soft popping sounds floated to them. After ninety seconds the mountains were silent again. "Fourteen or fifteen shots," he said, trying to sound bright. "That's good. Better than I had hoped."

The three women just stared at him in the darkness, grim-faced.

259

"Let's go," he said finally. He took Leslie's hand and they started downward again. He noticed that she held onto him more tightly than the steepness of the path required.

They had only gone another hundred yards when Bryce spun around. Someone was coming up behind them.

"Shhh!" Bryce whispered urgently. "Into the trees."

They had talked about this possibility, and the three women quickly obeyed. Bryce stepped behind a large pine tree and raised his rifle. The footsteps were getting louder, running toward them.

"Bryce, it's me. Lewis. Wait!"

Surprised, Bryce looked back up the path toward the dark shape that was approaching.

The voice called again in an urgent whisper. "Bryce! It's Lewis."

He stepped out.

"Thank heavens!" Lewis said, pulling up sharply and leaning over to catch his breath.

"What?" Bryce asked quickly, feeling a sudden fear.

"Something's gone wrong," Lewis panted. Bryce felt Leslie clutch at his sleeve.

Lewis straightened, looking back up the way he had come. "Hal's coming. Needs to talk to you."

Bryce turned and peered up the path into the darkness. As he did so, Lewis whipped a pistol out from beneath his jacket and put the muzzle against the back of Bryce's head. "Drop the rifle, Bryce," he said quietly.

Wesley Quinn drove slowly through the deserted streets of the inner city, circling and doubling constantly to make sure he was not being followed. Finally satisfied, he headed for a district of run-down factories and warehouses along the shores of the Potomac River. He glanced at his watch and grunted in satisfaction. He still had fifteen minutes before his rendezvous with Bryce and the women from the camp.

It had been a busy three days for Quinn. While the others became the bait in Elliot Mannington's trap, Quinn was putting the final touches on the jaws of their own. There was, of course, no word about the raid in the media. Nor would there be. The prime minister was not going to let anything spoil his dramatic little surprise. But Quinn had posted a watch on the radio until nine that morning, waiting for the call alerting him that something had gone wrong. It hadn't come, so the clock was running.

The plan was deceptively simple on paper, though the war council, as they had somehow started to call themselves, had gone over every detail meticulously again and again. The hardest part had been persuading the men and women who led the numerous factions of the resistance to send people openly into a trap set by the ISD. A few had refused, calling the whole thing insane. But most had agreed. Paul Adams had argued most persuasively, using again and again the point that if they ever wanted the struggle for freedom to succeed, they must strike one dramatic blow to win the hearts of the people.

The twenty-first of October was known as People's Day, an ironic euphemism if ever there was one, Quinn thought bitterly. Though he loved his work and was fiercely committed to what he was doing, life in CONAS was a depressing contrast to his life in the mountains of Oregon. When this was over, he was going to request a leave, go back, maybe find a wife. He sighed, knowing he had made that same promise to himself half a dozen times before.

People's Day commemorated the treaty of 1836 that ended the war between the Confederation of Canadian States, the New England Confederation, and the Atlantic States Alliance and created the Confederation of North American States.

And so, beginning at nine o'clock, day after tomorrow, the People's Day celebration would begin. There was to be a large military parade at 9:00 A.M. in the heart of Washington. As hundreds of thousands of citizens lined the streets and much of the military might of CONAS was passing the reviewing stand, five small assault teams would move into position around the city. At 10:30 A.M., the prime minister and his party would leave the reviewing stand and move nearby to the state-owned radio and television station. There, at 11:00, with great fanfare, the prime minister would begin his national broadcast. The people were expecting nothing more than the usual patriotic speech and glowing reports of all the state had accomplished. But this time, of course, there would be a surprise.

Quinn gave a short laugh to himself. More surprises than one, he thought in satisfaction. As the prime minister was announcing to the world the greatest triumph of his career, namely the arrest of the leading figures in the rebellion, mortar and rocket attacks would be launched against five targets within the city. The assault teams would strike quickly and move out, maximizing the shock value and drawing the military and police forces in the city away from the television station. The five targets had been chosen specifically with those two purposes in mind. They were the parliament building, the presidential palace, the building housing the offices of the prime minister and the Central Committee, the Ministry of Finance and headquarters of the national bank, and, finally, ISD headquarters. If all went well, in just under ten minutes the entire city would be thrown into panic. The streets would still be jammed with people from the parade, which would hamper the movement of police and military. Command centers would be paralyzed with the simultaneous strikes. And that was critical to what would happen next.

Quinn became very sober as he thought about the next phase. Already smuggled inside and hiding in the attics and storage rooms of the television station were a dozen of Quinn's best men. Precisely at 11:10 A.M., about the time the prime minister was triumphantly presenting his captives to the television cameras and announcing their public trial, those men would come out of hiding and make their move. Using tear gas, stun grenades, and total surprise, they would move into the studios swiftly, overpower the guards, and take the prime minister hostage. At the same time, Quinn, who would be waiting outside with another hundred heavily armed men, would launch an attack on the forces outside the station.

Quinn turned into a deserted alley, turned off the headlights and let the small truck roll to a stop. He sighed deeply, already starting to feel the churning in his stomach that always accompanied this kind of an operation. If all went well—and there were so many things that could fall apart—then at that point Paul Adams would take center stage, go before the cameras, and provide the millions watching a very different show than what the prime minister had promised. Ten minutes later, assuming Quinn had successfully controlled the outside forces, the "captives" would be gone, leaving the prime minister to pick up the pieces of his disaster as best he could.

There were a lot of ifs in this one, Quinn thought. And if they failed they had deliberately given some of their best people to Mannington and the ISD. As he unlocked the warehouse door and slipped inside, he shook his head. If they succeeded . . . Oh, man! If they succeeded, it was worth every risk they had taken, for they would have struck a blow that would ignite the fires throughout the entire land, his own as well as CONAS.

Quinn stopped, suddenly alert. No one was waiting for him inside the cavernous area. He reached inside his jacket and pulled the pistol from its holster, moving slowly now, every sense alert. He had left four men there earlier to guard the weapons cache and wait for the rendezvous. Now the warehouse was empty.

There was sudden noise behind him, and he whirled, pistol coming up fast.

"Hey, man," cried a voice, "don't shoot, it's me, Lewis."

Quinn straightened slowly as the familiar figure stepped out from behind a crate. "Lewis! What are you doing here?"

He lowered the gun as Lewis walked toward him. "Something went wrong, Wes," he said. "Bryce isn't coming."

"What? What happened?"

"This!" Lewis's arm whipped up, a pistol filling his hand. "Drop your weapon!" Two more men, rifles trained on Quinn, jumped out to join him.

Quinn was no fool. For a split second he debated, then slowly relaxed his fingers to let the pistol drop to the floor. Whether he hesitated a moment too long, or whether the one soldier saw the movement and thought he was going to try for it, would never be clear. There was a shattering blast, a flash from the muzzle. The bullet caught him full in the stomach, slamming him around hard into a pile of cardboard boxes. Quinn's body toppled to the cement floor with a sickening thud and jerked convulsively for a moment. Then it was still.

CHAPTER 31

Though Bryce's guards did not speak to him when they got him out of bed and marched him out of his cell block, he was not surprised when they came for him. As they marched down the corridor, he peered into the other darkened cells, but there was no sign of Leslie or the others.

They drove into the city, circled around the Mall, and started up what should have been Constitution Avenue but was now called Liberation Boulevard. The car slowed as it passed the squat, ugly building. Bryce looked once out of the window of the prison van, then sat back. MINISTRY OF INTERNAL AFFAIRS, proclaimed the granite sign on the lawn in front. He had expected nothing more.

It was the morning of the twentieth of October. A heavy overcast had moved in from the ocean and the day was gray with a misty rain just starting to fall. As they pulled into a stall in the underground parking terrace, his two guards were out instantly, weapons up. As he climbed out stiffly, he saw four others forming a perimeter around him. He smiled fleetingly. No more chances, he thought. As they moved toward the door to the building, it opened and Colonel Anthony Burkhart stepped out.

"Well, good morning, Bryce," he said cheerfully. "I think the minister is ready to see you."

Mannington leaned back, in a jovial and expansive mood, and took a long draw on his cigarette. Finally he turned to Bryce, who was still heavily manacled and cuffed to the chair.

"You see," Mannington said, waving toward Lewis, who sat relaxed and pleased in the chair across from Bryce, "Lewis, as you know him, is what in this profession we call a mole, a deep-cover mole. For the past six years he's been in place, working his way slowly up the resistance hierarchy, building trust, gaining confidence."

He smiled over at the commander of his Internal Security Division. Burkhart was sitting in the chair next to Lewis. "Even Anthony was not aware of this one. Like you, Lewis was hand-picked by me personally."

Bryce didn't answer. He was still half in shock, still filled with a burning fury for Lewis and the betrayal, still sick at the thoughts of Leslie and all the others, now with no hope.

"He did well, don't you think?" Mannington asked, still looking at Burkhart.

The colonel nodded, though he didn't seem nearly as amused as Mannington.

Mannington actually rubbed his hands together, relishing his moment immensely. "What a catch we have made. Hal Hoffman. Paul Adams and his daughter. Neal Lambert." He paused, then smiled briefly. "We are disappointed with the little ruse you tried to pull on us. Not that I blame you, of course. It was foolish to even consider putting every major leader of the opposition into our hands. When Lewis told us that for the most part you were going to slip in substitutes, brave volunteers who would stand in the place of their leaders, I was at first very angry. But the more I thought about it, the more I decided it would do. After all, through interrogation, I think we can still get the information we want."

"This will not only decimate the resistance movement to the point where they may never recover," Burkhart said with satisfaction, "but with what Hal Hoffman knows, we will hand the

United States government and its AIS agents the most severe blow they have ever had."

Mannington sighed, feigning deep sorrow. "In a way, it's a pity that Lewis had to surface now. Who knows how high he could have risen?" Then he chuckled and again looked at Bryce. "But I'd say it was worth it, wouldn't you?"

"It's not like you to gloat," Bryce said evenly. "Why am I here? You obviously know everything I know."

"Ummm," he murmured, "good question. You always were so perceptive, Bryce. It really is a shame to lose you."

"So?"

"We have need of your services."

Bryce laughed right out loud at that, scorn twisting his face.

"Oh, we think we can persuade you," Lewis said with a sneer.

"We want you to talk to Paul Adams," Mannington went on. "You know what he planned to say in his speech tomorrow, I'm sure. Something profoundly moving and inspiring, I suppose. Something to fire the minds and hearts of the people. I mean, after all, not only will all of CONAS be listening, but much of the Western Alliance as well. Right?"

Bryce just looked at him, his face expressionless, trying to fathom where this conversation was leading.

"We want you to persuade him otherwise," Mannington said, leaning forward, and all the banter was now gone from his voice. His eyes were hard and glittering. "He'll go on television as planned, but I don't want anything inspiring. He is to be dull, pedantic, boring."

Bryce was staring, his eyes wide.

"Perhaps," Burkhart said with a mirthless smile, "perhaps you need to tell Bryce what is going on. I think you have taken him by surprise."

"Of course," Mannington laughed. "I forgot. Lewis, would you like to enlighten him."

The agent known as Red Fox leaned forward, the triumph of the moment lighting his face. "You see, Bryce, your little plan was really quite brilliant. Even more so than you know. While we can't, of course, let the five assault teams launch their strikes at the five targets here in the city, we feel otherwise about the television station. The five teams have now been neutralized. But the attack on the station will proceed as planned." He shook his head sadly. "Except, of course, for the unfortunate demise of Mr. Quinn."

Bryce started.

"Yes, unfortunately, Wes was shot and killed last night at the place where you two were to have rendezvoused. Tragic, but we'll have to adapt. I guess I, who barely escaped from the raid on the logging camp, will now have to lead that team tomorrow."

Bryce's mind was whirling. Quinn dead. The whole plan blown. Then why this talk of attacking the television station?

"You still don't understand, do you, Bryce?" Mannington laughed right out loud.

"No, I don't."

"This public trial the prime minister has planned will be his finest hour. Several of us on the Central Committee have tried to persuade him that bringing all those prisoners into a place that cannot be adequately guarded, simply as a dramatic gesture, is very foolish, even dangerous." He clucked his tongue. "He just won't listen."

And suddenly Bryce understood very clearly. "And so the television broadcast goes on?"

Mannington seemed pleased. "But of course."

"And when the station is attacked, and Paul Adams takes over the camera and makes his speech, even if he never finishes, the prime minister, foolish man that he is, will topple from the throne."

"As I said, Bryce, you always were very clever."

"And you, who have saved the city, will step in at the last moment and turn the tide."

Mannington sat back, smiling. "Not, of course, in time to save the prime minister from a terribly embarrassing situation from which he may never recover." He laughed again, and the sound sent chills up and down Bryce's back. "Oh, Bryce, if only you knew what a wonderful opportunity you have handed us."

"Paul Adams must at least start his speech," Burkhart broke in now. "And it will have to go out over the airwaves. But he will say only what we tell him to say."

Bryce didn't answer, already knowing what was coming.

"You will talk to him, won't you?" Lewis said, with a wicked grin of satisfaction.

"Or else Leslie suffers?" he asked, already knowing the answer.

Mannington looked to the others. "Didn't I tell you he was quick?" he crowed with happiness. "Didn't I tell you?"

They were in separate cells, but across the corridor from each other. They were the only ones on the block, and the guard made it clear they had only a few minutes and then Paul Adams would be taken back to his own place.

The old man sat on the edge of his cot, his head in his hands as Bryce told him all that had happened. When he was finished, Paul didn't move for a long time. Then, finally, his head came up. The anguish in his eyes was unmistakable.

"There's really not much point in doing other than what they say, is there?"

Bryce had thought that through very carefully too. "No. If they were asking you to make a pro-government statement, or something that betrayed others, then it would be a different matter. But we've already lost. If you try to do something that will make a difference, they'll just cut you off the air."

"And Leslie will suffer for nothing."

"Yes."

He sighed, a deep, weary sound of pain. "Then you can tell them I will cooperate. They will have their dull, pedantic speech."

Bryce sighed and laid back on his own cot. He had been dreadfully afraid that Paul would not, could not, capitulate. And he had no illusions about Mannington's seeing to it that Leslie paid the price for her father's stubbornness.

269

"Do you really believe that?" Paul's voice floated to him as if from some vast void.

"What?"

"That we've lost."

Bryce sat back up. "Don't you?"

The old man shook his head back and forth slowly.

"If you know something I don't," Bryce said with bitter irony, "please tell me. I could use some good news right now."

"I know only one thing—that evil will never permanently triumph."

"Maybe not," Bryce retorted, "but right now, it's not doing too badly."

"To the contrary. What is happening proves just the opposite."

"Well, you'd better enlighten me then," Bryce said, "because with Elliot Mannington about to seize power, I'm having trouble finding much cause for hope."

"Ah, but that is the point," Adams said. "The thing you must remember is that evil is always self-consuming. Even as Mannington overthrows the prime minister, he must himself begin to fear for his own security." He gave Bryce a searching look. "Do you know who will be his greatest threat?"

The question surprised Bryce. Finally, he shook his head.

"Those who are at this moment helping him come to power."

"Burkhart and Lewis!" he breathed, knowing instantly that this man across from him was exactly right.

"Yes. And if they someday succeed in bringing Mannington down, then they will have to watch the hands of those who lift them up, and so on and so on forever. And all the while, they must keep the people at bay."

"Well," Bryce said with a soft laugh, "I've got to admit, the thought of Mannington fighting his own palace revolution is the first thing I've heard that cheers me up."

Adams stood and came to the bars of his cell. "Mannington's decision to let us go on the air is brilliant strategy for bringing down the prime minister. But for the people . . . for the people,

Bryce, it is the worst possible thing he can do, for they will know that we nearly won. And that will give them hope to try again."

Suddenly he glared upward at the ceiling of his cell. "Do you hear that, Mannington," he asked loudly, "with your microphones and secret police? Do you hear that? You know it's true. Even as you plot, you sow the seeds of your own destruction."

"You really don't believe it, do you?" Bryce asked, starting to feel a new surge of hope in spite of himself. "You really don't believe they've won, do you?"

"In a way we failed, Bryce," Paul said quietly, "but we penetrated right into the heart of their power structure. Right to the heart of it!" He breathed deeply, the fire of pride clearly ringing in his voice. "The world will know that, and whatever the setbacks, they will not forget. They will not!"

There was a clang of metal, then footsteps.

Paul Adams stood up quickly. "We have not lost, Bryce," he whispered fiercely. "Not so long as the desire for freedom burns in the heart of one person. We have not lost!"

They had taken everything from Bryce except his socks, pants, and shirt, so he had no idea what time it was or how long he had lain on his bunk staring at the ceiling. The light from the high barred window in the corridor had long ago died, so he knew it was night, but that was the only sense of time he had. Hour after hour he had lain motionless, his eyes open and blank, his mind churning like the sea in a hurricane.

When the answer came, it was so simple, so beautifully simple, that he shot to his feet. "Of course!" he cried, then instantly dropped his voice to a whisper. "Of course!"

He sat back down, his pulse racing, forcing himself to run over it again and again, probing every possible oversight, challenging every assumption. After fifteen minutes he stood slowly, knowing it could work. It could easily backfire and get him killed, but it could work! It wasn't a difficult choice. Who was it that had said not having any options greatly simplifies the decision-making process?

But it all depended on one thing. He looked around the darkness of his cell desperately, not knowing if there was a chance in a hundred that he could do the one thing that everything else hinged on.

He stood again, took a deep breath, let it out slowly, and then in a soft whisper called out into the darkness. "Gorham! Gorham, can you hear me?"

He waited. There was nothing. "Oh, Gorham," he murmured to himself, "don't fail me now. Wherever you are, I need you. Come now and I'll forgive you for everything."

"Would you consider putting that in writing?"

Bryce whirled and nearly shouted for joy. Nathaniel Gorham was standing just outside his cell door, head cocked inquisitively to one side.

CHAPTER 32

"So why do they call it the Presidential Palace if it's the prime minister who lives here?"

They were walking down a long, opulently furnished hallway, flanked on both sides by two armed guards. Bryce was dressed in his prison garb, Nathaniel Gorham was in the navyblue uniform of the ISD policeman. A picture ID, showing he was an official courier for the Signals Division, hung from one pocket.

Bryce spoke quietly out of the side of his mouth. "Because the prime minister is the head of state. He also happens to be the president of the Central Committee. How would I know? I'm a relative newcomer here, if you haven't forgotten."

Gorham gave him a quick grin. "For a relative newcomer, you sure have stirred up the pot."

Bryce didn't respond, for at that moment a man stepped from a doorway into the hallway in front of them.

"Okay, Laddie," Gorham said quickly. "Here you go, center stage."

"Yeah." Bryce's mouth set grimly. All the marbles in one bag. And if the bag broke . . . ? He shook his head, not wanting to think about it.

The man was dressed in a suit and had a thin, pinched face. He stepped back, inclining his head toward the open door. *Let's hope he always looks that sour,* Bryce thought, *and that this doesn't portend our reception inside.*

And then he came to attention, for sitting behind the massive desk was the prime minister, the man whose picture Bryce had seen everywhere he had traveled in the Confederation of North American States. It hung on the wall behind Elliot Mannington's desk. It was in post offices and bus stations, in the state-run stores, in classrooms and government offices. It was not a particularly striking face, with its broad features, but knowing who the man was and what he represented was impressive enough.

The prime minister didn't rise, just surveyed the five men who had entered his study. The guards had come to rigid attention. The pinch-faced man moved around, took a seat to his right, and took out a pad of paper and a pencil from a small stand.

The prime minister fixed his eyes first upon Nathaniel Gorham. "Sergeant Gorham?"

"Yes, Mr. Prime Minister."

"I understand from Carlson here that you have taken a considerable risk to bring this matter to our attention."

Gorham somehow managed to shrug that off as though it were nothing, yet without seeming to minimize his role in the matter.

"You have my assurance that no retaliatory measures will be taken against you by your superiors."

That would take some doing on the prime minister's part, Bryce thought with an inward smile.

"Thank you, sir. That's very good of you." He hesitated. "If there's nothing else, sir, I'd better get back."

"No. If we need you, we'll send for you."

Gorham turned, shot Bryce one quick glance, and exited.

"You may sit down, Mr. Sherwood."

Bryce did so, noticing that the guards stepped back but still stayed in a position where they could watch his every move and be on him in a split second if necessary.

There was no humor whatsoever in the prime minister's face as he leaned forward to peer at Bryce. "Be warned, Mr. Sherwood, that tomorrow is a very big day for me. I am not used to dealing with traitors, and especially not at this hour of the night. If this turns out to be some kind of a trick, things will not go well with you."

"I understand, Mr. Prime Minister," Bryce said evenly, "but if you do not deal with traitors tonight, tomorrow will be a far more significant day than you may wish it to be."

"Yes, yes," he said impatiently, "that's what Sergeant Gorham reported. That's why you're here. Now let's put aside the veiled threats and innuendos and get to what it is you have to say."

Bryce noted out of the corner of his eye that Carlson had his pencil poised now. Bryce took a deep breath. "There are some conditions."

"Somehow I figured there would be," the prime minister said dryly. "But it occurs to me that you are not in a very strong bargaining position. I can have you put under interrogation and find out whatever it is you think you have to offer me."

"You could."

There was a soft laugh, and what Bryce thought was a hint of admiration. "But?"

"But it could take most of the night, and if you are to intervene and stop this threat, you must act swiftly. Even now, it may be too late."

"Even now it may be too late," he intoned back in soft mockery. Then suddenly he slammed his fist down against the desk, causing both Bryce and Carlson to jump. "Enough of these games, Mr. Sherwood!" he roared. "What is it you have to offer me?"

"I ask nothing for myself," Bryce continued calmly. "I ask only three things."

The thick fingers were drumming rapidly on the desk, and Bryce knew the gamble could go either way momentarily.

"I want Paul and Leslie Adams released and allowed to escape to the United States of America, where they can join Vera Adams who is already there. And I also want Hal Hoffman set free."

275

Carlson was staring at him with open mouth. The prime minister's eyes had narrowed dangerously. "Is that all?" he asked softly.

The anger in his eyes sent a tiny chill up Bryce's back. "Yes."

"And what do *I* get for these small concessions?" The sarcasm was heavy.

Bryce proceeded to tell him, quietly and without dramatics. As he talked, Carlson's head would keep jerking up to stare at him before dropping back down to follow his furious scribbling. The prime minister simply sat back, his face becoming more and more stony, the mouth setting in a tighter and tighter line.

When Bryce finished, there was a long silence. Finally the prime minister stirred. "And you can prove all this?"

Bryce nodded solemnly. "Not only prove it, but I also have a way to solve it."

There was no answer.

"I could demand the release of every one of the prisoners," Bryce said slowly. "This information is worth that much to you, but all I ask is for the three."

The head of state for all of CONAS got to his feet slowly, watching Bryce with unseeing eyes. He walked to the window, parted the curtain, and stared out at the lights of the capital for a long time. The silence in the room became almost oppressive. When he turned, his face looked drawn and tired.

"And now that you have told me this, why shouldn't I simply take action on my own? Why should I deal with you?"

That was hardly an unexpected question. Bryce leaned forward. "Because Elliot Mannington is very clever. He has others who stand with him in this. He will have protected his back very carefully. I think I have a way to see that he is not allowed to wiggle out of the little situation he has created for himself."

The prime minister grunted. He knew his minister of internal affairs better than Bryce Sherwood did, and that was the very thing troubling him as well.

"Actually," he said, half musing, "losing Paul Adams and his daughter may not be all bad."

Bryce felt his heart leap.

"In fact, I have pondered what to do with them. I do not need martyrs." He paused, then shook his head. "Especially I do not need Paul Adams as a martyr. They will be an irritation to me in the United States, but not nearly as troublesome as here." He turned back, his voice hardening. "But I cannot allow Hoffman to leave. He is the key to the AIS networks in CONAS."

For one moment, Bryce was tempted to cut his losses and accept what he had won, for he knew it was a major victory. But then he shook his head. The United States would play a critical role in what happened next in this country, and Hal Hoffman was in an influential position to see that the role continued. He decided to push for the limits.

"Hal Hoffman is important to you, yes. But as far as being the key to AIS here, you know that won't be the case. You can bet that the moment word of his capture went out, the whole agency began scrambling to protect themselves." He shook his head again. "Hal Hoffman can tell you only what was as it relates to the AIS. He will no longer be able to tell you what is."

As the prime minister's head came up and he gave Bryce a long appraising look, Bryce tossed in the final chip. "Besides, he'll play a critical role in what happens if we're going to stop Mannington."

"Suppose I agree to these conditions," the prime minister said thoughtfully. "How will you know that I will carry out my part of the bargain?"

Bryce smiled faintly. "I have thought of that too, Mr. Prime Minister."

When Colonel Anthony Burkhart stepped into the prime minister's study and saw Bryce Sherwood sitting in the chair in front of his desk, his face went instantly white.

The prime minister nodded in satisfaction. "That," he said to Bryce, "is proof enough. I think you and I may have struck a fair bargain this night."

Then he swung around to Burkhart, whose hands were now visibly trembling. "Colonel?" he said roughly.

"Yes, Mr. Prime Minister."

"This prisoner has been making some allegations."

"Yes, Mr. Prime Minister."

"About your leader."

There was a quick flash of hope as Burkhart realized he had not been included in that statement.

"Would you like to save your career, or would you like to go down with Mr. Mannington?"

Burkhart's eyes darted nervously to Bryce, then to Carlson, then back to the prime minister. He licked his lips, then his shoulders sagged. "What would you like me to do?" he whispered.

Bryce had moved to the sofa in one corner and was fighting heavy eyes when the phone rang. Carlson snatched it up, listened for a moment, then handed it to the prime minister, who was still at his desk, smoking a cigarette.

"Yes. Mr. Hoffman?"

Bryce straightened, watching this cunning old fox very carefully as he listened into the phone.

There was a soft exclamation of satisfaction. "You'd better tell that to Mr. Sherwood."

Bryce came over to the desk quickly. "This is Sherwood."

"Bryce, this is Hal."

There was no mistaking the voice, but Bryce had demanded something more than the voice. He must give me something that only he and I would know, Bryce had insisted. Something so I know he is who he says he is and that he really is clear.

"Are you free?"

"That's affirmative, my friend. And we are deeply in your debt. Greatly in your debt."

"What about the others?"

278

"The man who calls you his young firebrand, and the woman who kindles that fire in you, are now on their way."

Bryce felt a surge of relief. Only Hoffman would know the significance of the firebrand wording. He sat down slowly, the relief cascading over him. "Are you sure?"

"Positive. They should be arriving in America within the hour."

"Thank you."

"Leslie wanted to stay long enough to talk to you."

Bryce smiled sadly. "Thank you for not letting her."

"You know what she wanted to tell you."

"Yes."

There was a short pause, then Hoffman's voice became softer. "We won't forget you, Bryce."

He looked up at the prime minister, who was watching him closely. "I hope not."

"We owe you," Hoffman said again. "Take care."

"Take care."

As he handed the phone back to Carlson, the prime minister grunted. "Satisfied?"

Bryce looked up. "Yes. Thank you."

It was 4:00 A.M. when the man Bryce Sherwood and many others called Lewis entered the old deserted factory building escorted by two armed men. Men with blackened faces looked up from their weapons, some in surprise. A man standing near the back of one of the trucks, checking the loading of some mortars and shoulder-held rockets, looked up. Then his jaw dropped.

He rushed over. "Lewis," he blurted. "What are you doing here? I thought you were captured—"

"I got away," Lewis said bluntly. "Wes Quinn didn't. He's been killed. I'm now in command."

"Killed!" echoed the other, his face shocked.

"Yes. I'll explain later. Get the other platoon leaders together. We'll have a briefing in five minutes."

279

"Why not right now, Lewis?"

Lewis whirled at the sound of the familiar voice.

Hal Hoffman had stepped out from behind the truck, a rifle held low in his hands but pointing steady as a rock at Lewis's stomach.

Elliot Mannington and Colonel Anthony Burkhart sat in Mannington's office in front of the television. It was 11:00 A.M. on the morning of October the twenty-first. Though Mannington was outwardly cheerful, almost jovial, one could sense his inner tension. As the announcer proclaimed the arrival of the prime minister at the television station, Mannington began to tap on his leg with the fingers of one hand.

Then he frowned. The face Elliot Mannington had come to loathe appeared on the screen, smiling and waving to the small but enthusiastic audience privileged to be in the station's small auditorium. A hush fell as the prime minister set aside his sheaf of papers and proceeded to stun the audience and the nation by announcing in triumph what had happened two days previously in the mountains of West Virginia.

One could almost sense the shock that swept through the watching millions as the camera turned and followed the manacled group of men being led into the studio. As the prime minister grimly began to recount who and what these men were, the camera zoomed in for a closer look, panning their faces one by one as they took their seats.

Mannington suddenly lurched forward. "Where is Paul Adams?" he cried. "And Hoffman?"

Burkhart straightened. "Perhaps the camera missed them."

But the camera was pulling back now for a wider shot, lingering on the group. Mannington leaped to his feet. "They're not there!" he shouted. "*They're not there!*"

He spun around to stare at Burkhart, who shrugged helplessly.

"Come on!" he shouted, starting for the door. "Something's wrong."

Burkhart came to his feet slowly as Mannington reached the door and flung it open. Two guards swung around, rifles coming up to block the doorway.

Mannington stared, stunned at their presence. Angrily he started to push through but was shoved back roughly.

Burkhart joined him then. "I regret to inform the honorable minister of internal affairs that by direct instructions of the prime minister, you are hereby charged with activities subversive to the state. You are under arrest."

Bryce had been placed in a small room somewhere in the basement of the presidential palace to avoid any chance that Mannington would learn of his absence from the prison and call for an explanation. In the morning, he would go back to his cell. People's Day had come to an end and the events that had filled it were now history, though most of the people would know nothing of the inner struggles that had shaken the government.

The sweet taste of victory and his joy at knowing that Leslie was now safe had gradually faded away and the reality of his own situation settled upon him. He was left with nothing but a profound sense of depression. Hoffman had said they wouldn't forget him, but Bryce was realist enough to know that his chances of seeing Leslie again were very slim.

Suddenly he heard a soft rustling behind him. Even before he turned, he knew who it was.

"Good evening, to you, Laddie."

"Good evening, Nathaniel."

The old colonialist moved over and sat down on the narrow bed beside him.

"Taking stock of the day?"

Bryce nodded.

"It was a great one, Son. You've every reason to be proud."

"It was a salvage operation."

"True, but a brilliant one nevertheless."

Bryce looked away, and Gorham sighed. "I know what you're thinking, Lad. And you're right, of course. Had I warned you sooner of who Lewis was, all of this could have been avoided. But again I must tell you. I am not omniscient. I can't read the future. And I can't be everywhere at once."

"I know."

"I was gone during all that."

Bryce looked up in surprise. "Gone! Where?"

"With the council."

"Oh."

There was a long silence, then finally, "This will be my last visit with you."

"No!" Bryce cried.

"Yes." Again the long pause. "I wish I could shake your hand. You've come to mean a lot to me, Laddie."

Bryce blinked, his eyes suddenly burning. "And you have to me, Nathaniel."

He smiled. "You always used to call me Gorham."

"I know."

"Is there anything I can do for you before I leave?"

Bryce looked at him. "You're not into teletransportation, I guess?"

"Teletransportation? What is that?"

"You point your finger at me, say 'Presto!' and instantly I'm transported to wherever it is in the United States that Leslie Adams is right now."

"I understand." There was a deep sigh. "Is that really what you would have me do?"

Bryce gave him a sharp look. "Of course. You can't, can you?"

Sadly he shook his head. After a moment he looked up. "I can do very little."

"You have done much," Bryce said earnestly. "For that I will always be grateful."

The old figure in long coat, breeches, kneesocks, and buckle shoes was suddenly fading. "Wait?" Bryce cried. "Not yet!"

He was barely discernible now. "Good-bye, Bryce Sherwood. Find Leslie."

"Find her!" he shouted. "How can I find her?"

The room was empty now except for Bryce. "Nathaniel. Help me. Help me get out of here so I can find her."

"I can do but little," came the echoing reply. "You must do the rest yourself."

"The rest of what?" Bryce cried at the nothingness.

But there was no answer, and he knew with sudden finality that there would be no more answers. He sat down on the narrow bed, head in his hands.

Suddenly his nose wrinkled. He sniffed once, then again. Smoke. He could smell smoke. He leaped to his feet. The blanket folded up on the foot of the bed was smoldering, curls of smoke rising slowly. Even as he stared there was a soft puff, and the blanket burst into flames.

He grabbed at it wildly, threw it on the floor, stamping hard on the flames, but suddenly the mattress exploded into a sheet of fire. Instantly the room was filled with a dense, strangling smoke.

Bryce leaped to the door, one arm thrown across his face. "Fire!" he screamed. He pounded against the wood. "Fire! Open the door!"

The lock rattled and the door was jerked open. The guard stared past him as Bryce stumbled out.

"Fire!" the man screamed. "Fire!" He turned and ran down the corridor, shouting for help.

Opening the door on the room fed oxygen to the flames. Bryce fell back, still choking and gasping for breath, as the flames snaked across his floor and caught the carpet in the corridor. There was a loud whoosh, and the whole hallway was blazing.

Two things hit Bryce at the same moment. First, that he was rapidly being cut off by the fire; and second, he stood in the corridor alone. He stared in the direction the guard had run, then turned and darted up the hall in the other direction. He came around a corner and yanked on the nearest door. It was a room identical to the one he had been in. He leaped to the next door. A storage room, filled only with old furniture. The third and last door was locked.

He spun around and started back. Thick black smoke was rolling toward him now, and he dropped to his hands and knees and crawled blindly, feeling the heat rising sharply with every yard of progress he made.

The corridor in front of him was now a mass of flames, and the roar of the fire was deafening. He heard someone screaming and came up on one knee to peer through the fire. Dimly he could see the figure of his guard through the flames, shouting to him, waving wildly at him with both arms.

Bryce hesitated, feeling the heat searing into his lungs, knowing that he had only moments to save himself. He made a quick decision, dropped down on all fours again, and scuttled back the way he had come. He opened the first door and dove into the room, sucking in the cleaner air in huge gasps. One, two, three—he sucked in the air hungrily, storing as much as possible in his tortured lungs. Then he grabbed the blanket off the bed.

Moving swiftly now, he wrapped the blanket around his head, leaving only a slit for his eyes, wishing that he had even so much as a glass of water to wet it with. Then one more deep breath of air, and he stepped back out into the corridor. This time he did not go down on his knees. He peered for an instant into the thick smoke to get his bearings, then hurtled forward, running hard. As he reached the wall of flames, he threw himself through the air, into the wall of fire. There was the searing sensation of scorching flesh along his arms, the sensation that the inside of his throat was being cauterized, then blackness—instant, all-encompassing blackness.

CHAPTER 33

The first thing Bryce was aware of was the cold wetness along the whole back side of his body. The next was the incredible glitter of stars that filled his vision. Gradually, other things began to impinge upon his consciousness—the rhythmic droning of crickets, the deeper harmony of croaking frogs farther away. He turned his head, felt the wetness hit his face.

He sat bolt upright, the memory of the fire slamming back into his mind like the bolt of a rifle being shot home. He rubbed his hand along his other forearm. There was no pain. He breathed deeply. His throat felt fine.

Suddenly there was a sound behind him, faint, but growing rapidly louder. He stood, still half dazed, groping to pull everything into some kind of meaning. Then the headlights of a car came into view, flickering ghostlike through the trees. The car whipped past him about thirty yards to his right, the hiss of tires on wet pavement rising then falling rapidly in volume.

Bryce stared in shocked disbelief. He was in the meadow. It was night, and he was in the meadow. With a cry of surprise he broke into a stumbling run toward the highway.

The BMW was parked alongside the road. There were deep tire marks in the soft mud of the shoulder where he had slid off the pavement, tires locked in a hard skid. He rubbed his hand softly along the sleek metal of the automobile, unable to believe, not daring to hope.

He opened the door and slid inside, feeling the softness of the velvet upholstery, reaching out to finger the cassettes in the box he kept below the tape deck. It was all so familiar and yet strange, as though he had been away a long, long time. He shook his head in amazement. He *had* been away a long time!

The keys were in the ignition, and the engine started with a roar, then settled into its familiar low rumble. Was this why Gorham had said he couldn't see him again? Had he brought him back? Still shaking his head in disbelief, Bryce shut the door, put the car in gear, and spun the wheel. The sports car made a sharp U-turn and headed south.

The town was small, and there was a road sign. Bryce slowed, letting the headlights flash on it, holding his breath. It was not Bollingbroke. Cannondale, said the sign. But the motel was right where he had expected it to be. He smiled inwardly. At least they didn't call it the Dew Drop Inn, he thought. Cannondale Motel, the flashing neon announced. He pulled into the parking area and let the car come to a stop.

One other car was parked in front, and as he got out, he saw that the cafe was open. There was a woman behind the counter, and two men sitting in front of it drinking coffee. He changed directions and moved past the motel office and into the cafe. Jessie Lambert looked up and smiled at him as he entered. He stopped, unable to make himself quit gaping at her. The two men glanced around at him and then went back to talking in low voices.

"Hello," Jessie said pleasantly. "May I help you?"

Bryce shook it off, forced a smile in return. "Uh. . . I've had a little car trouble. Do you happen to have a phone?"

She pointed to the far wall.

"Thanks." He pulled his eyes away from her, noting that she was starting to get uncomfortable with his scrutiny. *Déjà vu* was one thing, but this was eerie, almost as disconcerting as when he had gone in the other direction.

He moved to the phone, reaching into his pocket without thinking. Then as he withdrew his hand, it hit him. He had coins. American coins! He patted his back pocket, then took out his wallet. He opened it, fingered the driver's license slowly, feeling the dreamlike aura coming over him again. Bryce Sherwood, 435 Winwood Drive, Apartment 4A, Chevy Chase, Maryland. Was there really such a person? That seemed so long ago now. But there was his Diner's Club card, American Express, and VISA.

He punched a quarter into the coin slot quickly and hit the 0 button.

"Yes, may I help you?"

He hesitated, holding his breath.

"Operator. May I help you?" the voice said again.

"Yes, uh. . . I'd like to make a long-distance call to Boston, please."

"And how would you like that billed, sir?"

He let out his breath in a sigh of relief. "Credit card."

"Number you are calling and your credit card number?"

He gave her the phone number as he flipped to his credit card, then read her those numbers too.

"Thank you for using AT&T."

"You are most welcome," he said, more loudly than he intended. He saw Jessie turn and give him a curious look. He smiled at her, and turned back as the call clicked through and started to ring.

"Hello." The voice was muffled and very sleepy sounding.

"Mom?"

"Yes? Is this Bryce?"

"Hi, Mom!" He leaned against the wall, suddenly no longer trusting his voice.

"Bryce, is everything all right?"

He laughed. "Everything's fine, Mom."

"Bryce, it's nearly midnight. Are you okay?"

"I've never been better."

"Are you sure?"

287

There was a sudden audible sigh. "You're not coming tomorrow."

That caught him off guard. "Tomorrow?"

"Yes, are you still coming?"

"You mean for Labor Day?"

"Of course." There was a pause. "Are you sure you're all right, Bryce?"

He smiled, wishing he could reach out and put his arms around her. "Yes, Mom. I'm fine. Is Dad there?"

"Yes, he's right here."

There was a pause, then his father came on. "Son, is that you? Is everything all right?"

"Everything's fine, Dad. Did I wake you?"

"Oh, no," he said, then, "well, not really."

"I'm sorry. I just wanted to say hi, hear your voices."

This time the pause was considerable.

"You sound a little bewildered."

"I . . . I guess I am. What day is it?"

The silence stretched out for several seconds. "It's Thursday."

"What date?"

"August twenty-eighth."

So he was back to the same night he had left! He leaned back against the wall.

"Bryce, are you sure you're okay?"

"Yes. Really. I just came from a long meeting. Look, tell Mom I won't be able to come up tomorrow. Something's come up, but—"

His mother's voice cut in from another extension. "Bryce, you promised!"

"Mom, I know. And I'll come up in the next week or so. You have my word. And for Thanksgiving."

"You said you weren't coming for Thanksgiving."

"I know what I said, but I've changed my mind. I'll be home."

"Wonderful." Then almost instantly, "Are you still bringing this Leslie?"

He laughed. "Yes, Mom. I think for Christmas too."

"Really!"

He really chuckled now. "You and Dad will like her. Very much."

"Wonderful! No wonder you're not making sense."

Suddenly tears welled up in his eyes as he realized how much he would give if he could sit down with these two wonderful people and just talk.

"I've got to run, Mom. Sorry I woke you."

Now she laughed, teasing him. "If you bring a young lady home with you for both Thanksgiving and Christmas, you can call me any time of the night you want to."

"Good night, Mom. Good night, Dad." He hung up the phone and sat there for some time, just looking at nothing.

He drove all night, stopping only once for gas and a large soft drink with lots of ice to keep him awake. Dawn was just lighting the sky as he pulled into the carport stall beneath his apartment, unloaded the car, and took his things upstairs. He looked around, still half unable to comprehend that he was back. Then he walked to the phone, picked it up, hesitated. For a long moment he just stood there. Then he set the phone down, went into the bathroom, and started the water running in the shower.

He slept until ten, got up and dressed, then forced himself to jam down some breakfast. Twice the phone rang, but he ignored it. He had two people he wanted to talk to, but in circumstances of his own choosing. Until then, there was no one else he felt like speaking to. Six weeks had been wiped off the slate. He couldn't go charging back into life as though nothing had changed.

While he started into the city with the intent of going directly to the office of Elliot Mannington, as he came down Sixth Street, on sudden impulse he turned right onto Constitution Avenue and drove slowly west, past the Ellipse, past the Washington Monument and the White House. The haze was thick and the late summer air heavy. Traffic slowed to a crawl, horns honked angrily as tempers flared, but Bryce rolled down his windows, savoring it all like a hungry man savors the smell of hot bread cooking in the oven.

He went all the way around the Mall, circling the Lincoln Memorial twice, then finally pulled in next to the Jefferson Memorial. He got out and walked slowly around the gleaming white columns, letting the sea of tourists and schoolchildren ebb and flow around him. He went inside and stood for a long time, staring up at the statue of the nation's third president. And then, finally, he let his eyes move upward to the frieze that ran all around the inside of the dome. Taken from a letter written to Benjamin Rush in 1800, it said simply: "I have sworn upon the altar of God eternal hostility against every form of tyranny over the mind of man."

He straightened, looked up again into the bronze face of the man from Monticello, then turned and walked swiftly to the car.

"Well, well," Mannington said, getting up from his desk to come around and shake Bryce's hand. "I've been trying to call you."

Bryce inwardly recoiled at the presence of the man, then caught himself. *This is not the same man*, he repeated to himself. *This is not the same time, nor the same circumstances. You cannot react as though it were.* He stuck out his hand. "Hello, Elliot."

Mannington ushered Bryce to a chair, picked up the golden cigarette case, started to offer it to Bryce and then remembered he didn't smoke. He took one out, lit it, then sat back.

"Senator Hawkes called. He thought you had agreed that you would meet with that delegation from the Iowa legislature this morning."

There was no mistaking the chiding in the tone as he waited for his star pupil to provide an explanation. Bryce sat back. There was no point in trying to sidle into this one. "Look, Elliot," he

290

said quietly, "I'm sorry, but I'll be turning in my resignation this afternoon."

If he had pulled a pistol out and put it to his head, he couldn't have stunned him more. Mannington's hand froze in midair, leaving the cigarette dangling. His mouth dropped. The dark eyes widened perceptibly. "You what?" he cried.

"I know this is totally unexpected, but some things have changed."

Mannington lowered the cigarette slowly, the eyes narrowing and the line along his jaw hardening. "Say that one more time."

"I've learned some things in the last few days, Elliot. I can no longer support the twenty-seventh amendment to the Constitution. You'll have my letter of resignation within the hour."

The dark eyes were suddenly chilling, and Bryce saw in them the same look he had seen in the eyes of the minister of internal affairs. "If this is your idea of a joke, Bryce, I—" He jerked forward. "Did Senator Hawkes put you up to this?"

"No. I'll not be going back with Senator Hawkes either."

Mannington got up from his desk slowly, the muscles in one cheek twitching. "Are you telling me that after all I've done for you, you're just going to up and quit on me?"

"I am resigning as national chairman for passage of the twenty-seventh amendment. Yes, that is what I am saying."

Mannington swung around, his hand coming down in a sweeping arc to catch a stack of papers on the corner of his desk and send them hurtling across the room. "Do you know who you're talking to?" he shouted.

"Yes, I certainly do," Bryce responded calmly.

"After all we've promised you? The senatorship, a shot at the White House? And you walk in here and tell me you're resigning?"

"I guess that's about it."

"You . . ." He swung around again, livid, swearing as he slammed down his fist on the desk. "I'll see that you never work in this town again."

291

He was up on the balls of his feet, rocking back and forth, fists clenched. "Is that clear, Mr. Bryce Sherwood?" he shouted. "You're through!"

Bryce stood up and smiled faintly. "No, actually, I think I'm just beginning."

He stopped in the hallway of Arlington High School outside the door that said "Leslie Adams" on the nameplate. He looked through the small window with the triangular wire mesh embedded in the glass. She was at the blackboard, chalk in hand. He could hear her voice coming softly through the door. He straightened his tie, pulled at his sports jacket, then opened the door and walked in.

Leslie was just turning to write something on the board when she heard the sound behind her. She turned back, a tentative smile just starting to form. This seemed to be Bryce's day for stopping people in midstride. Like Mannington, she too froze in position, chalk half raised, her body partially turned toward him.

"Bryce?" she blurted.

A quick murmur of interest and surprise rippled through the classroom as he nodded. "Hello, Leslie."

"What are *you* doing here?"

"Well, actually, I came to give you something."

And with that he stepped forward, swept her up in his arms, and kissed her, long and hard.

Instantly the class erupted. There were oohs and ahs, catcalls, whistles, and applause, and one student near the back punched his fist into the air and shouted "All right!"

Bryce ignored it all, just held her tight, even as she started to struggle. Finally he let her go and stepped back. One hand flew to her mouth, her face turned instantly scarlet, and her eyes looked as his must have on the night he first saw Nathaniel Gorham.

292

Bryce swung around to the class, bowed slightly to the now-wild applause, then raised his hands. "Class dismissed!" he shouted.

For an instant they just stared at him in disbelief, then bedlam really broke loose.

"Wait!" Leslie cried. Students half out of their chairs or already on their way to the door, stopped.

Bryce turned to face their teacher.

"You. . . You can't do that."

"Why not?"

"School isn't out for another half an hour."

He smiled at her. "It is for these kids."

"All right!" the same kid hollered again, and this time there was a stampede for the door.

"Hold it!" Bryce hollered. The first one, just opening the door, stopped short. The others bumped up against him like freight cars behind a switch engine.

"What class is this?" Bryce demanded.

"U.S. history and government," one of the girls shouted back.

He swung around and pointed to the small flag hanging from a holder in one corner. "Do you know the Pledge of Allegiance?" he asked them.

There was a chorus of yesses.

"C'mon back in here. If you can say the Pledge of Allegiance properly, you're excused."

Leslie grabbed his arm. "Are you crazy?" she hissed. "You can't do this!"

"I really can, trust me." He turned back to the kids. "C'mon, c'mon, do you want to get out of here or not?"

They shuffled back in, not sure if he was serious, and formed a rough semicircle facing the flag. A few hands tentatively came up and over the heart. Most of them had not done this since elementary school.

Leslie was looking up at him strangely now.

"You too, Miss Adams," he said soberly. "Hand over your heart."

293

She turned, her hand coming up slowly, still staring at him.

"If you don't mind," Bryce said to the class, "I'd like to say it first, then we'll all do it together. Okay?"

He turned back and faced the red, white, and blue banner hanging limply in the corner. Then he put his hand over his heart, took a deep breath, and began.

"I pledge allegiance to the flag of the United States of America . . . "

There were a few nervous giggles, some feet shuffling, but Bryce heard none of it. His mind was in another time and and another place.

" . . . and to the republic for which it stands . . . "

His breath caught, and he blinked quickly, eyes burning. "And to the republic for which it stands," he said again, "one nation under God, indivisible—" The image of a red slash marked "demilitarized zone" running down the middle of the map of the North American Continent flashed into his mind, and he had to stop.

Leslie stepped up beside him. " . . . one nation under God, indivisible, with liberty and justice for all."

The class was totally silent now, watching the two adults standing shoulder to shoulder in front of them. Leslie turned her head. "All right, all together now."

They spoke in unison, these bright-faced, coddled kids, born of the permissive generation, suckled in the land of the free and barely aware of what they had. But at that moment something in the face of the handsome young man who had swept into their classroom and kissed their teacher touched their hearts, just as his heart was touched. And as they went through the words again, they spoke them with feeling and with commitment, many of them in that way for the first time.

"I pledge allegiance to the flag of the United States of America and to the republic for which it stands, one nation under God, indivisible, with liberty and justice for all."

For fully ten seconds no one moved, then Bryce turned slowly. "Thank you," he said. Then he smiled. "Now get outta here!"

And in fifteen seconds he and Leslie were left standing in the classroom alone.

About the Author

Gerald N. Lund's numerous books include *The Work and the Glory* series; *One in Thine Hand*; *The Alliance*; *Jesus Christ, Key to the Plan of Salvation*; *Leverage Point*; and *The Coming of the Lord*. He received his B.A. and M.S. degrees in sociology from Brigham Young University and has been a seminary teacher, an institute of religion teacher and director, and director of college curriculum for the Church Educational System of The Church of Jesus Christ of Latter-day Saints. He and his wife, Lynn, have seven children; they reside in Bountiful, Utah.